Jack fired, but the rocket went wide. "Can't you hold this nag still?"

Bela almost laughed. "Would you like that?"

What do you say to a wildwoman who rides through the air on a winged Robosteed firing a pistol with one hand and waving a *sword*, for god's sake, with the other?

"Yeah!" he answered. "Looks like the only way I'll hit anything."

Bela complied, and the Robotech Pegasus hovered. As the Enforcer ship began a new attack run, Jack wrestled the launcher around and lined up his shot with the tube resting on Bela's shoulder.

He fired his last two rockets. "Let's get outta here!"

Published by Ballantine Books:

The ROBOTECH™ Series

The SENTINELS ™ Series

THE SENTINELS™ #2

DARK POWERS

Jack McKinney

A Del Rey Book

BALLANTINE BOOKS • NEW YORK

THIS ONE'S FOR THE MEN OF THE "BIG E,"
THE AIRCRAFT CARRIER USS *ENTERPRISE*,
WITH THANKS FOR THE KIND WORDS.

A Del Rey Book
Published by Ballantine Books

Library of Congress Catalog Card Number: 87-91852

ISBN 0-345-35301-3

Manufactured in the United States of America

First Edition: May 1988

ROBOTECH CHRONOLOGY

1999	Alien spacecraft known as SDF-1 crashlands on Earth through an opening in hyperspace, effectively ending almost a decade of Global Civil War.
	In another part of the Galaxy, Zor is killed during a Flower of Life seeding attempt.
2002	Destruction of Mars Base Sara.
2009	On the SDF-1's launch day, the Zentraedi (after a ten-year search for the fortress) appear and lay waste to Macross Island. The SDF-1 makes an accidental jump to Pluto.
2009-11	The SDF-1 battles its way back to Earth.
2011-12	The SDF-1 spends almost half a year on Earth, is ordered to leave, and defeats Dolza's armada, which has laid waste to much of the planet.
2012-14	A two-year period of reconstruction begins.
2012	The Robotech Masters lose confidence in the ability of their giant warriors to recapture the SDF-1, and begin a mass pilgrimage through interstellar space to Earth.
2013	Dana Sterling is born.
2014	Destruction of the SDFs 1 and 2 and Khyron's battlecruiser.
2014-20	The SDF-3 is built and launched. Rick Hunter turns 29 in 2020; Dana turns 7.

Subsequent events covering the Tiresian campaign are recounted in the Sentinels series. A complete Robochronology will appear in the fifth and final volume.

CHAPTER
ONE

All I have learned of the Shapings of the Protoculture tell me that it does not work randomly; that there is a grand design or scheme. I feel that we have been brought here, kept here, for some reason.

Yet, what purpose can there be in SDF-3's being stranded here on Tirol for perhaps as long as five years? And during that time will the Robotech Masters be pursuing their search for Earth?

Since tempers are short, I do not mention the Shaping; I'm a little too long in the tooth, I fear, for hand-to-hand confrontations with homesick, frightened, and frustrated REF fighters.

Dr. Emil Lang, personal journal of the SDF-3 mission

ON CAPTURED TIROL, AFTER A FIERCE BATTLE, THE Humans and their Zentraedi allies—the Robotech Expeditionary Force—licked their wounds, then decided it was time to mark the occasion of their triumph. It was, as nearly as they could calculate, New Year's Eve.

But far out near the edge of Tirol's system, a newcomer appeared—a massive spacegoing battleship, closing in on the war-torn, planet-sized moon.

Our first victory celebration, young Susan Graham exulted. *What a wonderful party!* She was just shy of sixteen, and to her it was the most romantic evening in human history.

1

She was struggling to load a bulky cassette into her sound-vid recorder while scurrying around to get a better angle at Admirals Rick Hunter and Lisa Hayes Hunter. They had just stood up, in full-dress uniforms, clasping white-gloved hands, apparently about to dance. There had been rumors that the relationship between the two senior officers of the Robotech Expeditionary Force was on shaky ground, but for the moment at least, they seemed altogether in love.

Sue let out a short romantic sigh and envied Lisa Hunter. Then her thoughts returned to the cassette which she was bapping with the heel of her hand. A lowly student-trainee, Sue had to make do with whatever equipment she could find at the G-5 public-information shop, or Psy-ops, Morale or wherever.

At last the cassette was in place, and she began to move toward her quarry.

In Tiresia, the moon's shattered capital city, the Royal Hall was aglow. The improvised lighting and decorations reemphasized the vast, almost endless size of the place.

The lush ballroom music remained slow—something from Strauss, Karen Penn thought; something even Jack Baker could handle. As she had expected, he asked her to waltz a second time.

And he wasn't too bad at it. The speed and reflexes that made him such a good Veritech pilot—*almost as good as I am*, she thought—made him a passable dancer. Still, she maintained her aloof air, gliding flawlessly, making him seem clumsy by comparison; otherwise, that maddening brashness of his would surface again at any second.

They were about the same height, five ten or so, he redheaded and freckled and frenetic, she honey-blond and smooth-skinned and model-gorgeous—and long since tired of panting male attention. Jack had turned eighteen two months ago; Karen would celebrate her majority in three more weeks.

They had been like oil and water, cats and dogs, Unseducible Object and Irrepressible Force, ever since they had met. But they had also been battle comrades, and now they swayed as the music swelled, and somehow their friendly antagonism was put aside, at least for the moment.

The deepspace dreadnought was a bewildering, almost slapdash length of components: different technologies, different philosophies of design, even different stages of scientific awareness, showed in the contrasts among its various modules. From it, scores of disparate weapons bristled and many kinds of sensors probed.

With Tirol before it, the motley battlewagon went on combat alert.

On the outer rim of the ballroom, members of General Edwards's Ghost Squadron and Colonel Wolff's Wolff Pack traded hostile looks, but refrained from any overt clashes; Admiral Lisa Hunter's warnings, and her promises of retribution, had been very specific on that point.

Edwards was there, a haughty, splendidly military figure, his sardonic handsomeness marred by the half cowl that covered the right half of his head.

Per Lisa's confidential order, Vince Grant and his Ground Mobile Unit people were keeping an eye on the rivals, ready to break up any scuffles. So far things seemed to be peaceful—nothing more than a bit of glowering and boasting.

Hanging in orbit over the war-torn ruin of Tirol, Superdimensional Fortress Three registered the rapid approach of the unidentified battleship.

SDF-3 had been tardy in detecting the newcomer; the Earth warship's systems had been damaged in the ferocious engagement that had destroyed her spacefold apparatus, and some systems were still functioning far short of peak efficiency.

But she had spotted the possible adversary now. According to procedure, SDF-3 went to battle stations, and communications personnel rushed to open downlinks with the contingent on Tirol's surface.

Perhaps the strangest pair at the celebration was Janice Em, the lovely and enigmatic singer, and Rem, assistant to the Tiresian scientist Cabell.

Janice was Dr. Lang's creation, an android, an artificial person, though she was unaware of it.

Lang shook his head and reminded himself that the Shapings of the Protoculture were not to be defied. He was really quite happy that the two were drawn together.

He turned to Cabell, the ancient lone survivor of the scientists of Tirol.

What were once the gorgeous cityscape of Tiresia and magnificent gardens surrounding the Royal Hall, were now only blasted wasteland.

Above was a jade-green crescent of Fantoma, the massive planet that Tirol circled. Its alien beauty hid the ugliness that Lynn-Minmei knew to be there in the light of Valivarre, the system's primary. The green Fantoma-light cast a spell with magic all its own. How could the scene of so much death and suffering be so unspeakably beautiful?

She shivered a bit, and Colonel Jonathan Wolff slipped his arm around her. Minmei could feel from the way he had moved closer that he wanted to kiss her; she wasn't sure whether she felt the same or not.

He was the debonair, tigerishly brave, good-looking Alpha Wolf of the Wolff Pack—and had rescued her from certain death, melodramatic as it might sound to others. Still, there was a danger in love; she had learned that not once but several times now.

Wolff could see what was running through Minmei's thoughts. He feasted his eyes on her, hungered for her. The Big, Bad Wolff, indeed—an expression he had never liked.

Only this time, the Big Bad was bewitched, and helpless. She was the blue-eyed, black-haired gamine whose

voice and guileless charm had been the key to Human
victory in the Robotech War. She was the child-woman
who, unknowingly, had tormented him with fantasies he
could not exorcize by day, and with erotic fever-dreams
by night.

She hadn't moved from the circle of his arm; she looked
at him, eyes as wide as those of a startled doe. Wolff
leaned closer, lips parting.

I love her so much, Rick thought, as he and Lisa went to
join the dancing. His wife's waist was supple under his
gloved hand; her eyes danced with fondness. He felt himself
breaking into a languorous smile, and she beamed at him.

I can't live without her, he knew. *All these problems
between us—we'll find some way to deal with them. Because otherwise life's not worth living.*

The music had just begun when it stopped again, rag-
gedly, as Dr. Lang quieted people from the mike stand.
The ship's orchestra's conductor stood to one side, looking
peeved but apprehensive.

Everyone there had already served in war. Something
inside them anticipated the words. "Unidentified ship...
course for Tirol ... Skull and Ghost squadrons ... Admiral
Hayes and Admiral Hunter..."

The war's come between us again.

Rick started off in a dash, but stopped before he had gone
three steps, realizing his wife was no longer with him.
Fortunately, in all the confusion, only one person noticed.

He looked back and saw Lisa waiting there, head erect,
watching him. He realized he had reacted with a fighter
jock's reflexes, the headlong run of a hot scramble.

It was the argument they had been having for days, for
weeks now—tersely, in quick exchanges, by day; wearily,
taxing to the limit their patience with one another, by
night. Rick was a pilot, and had come to the conclusion
that he couldn't be—*shouldn't* be—anything else. Lisa
insisted that his job now was to command, to oversee

flight-group ops. He was to do the job he had been chosen to do, because nobody else could do it.

Rick saw nothing but confidence in his wife's eyes as she looked at him, her chin held high—that, and a proud set to her features.

Sue Graham, wielding her aud-vid recorder, had caught the whole thing, the momentary lapse in protocol, in confidence—in love. Now, she rewound the tape a bit, so that the sight of Rick Hunter dashing off from his wife would be obliterated, and began recording over it.

Just as people were turning to the Admirals Hunter, Rick stepped closer to Lisa. In that time, conversation and noise died away, and the Royal Hall itself, weighted by its eons of history and haunting events, seemed to be listening, evaluating. Rick's high dress boots clacked on an alien floor that shone like a black mirror.

He offered her his arm, formal and meticulously correct, inclining his head to her. "Madam?"

She did a shallow military curtsy, supple in her dress-uniform skirt, and laid her hand on his forearm. The whole room was listening and watching; Rick and Lisa had reminded everyone what the REF was, and what was expected of it.

"Orders, Admiral?" Rick asked his wife crisply, loudly, in his role as second-ranking officer present. By speaking those words, he officially ended the ball and put everyone on notice that they were on duty.

Lisa, suddenly their rock, gazed about at them. She didn't have to raise her voice very much to be heard. "You all know what to do, ladies, gentlemen.

"We will treat this as a red alert. SDF-3 will stand to General Quarters. GMU and other ground units report to combat stations; all designated personnel will return to the dimensional fortress."

There was already movement, as people strode or hurried to their duties. But no one was running; Lisa had given them back their center.

"Fire-control and combat-operations officers will insure

that no provocative or hostile acts are committed," she said in a sharp voice. "I will remind you that we are *still* on a *diplomatic mission*.

"Carry on."

Men and women were moving purposefully, the yawning hall quickly clearing. Lisa turned to an aide, a commo officer. "My respects to the Plenipotentiary Council, and would they be so gracious as to convene a meeting immediately upon my return to SDF-3."

The aide disappeared; Lisa turned to Rick. "If you please?"

Rick, his wife on his arm, turned toward the shuttle grounding area. REF personnel made way for them. Rick let Lisa set the pace: businesslike, but not frantic.

When the shuttle was arrowing up through Tirol's atmosphere for SDF-3 rendezvous, and the two were studying preliminary reports while staff officers ran analyses and more data poured in, Rick paused for a moment to look at his wife as she meditated over the most recent updates.

He covered her hand with his for a moment; squeezed it. "We owe each other a waltz, Lisa."

She gave him a quick, loving smile, squeezing his hand back. Then she turned to issue more orders to her staff.

To Rem, the Humans and their REF mission had been bewildering from the beginning, but never more so than now.

With this news of an unidentified warship, he and Cabell—who had been a father to him, really, and more than a father—were hastened toward the shuttle touchdown area, to await their turn to be lifted up to the SDF-3. Their preference in the matter wasn't asked; they were an important—perhaps crucial—military intelligence resource now, even though they were just as mystified as anybody else.

There were confused snatches of conversation and fragments of scenes as Rem guided Cabell along in the general milling.

There were the two young cadets Rem had come to

know as Karen Penn and Jack Baker. They had been pressed into service as crowd controllers and expediters of the evacuation. Jack kept trying to catch Karen's eye and call some sort of jest or other; she just spared him the occasional withering glance and concentrated on her duties.

Rem couldn't blame her. What could be funny about a situation like this? Was Jack psychologically malfunctional?

Then there was the singer, Minmei, Janice Em's partner, possessed of a voice so moving that it defied logic, and a face and form of unsettling appeal. The one they called Colonel Wolff seemed to be trying to usher her along, seemed to be proprietary toward her, but she wasn't having any of it. In fact, it appeared that she was about to burst into that startling and alarming human physiological aberration called tears.

The Ghost and Skull and GMU teams were cooperating like mindlinked Triumvirates, though Rem had seen them ready to come to blows only a short time before.

He look about for Janice Em, Minmei's partner and harmony and, in some measure, alter ego, but couldn't see her. She had been with Lang only moments before, but now Lang was gone, too. Rem tried to push troubling thoughts from his mind, such as the rumors that were rife about Lang and Janice. Lang was supposed to be like an uncle to her, though some said he was "much more."

But *what*? Rem barely understood the concept "uncle," and had no idea what "much more" might mean. Yet his cheeks flushed, and he felt a puzzling rage when he thought of Jan having some nebulous relationship to Lang that would make the old Human scientist more important to her than, than . . .

Then all at once Rem and Cabell were being rushed into a shuttle, and a sliding hatch cut off the haunted nighttime view of ruined Tiresia.

CHAPTER
TWO

I never got tired of covering the Hunters, the admirals. To me,
they were a perfect couple, the best the Earth could field.
But in another sense, the enemy had fielded his worst.

Susan Graham, narration from documentary *Protoculture's*
Privateers: SDF-3, Farrago, *Sentinels, and the REF*

O N THE BRIDGE OF THE SUPERDIMENSIONAL FOR-
tress Three, Lisa Hayes surveyed the preparations for battle
and despaired, thinking the REF diplomatic mission might
be doomed to find nothing but war.

Approximately twenty minutes had passed since the unidentified dreadnought was spotted, and it was nearly upon
them. Yet it had not responded to any visual or electromag-
netic signal. Peace was important to her, but so were the
lives of her crew and the survival of her command. She
was as edgy as any enlisted-rating gunner, but didn't have
the luxury of simply hoping she could shoot first.

And, the SDF-3 was only partially combat-worthy; letting the enemy get to close range might mean ultimate disaster. Still, the REF mission *had* to mean something more than crossing the galaxy only to fight battle upon battle, had to mean more than war without end.

She went over every detail, to see if there wasn't one more preparation she could make. Lisa looked around the bridge. There was the same small bridge watch-gang setup that her mentor, Captain Gloval, had used, except that the three enlisted-rating techs were male, as were the watch officer and Lisa's exec, Commander Forsythe.

Rick and the other officers from the Tactical Information Center—the ship's cavernous command, communications, and control facility—kept up the flow of information, but none of it was very helpful. The Plenipotentiary Council, the civilian body in overall control of the Robotech Expeditionary Force, had convened just long enough to give Lisa operational control over the situation; they were satisfied that she wasn't trigger-happy, and that she was well aware of the dicey tactical dilemma.

Veritechs were scrambled, sent out to block the newcomer's way, and intercept and engage if necessary. Alphas, Betas, and Logans were deployed to their appointed places. Lisa's eye found the tactical display symbol for the Skull team for a moment, and she thought of Rick—trapped down there among the rows of consoles and techs' duty stations, monitors, and instruments. She knew he was longing to be out there with his beloved former outfit.

She supposed his heart was even more with them in this moment than it was with her. If so, that was something she could understand, could forgive, as long as he carried out his current assignment.

She thrust the thought aside; the Veritechs were coming within range of the unidentified dreadnought. Although the ship was as big as any Earth battlecruiser, it was still far smaller than the mammoth SDF-3. It maintained its worrisome silence.

According to the rule book, the next step should be a

close flyby, performed by VTs—a warning to the intruder. If there was still no acknowledgment, it would be time for a shot across the battlewagon's bow.

She found herself about to order Ghost in for the flyby, avoiding the use of Skull, but stopped herself. Although Rick would want to be with his old outfit in the thick of things, he would just have to maintain his duties as a commander. Edwards was too rash—he might even enjoy goading the newcomers into a shooting incident. Max Sterling, who had taken over Skull, was a more reliable man and the best flier in the REF.

She opened her mouth to give the command to Skull, when one of the male enlisted-rating techs said, "The incoming ship is decelerating, Captain. Changing course for possible insertion to Tirol orbit. It's deactivating its weapons systems."

As soon as the tech relayed the information, a female voice from the Tactical Information Center came up. TIC commo instruments were intercepting radio transmissions from the newcomer.

When the transmissions were patched through to the bridge, Lisa found herself listening to a strange, voice-processed-sounding garble. But bit by bit, she began to recognize syllables.

"Zentraedi," Lisa's bridge officer, Mister Blake, said softly, but Lisa was already turning to have a comline opened to Dr. Lang's science/research division.

"Respond, please," the transmissions came, in that strange, processed-sounding voice that might have been computer generated. "Alien vessel, please respond."

Alien? Lisa pondered as Lang came onscreen. He was flanked by Breetai, and Exedore. Once Humanity's greatest enemies, these two Zentraedi were now staunch allies.

"Can you speculate on what this means, Doctor?" Lisa asked. "Or Commander Breetai? Lord Exedore?"

It was Exedore who answered, his voice still holding something of the weird Zentraedi quaver, even though he had been Micronized to Human size.

His was the greatest mind of his race, and the storehouse of its accumulated—in some cases, fabricated—lore and history. "The language is Tiresian," he confirmed, "with loan-words from our own battle language and some elements of the Robotech Masters' speech. But it is being spoken by a non-Zentraedi, non-Tiresian.

"As for the ship, it fits no profile known to my data banks, although certain portions of it bear resemblances to the spacecraft of various spacefaring cultures."

"But this is no Zentraedi ship," boomed Breetai. "Of that I feel sure. Our race conquered thousands of worlds, contacted tens of thousands of species. The language of Tirol became the lingua franca of much of this part of the galaxy. This warcraft might come from anywhere in the entire region, or even beyond."

All of them heard the next transmission from the battleship. "We come in peace," that eerie voice said. "We come in friendship. Do not fire! We are desperately in need of your help!"

"Identify yourselves," a commo officer transmitted in her clear contralto. "Incoming vessel, who are you?"

"We are the Sentinels," the eldritch voice answered. "We are the Sentinels."

Down in the TIC, Rick Hunter had a sudden vision of black obelisks and dire events to the tune of *Also Spracht Zarathustra*.

Lisa looked at the bridge's main viewscreen.

Suddenly Edwards's face appeared in an inset at one corner of it. "It's some kind of trick! Admiral, you can't let them—"

"General, that . . . will . . . *do!*" Lisa thundered, and blanked him from the screen. A moment later she was talking to the Plenipotentiary Council.

"Ladies and gentlemen, I recommend that we allow the, er, alien ship to land under close escort by our VTs and with its weapons systems inert. We can track it with the SDF-3's main gun, and cover it with the GMU's as well, once it's down. If it turns out that they want to fight, let it be from a position of such tactical disadvantage."

That touched off a hectic, bitter debate in the council. Some members shared Edwards's attitude after the almost mindless hatred with which the SDF-3's arrival had been greeted by the Invid.

It was Lang who cut through the rancor with a single quiet plea, perhaps the most *Human* thing he had said since that Protoculture boost so long ago.

"My dear companions, we've traveled across the better part of the Milky Way galaxy with the express hope of hearing the word they've just used: friendship."

Permission to land was carried unanimously.

Exedore was less the frog-eyed, misshapen dwarf he had once been, thanks to Human biosurgery and cosmetic treatments. It seemed to make people more at ease in his presence, but other than that it meant little to him.

Now he pushed back his unruly mass of barn-red hair and squinted at the readouts as his own data banks interfaced with those of the SDF-3 mainframes, with input from the detectors tracking the newcomer battleship's descent. As had happened so often in the past, he could feel great Breetai looming nearby.

Exedore, Breetai, and many of the star players of the REF were in the Tactical Information Center. Techs, intel, and ops officers were scurrying around the compartment, which was two hundred feet on a side and half as high, crammed with screens and instrumentation. A main screen fifty feet square dominated the place.

Exedore was matching disparate parts of the newcomer's hull features with profiles in Zentraedi files. "You see? That portion toward the stern, starboard—it's Praxian! A-and the section there just forward of midship's starboard: is that not a Perytonian silhouette, I ask you?"

Nobody there was about to argue with him, but nobody understood what it meant—and neither did Exedore. "It's as if these Sentinels slapped together a variety of space vessels and united them with a central structure—you see?

—to form, oh, I don't know—a sort of aggregate. Certainly, it's not a design well suited to atmospheric entry."

Exedore was correct. The assemblage ship, asymmetrical and unbalanced in gravity and atmosphere, was already being battered as it fought its way down toward Tirol's surface.

But by some miracle the lumbering vessel held together. Rick Hunter found himself rooting for the Sentinels, whoever they were. He felt emotions he hadn't felt in years—buried exaltation from his days in his father's air circus.

"Our analyses of their power systems don't make any sense," a female tech officer reported to the bridge. "Some indications are consistent with Protoculture, but other readings are totally incompatible. We're even picking up systemry that appears to be—well, like something from the steam age, Captain."

"Thank you, Colonel," Lisa said, and the woman's image disappeared from the bridge's main screen.

She turned to Exedore and Breetai. "Gentlemen—*friends*—can you tell me what we've encountered?"

Breetai drew a breath, expanding his massive chest, then crossed his tree limb arms across it. "It is galling to us, Lisa, and so we were slow to bring it up, but many of the memories of the Zentraedi are false—constructs of the Robotech Masters, implanted when they—"

For once she saw Breetai's head, as huge and indomitable as a buffalo's, hang in dejection. Lisa could feel immense grief and loss coming from him. "They deceived us; made a mockery of our loyalty, our valor, our sacrifices . . ."

Exedore hastened to fill the ensuing silence. "We know less of this local star group than we do of far-distant ones; the Zentraedi were expanding the Masters' empire—the outer marches, as your ancient Romans might put it. But you must understand, Mrs. Hunter—um, Captain!—that we *cannot trust our own memories* in matters like these."

Breetai's chin had come up again. "Still, we'll tell you what we know. Praxis, Peryton, Karbarra, and the other planets whose technology you see mingled there—they were all valued parts of the Masters' empire. Planets of the local star group, easily reached, they were allowed to keep a large measure of their self-determination so long as they subordinated themselves to the Robotech Masters' ambitions. They survived, in their fashion, in the eye of the storm."

"So—they would be the last to fall to the Invid," Lisa said slowly.

Exedore nodded. "The last, except for Tirol. And worlds upon which the Invid Regis and Regent might wish to vent their anger, or as much of it as they can mount, now that both sides have been so reduced in numbers."

It was true that the Invid were victorious in the long war against the Masters, but in many cases what they ruled was an empire of ash. Planets, even suns, had died. What was left in that region of the galaxy seemed scarcely worth taking.

Rick's face appeared on the main screen. "Landing party standing by, Cap'n." He saluted his wife. He showed nothing but an unerring precision, aware that his demeanor and expression would be studied on a thousand other screens throughout the SDF-3. Behind him were the two heavily armed landing craft that would fly down with the expedition's envoys to greet the Sentinels. Max's Skulls were forming up to fly escort and cover. The GMU had already churned into position, its titanic cannon trained on the grounded space-battleship.

Lisa returned Rick's salute. They cut their hands away from their brows smartly, just like the manual said. She wondered if anyone who was witnessing the exchange could tell how *happy* he was, now that he was once more venturing into danger. She wondered if he knew it himself.

The Sentinels' ship had chosen a big patch of ground that would serve as its landing pad. VTs and ground units came in to cover; fearsome armored vehicles clanked and wheeled on their tracks. The descent of the landing craft kicked up clouds of sand and dust that settled quickly.

The protocol had been argued a bit, but nobody on the council wanted to be the one to go up and knock on the Sentinels' door. So it was Lisa and Rick, flanked by Breetai and Exedore and Lang, who approached the ship unarmed. The group walked under Fantoma's light and the glare of a hundred of the two-legged Tiresian Ambler spotlights, to what appeared to be the main hatch of the Sentinels' starship.

But when the main hatch of the ship rolled open, there were none of the dramatics Lisa had unconsciously braced herself for. Instead, a robed figure stood there, at the top of a ramp extended like an impudent tongue from the side of the Sentinels' ship.

Actually, the figure *floated* there; the hem of its robe billowed gently an inch or two above the ramp.

Lang had been elected to speak for the REF. He coughed a bit in the swirling dust, one foot on the ramp where it met the sand. "If you come in friendship, I offer you my hand, on behalf of all of us, in friendship."

The being looking down on him was virtually smooth-faced, like some blank mask. "I cannot offer mine," it said in the same voice they had heard over the commo.

Other figures, larger, loomed up behind it. Still more crowded at the sides, lower and surreptitiously slinky. Outgassing from the Sentinels' ship's atmosphere put a sudden mist in the air of Tirol, and it got even harder to see.

Then Rick heard Lisa's scream, and he cried out her name. All at once he was grappling hand-to-hand with the devil.

CHAPTER
THREE

I suppose we shouldn't have been surprised. We had already discovered, back during the Robotech War, that wherever the basic chemical building blocks of life coexisted, they linked preferentially to form the same subunits that defined the essential biogenetic structures found on Earth. In other words, the ordering of the DNA code wasn't a quirk of nature.

The formation and linking of amino acids and nucleotides was all but inevitable. The messenger RNA codon-anticodon linkages seemed to operate on a coding intrinsic to the molecules themselves. We knew that life throughout the universe would be very similar, and that some force appeared to dictate that it be so.

But that didn't keep the sight of the Sentinels from knocking most of us right off our pins.

Lisa Hayes, *Recollections*

THE DEVIL WHO WAS FENDING RICK OFF WASN'T QUITE the one from Old Testament scare stories. At least he seemed to lack the power of fire and brimstone, and was trying to reason in accented Tiresian rather than condemning Rick to the Lower Depths and Agony Everlasting.

"Release me! Unhand me!"

All Rick could see was a grinning, slightly demonic face from which horns grew. Then Rick felt himself pulled away with such strength that he thought the massive Vince Grant or even Breetai himself had laid hands on him.

To Rick's astonishment it was Lang, carefully but forcefully preventing a diplomatic catastrophe.

The Protoculture, working through him? the young admiral wondered.

The air was clearing and a riot had been averted. The Humans' jaws dropped in wonder as the Sentinels presented themselves.

"I am Veidt, of Haydon IV," the robed one—the one who had refused Lisa's hand—said. "And as I was about to say, I cannot offer you my hand, for I have none, nor have I arms, as you understand the concept. Yet, I welcome your words of friendship, and reaffirm mine." Veidt floated down the ramp toward them and inclined his head solemnly.

Lisa, finding no words, returned the gesture.

The envoys from the Sentinels adjourned with those of the REF to a big, round table, set out at the council's decree, under the jade glow of crescent Fantoma in the long Tiresian night. The area was lit by banks of illuminator grids, and by the odd-looking, two-legged Tiresian searchlights.

Human servitors brought trays of food and drink, and some of the Sentinels showed no reluctance about helping themselves, though others declined, having different nutritive requirements.

Great Breetai, his oversized chair creaking ominously beneath him, noticed figures pressed against viewports and observation domes in the thrown-together battleship. At his suggestion, a wide assortment of provisions was placed in the airlocks; the Sentinel envoys were loud in their thanks, and mentioned, almost as a matter unworthy of discussion, that they had been on near-starvation rations.

The beings who looked like male and female bears walking around on broad, elephantine feet—and wearing harnesses that supported cases and pouches and hand weapons of some sort—were Karbarrans.

Veidt and his mate Sarna were from Haydon IV, a revelation that made Cabell and Rem exchange significant glances that Lang and the others didn't have time to question them about. All of a sudden, Micronized Zentraedi seemed about as Human as most in-laws, Jack Baker reflected, looking on from the sidelines.

The couple who looked like they were made of living crystal were from a world called Spheris. And the big, supremely proud and athletic women in the daring, barbaric gladiatorial outfits, Gnea and Bela, came from the planet Praxis.

Karen Penn, watching from her vantage point on the roof of a commo van, stared in fascination at a foxlike pair, known as "Gerudans." They had feet whose tripartite structure reminded her of a hat-rack's base, and their mouths and snouts were hidden by complex breathing apparatus. Gerudans liked to thrash their long, luxuriant tails when they talked, and on-the-spot adaptations had to be done on their chairs to accommodate them.

Cabell and Exedore had helped Lang and a scratch task force from G-2 Intel and G-5 Community Affairs prepare translation programs for interpreter computers, but in general the envoys managed with broken Tiresian. Most of the REF spoke a Zentraedi-modified version of the language, and virtually everyone in the SDF-3 had had some exposure to it, while all the Sentinels spoke it—as Breetai had said, a lingua franca.

One of the first things to become clear was that the Sentinels weren't an army, or a governmental body—they were fugitives.

"Fugitives from the Invid tyranny," Veidt said in his whispery, processed-sounding voice. The voice came from no source Lisa could detect; Veidt and Sarna did not have mouths, but they could be heard and they were being recorded.

"Haydon IV, Karbarra, Peryton, Geruda, Praxis, Spheris—our homes are worlds under the Invid heel, to one degree or another. The ship in which we arrived was to be our prison, a sort of—zoo? No, what's the word?— trophy case! Yes, and the hundreds and hundreds of us aboard, its artifacts—all for the pleasure of the Invid Regent."

"And what happened?" inquired Justine Huxley, former United Earth Government Superior Court Judge, now a council member. Her tone was neutral, from years of habit. "What changed your circumstances?"

Lang noted that Burak of Peryton—the devil-horned one—the only Sentinel with neither mate nor companion, had looked fretful throughout the getting-acquainted proceedings. Now he slammed a six-fingered hand—equipped with a second opposable thumb where the edge of a human's hand would be—on the table and raised a whistling, furious voice.

"What do the details matter? We overcame our captors, and took the ship! And for every minute we delay here, every minute we wait, sentient beings suffer and die under the Regent's savagery! Our instruments have shown us your battles; you should recognize by now that the Regent will never offer you peace, or even a truce!

"Here you sit with your dimensional fortress all but disabled. You don't dare wait for the Regent to bring the battle to you, do you deny it? Very well! Help *us* bring it to *him*! Join us, for our sake and your own survival!"

The wicked points of Burak's horns seemed to be vibrating. He glared at them with pupilless, irisless eyes from beneath heavily boned brows. "Help us for the sake of those who are in slavery and anguish, and dying, even at this moment!"

Something was plainly tearing at Burak's guts, and Rick was afraid the Perytonian was going to come across the round table at somebody. But Lron, the big male of the two bearish Karbarrans, laid a weighty hand on Burak's shoulder, and he quieted.

Nearly Breetai's height, but far heavier, Lron looked around with what he perhaps meant as an amiable smile. On him, though, it was rather scary, at least as far as Rick was concerned—with those ferocious teeth, so long and white and keen.

Lron had lowered his heavy goggles, leaving them to hang loosely at his throat. He said in his gruff, moist, somehow mournful growl, "What Burak has said, we've all made a solemn pledge to carry out. No matter what the cost, we will fight until we win or the very last one among us is dead. Maybe you, in this REF, don't understand, but you would, I think, if you spent weeks or months in cages —animals, exhibits for the Invid's pleasure."

Lron's mate, Crysta, uttered a deep, gurgling snarl, a noise like the draining of some underground lake system. Like her husband/mate, she had horns suggesting diminutive mushrooms sprouting from her forehead.

Crysta added, "We buried at space many more of us than survived; such was the care the Invid meted out to us. You may ask why we survivors made a *pact*, to call ourselves the Sentinels—a Zentraedi term, and we hope you comprehend it.

"Sentinels. The Watchmen. The sentries who say, 'This place, I protect! *Protect with my life!* Meddle here, and you start a war only one of us can survive!'"

Crysta was in full roar now. The Humans could smell her fur and muskiness. Lisa was pale, mesmerized, wondering if anything the universe could create was more awesome than an angry she-bear.

Crysta lapsed into her own language, and computers supplied the translation. "The Regent and his Invid have had their way! And now here is a war only one side can survive!"

Crysta deliberately drew her paw-hand toward her over the gleaming Tiresian wood of the round table, her nonretractile claws digging in. Corkscrew shavings of wood curled up between her fingers, lacquered on one side, naked and unfinished on the other.

When the squeal of the tortured wood had died away, Baldan, the living gemstone from the planet Spheris, spoke to fill the silence. "Will you help us? We need supplies, weapons, and allies."

"What is your plan?" Justine Huxley asked. She maintained that neutral voice, but Rick could see compassion on her face.

"First, to liberate Karbarra. There, we can reactivate the weapons mills and arm ourselves completely. Next, open the prison camps of Praxis, where thousands upon thousands of warriors wish only to exact revenge for what has been done to them."

"Then we liberate Peryton!" Burak said, pounding his strange fist.

Baldan ignored him, and Rick saw that the Sentinels weren't all of a single mind. "Eventually, after Geruda and Spheris are freed, we'll have certain knowledge we require to free Haydon IV—and then we'll be ready for the campaign to liberate Peryton. In the course of this war, we will battle the Invid, of course—perhaps we will even defeat them.

"But if not, our united planets will hunt down the Regent, and force him to surrender or die."

While the Plenipotentiary Council withdrew to discuss the Sentinels' request, Lisa, Rick, and a few others were offered a tour of the peculiar spacecraft.

Poor Lang seemed torn in two, as his determination to sway the council fought against his passionate desire to examine the ship. As it turned out, though, there was something much more immediate to worry about.

"Confirmed enemy spacecraft approaching on definite attack vector, I say again, definite attack vector," a loudspeaker announced. Sirens and warning whoopers were sounding. Humans and Zentraedi looked to the Sentinels suspiciously.

"It must be the Invid Pursuer," Burak grated.

"But we destroyed the Pursuer!" Baldan cried. "Our instruments confirmed it!"

"Then they were in error," Burak shot back. "We destroyed a decoy, perhaps."

"What's this all about?" Rick demanded. "What's a

Pursuer?" Lisa was busy on a commo patch, making certain that the SDF-3 was at battle stations.

Exedor explained, "The Pursuer is a weapon the Invid used in the days when their empire was vast and powerful; I am surprised that there are any left."

"Perhaps this is the last," Lron grunted. "When we rebelled and took the ship, we destroyed its escort vessel, but not before it loosed its Pursuer at us. For two days we dodged and fought the Pursuer, and thought we'd obliterated it, but now it has found us once more."

Edwards had come up, his skullpiece throwing back Fantoma's glow and the glare of the Ambler searchlights. "Well, it's not going to trouble anybody much longer; not when my Ghost Riders are through with it."

"No!" Exedore barked. He turned to Lisa. "Admiral, mere Veritechs haven't the firepower to deal with a Pursuer. This is a weapon even the Zentraedi feared! Your GMU cannon, even the SDF-3's primary weapon—none of these have sufficient power to penetrate its shields! It is relentless, and once it finds its target . . ."

He gazed up at the Sentinel ship. "It will detonate with enough force to rupture Tirol's crust."

"Yes," Baldan the glittering Spherian said sadly. "Since its seeking mechanism is locked onto our ship, there is only one answer: we shall lead it away, into deepspace once more, and try to deal with it there."

"Is that any way for allies to talk?" Judge Huxley frowned, coming over to them from where the council had abruptly adjourned. She smiled at the surprise on their faces. "The Sentinels and the REF are now officially *involved*. The vote was five to four."

"Madam," Exedore got out, unable to express himself, knowing hers had been the swing vote. In a wave of emotion, he took her hand, pressing his lips to it, as he had seen Humans do. When he realized what he was doing, Exedore nearly swooned.

"If the SDF-3's main gun and the GMU's and the VT ordnance isn't enough to zap this Pursuer," Rick was saying, "what about throwing everything at it at once? We can lead it into the crossfire with the Sentinels' ship."

There was no time to try to come up with a better plan; the Pursuer was only minutes away. Once again, Lisa found herself in overall control; she was on the SDF-3 patch-in right away, ordering the dimensional fortress to leave orbit and swing low for the ambush.

There was no time to process orbital ballistics and computer data; she calculated variables and unknowns and, with a guess and a prayer, set the moment when the trap would be sprung. It was not far off.

"Somebody'll have to go along with our new *friends*," Edwards said with a sharkish grin. Plainly, he meant to be that one; to make early inroads with these creatures. Privately, he saw it as a possible means toward his own ends.

But Rick Hunter said, "Forget it, General. You look after the TIC and your Ghost Team." He turned to Lisa. "Admiral, I'm the logical one to go."

He had her there; Rick knew how the SDF-3's nerve centers operated, how the strikes would be coordinated and carried out, the proper command procedure for orchestrating the whole business from the Sentinels' end . . .

And he looks so happy at the chance to risk his life, Lisa thought. She almost hated him at that moment, but she was a flag-rank officer with more important things to do.

"Carry on," she said, her jaw muscles jumping. Rick saluted, turned, and dashed up the ramp along with the Sentinels.

CHAPTER
FOUR

With the death of Zor, the grand Tiresian design to sow the Flower of Life among the stars came to a stop. In fact, in most cases it was reversed. The Flower couldn't be made to prosper where it didn't wish to, and couldn't be coerced. The shrinking, embattled Tiresian empire was forced to divert its resources to its fight for survival.

The Invid/Robotech Masters conflict that had promised to engulf the galaxy collapsed. The fighting on that side of the Milky Way shrank to the few remaining Haydon's Worlds, where a handful of Flower-viable spots still remained.

There was a pattern at work, but none of the combatants had eyes with which to see it.

Jan Morris, *Solar Seeds, Galactic Guardians*

ONE OF THE PRIME SELECTIVE CRITERIA FOR REF personnel had been a capacity to function in crisis and under severe stress. As hasty preparations were made to bushwhack the Pursuer, the Ref showed its mettle.

Not only did arrangements have to be made to have the SDF-3 and the GMU in precisely the right place at precisely the right time, but a makeshift commo/data link to the Sentinels' ship had to be established. In addition, large numbers of Humans and Zentraedi had to be redeployed, Protoculture weapons fire missions had to be laid on, and VTs had to be hot-scrambled and correctly positioned.

Lisa, being shuttled to the GMU with the council because there was no time to rejoin her ship, was even too busy to think about how things might never be the same again between her and Rick.

Entering the Sentinels' ship, Rick was assailed by strange sights and even stranger smells.

He had little time to look around as he pounded along behind Lron and Burak and the rest, but from what he could see, the vessel was anything but sophisticated. The air was thick with a solvent smell. Welds and power routing and systemry interfaces, even accounting for the fact that it was alien, all seemed so *makeshift*.

Lron had howled orders back at the ramp, and now the ship tremored as its engines came up. Rick fought down a flood of doubt; maybe this wasn't as good as being in the cockpit of an Alpha, but it sure beat vegetating down in the SDF-3's Tactical Information Center!

Still, this alien scow was a strange piece of machinery; there were safety valves venting steam, bundles of cable looping overhead in different directions, mazes of ducting and conduit everywhere he looked, and even—

He skidded to a stop as Lron and the rest made a sharp right turn at a junction of passageways. Rick found himself staring into what appeared to be a Karbarran version of perdition.

Or at least something close enough to pass. Rick saw dozens of Karbarrans shoveling tremendous scoops of some kind of fuel into furnaces that seemed to be burning in colors of the spectrum Rick had never seen before. Whatever the fuel was, it was piled high in bunkers nearby; the Karbarrans might have been stokers in a nineteeth-century ironclad, allowing for their thick goggles and long, gleaming teeth.

Rick stood transfixed, breathing the stench of singed fur.

Suddenly, Lron's enormous paw closed around his arm, and he was yanked off toward the bridge. The trip showed him more of the same mismatched machinery. He recalled

Lron saying that the Sentinels' ship had been put together as a sort of aggregate trophy for the Regent, but this was carrying things rather far.

Then he was shoved into a cramped elevator thick with the odor of machine lubricants and metal filings. Whatever the occupancy limit was, the group exceeded it, and Rick found himself pressed up against Bela, the taller—six foot eight or so, he estimated—and brawnier of the two amazons from Praxis.

Her body showed the definition of a bodybuilder's; the pleasant scent of some kind of skin oil or balm emanated from her. While most of her definitely looked Human, Bela's eyes resembled those of an eagle.

He was acutely aware that her skimpy ceremonial fighting costume left a lot of skin exposed, and that a good deal of it, along with metallic bosses and leather-set gems, was pressed up against his uniform. To the primary mission of dealing with the Pursuer a most important secondary one was added: making sure Lisa never found out about the elevator ride.

Bela smiled at him, showing white, even teeth and deep-dish dimples. "Welcome aboard the—" Here she used a word that his translator chip rendered as *Farrago*.

"Thanks for throwing in with us, Admiral," Bela added. "You're as brave as any woman I ever met."

"Um. Thanks . . ." was all Rick managed to say before the lift door spiraled open and the group charged out onto the bridge. The bridge was a blister of transparent material, a few hundred feet through its long axis, fifty across, set high up and forward on the bizarre megastructure of the *Farrago*.

In the few seconds he had to look around, Rick noticed the same design contrasts he had seen on the rest of the ship. Then he spotted the command station of the *Farrago*.

"Why am I not surprised?" Rick asked himself aloud, walking toward it slowly, almost unwillingly.

"Gorgeous, isn't it?" Lron grunted heartily. "It's Karbarran, of course."

Of course. Who else but the hulking bears could spin a wooden ship's wheel ten feet in diameter? The wheel was made of polished purple wood, set with fittings of white brass. It looked like a giant carved spider with extra legs that had suffered rigor mortis and had an enormous hoop affixed to all its ankles.

"Sentinels' flagship, do you copy?" Lisa's voice was saying over the commo. The Praxians and Karbarrans and Gerudans and others who had been manning the communications consoles made way for Rick as he walked over, in a daze, to respond.

The mike resembled an old-fashioned gramophone horn. A beautifully luminous Spherian woman showed him how to throw the beer-tap lever so that he could transmit. "This is the *Farrago*, reading you five-by-five, Admiral. When does the party start?"

That drew a low chuckle from Gnea, Bela's younger sidekick—who looked like a giant sixteen-year-old—and an amused rumble from Lron. Lisa answered, "We're ready when you are. Lift off, meet the Pursuer at altitude one hundred thousand or so, and bring him back here in a pass from magnetic east to west, altitude three thousand feet, is that clear? We've accessed old Zentraedi battle tapes; maintain a distance of at least ten thousand feet from your attacker at all times! Do you roger, *Farrago*?"

Rick repeated the instructions word for word, then it seemed like there was nothing to say. The Sentinel ship rumbled and quaked, then it was airborne, blasting away into the sky, and still he couldn't decide what it was he wanted to say to his wife. "We still owe each other that waltz, Lisa," he finally blurted.

There was a silent hesitation at the other end of the link, then the brief throb of her laughter. "You rat! Watch your tail."

* * *

The Pursuer was the last of its kind.

Deployed now for a kill in atmosphere, it resembled an umbrella blown inside out by the wind, its fabric stripped away. It plunged toward its prey only to find that its prey was rising to meet it.

It hadn't been an easy hunt; the Pursuer had been created to home in on the Protoculture systemry of an enemy and eliminate the target, but the bizarre ship it had been stalking fit no known profile. Sometimes *Farrago* was a target; sometimes it simply wasn't.

And so the silent duel had been waged across the light-years, the Pursuer stymied again and again, frustrated by the lifethings in the ship it hunted. But now the kill was near; soon the Pursuer would know the detonation/orgasm/death for which its guiding AI sentience longed.

But now its prey seemed to be coming directly toward it, and that felt wrong. But then the Sentinels' ship did a shuddering wing-over, and plunged back toward the low-hanging pall of Tirol's atmosphere. The Pursuer plunged after, ardently.

"They track Protoculture, y'see," Lron was bellowing above the noise of reentry, holding Rick down with one hand and spinning the cyclopean wheel with the other—and a little help from Crysta. "That's how we could keep the Pursuer at bay for so long: we don't *run* on Protoculture!"

The atmosphere was giving *Farrago* a radical case of the shakes; crewbeings smaller than the Karbarrans were being jostled around just like Rick. The bridge was bedlam. "W-what *do* you run on?" Rick managed to ask.

The word Lron snarled in his guttural basso wasn't one Rick had heard in Zentraedi before, and he managed to query the thin, chip-size translating package clipped to his dress uniform lapel.

"Peat!" it rendered. Rick tapped the transmitter a few times to make sure it was not malfunctioning. He was about to ask for another translation when the bridge screens were filled with the horror of the Pursuer plunging down at them. The *Farrago* turned over and dove back toward Tirol's surface.

Rick was feeding course information through to the TIC, and trying not to calculate his own chances. The Sentinels' ship had risen high into the light of Valivarre and Fantoma, but it was falling back quickly. One good thing Rick noted was that the Sentinels' vessel, like the SDF-3, had artificial gravity, and so he wasn't likely to get sick before the Pursuer vaporized him.

Suddenly the Pursuer appeared again, looking like an enormous squid about to swallow a minnow. Rick shook off his sense of unreality and slugged Lron in the arm to get his attention. "How come it can track us now?"

Lron made *wuff*ing sounds of amusement. "We set up a Protoculture homing device in the center of the ship, see?"

Rick saw; it was a beacon on the computer-driven schematics off to one side. "Listen, Lron: I've been doing some thinking, and—"

He was interrupted as an especially heavy blow from the Tiresian atmosphere nearly sent him sprawling; Lron had caught him. Amazons and crystal people and foxlike Gerudans were struggling out of the heap they had ended up in.

"—and if this Pursuer of yours had the kind of warhead you're talking about, we're gonna end up fried right along with it when the SDF-3 and the GMU start blazing!"

Lron's muscles stood out against his pelt as he wrestled the wheel around, while holding Rick in place with his free hand. "Do you think we're *stupid*?"

"No-no-no," Rick responded weakly, as Lron spun the gargantuan wheel and the ship took up its approach.

The Pursuer had its target at last: a bright, strobing Protoculture marker at the center of *Farrago*. It plunged down. It knew its opponent's performance profile from computer analysis and hard experience, knew that the lumbering Sentinel vessel couldn't possibly pull out of its dive or avoid the final destruction of Pursuer's detonation.

The guidance AI's death was near; it cut in auxiliaries, eager for that moment.

Rick clung to the wooden wheel, looking back through the bridge's clear blister to where the Pursuer was already a discernible speck in the cosmos.

Lron virtually *handed* Rick over to Crysta. "You're right!" Standing at the wheel, the bear-being pressed the titanic circle against its stem, deepening the dive. "It's almost time to go! Well? Tell your mate and your people! That thing will be in their laps in another minute!"

Rick struggled to be heard over the winds that bucked and jostled the ship. "What're you talking about? It's following *us*!"

Lron made a sawing sound that Rick took as laughter. "No time to explain! Hold on!"

Rick didn't have to, because Crysta scooped him up. The smell of her fur was actually rather pleasant, rather relaxing.

Rick, seeing parts of *Farrago* fly in separate directions, suppressed a certain sadness that he and the REF hadn't been able to do much to help the Invid's victims. It was just bad luck; he waited to die.

Then he saw that the bridge was *ascending*.

Lisa saw it, too, from her place in the GMU: the *Farrago* was an amalgamation of the prizes of war, and now the components had broken away.

A module like a streamlined, art-deco grasshopper arced away in one direction; a thing like a glittering bat deployed wings and banked in another. Diverse segments headed toward every point of the compass.

Suddenly, the only thing remaining where the Sentinels' ship had been was a blinking transceiver package attached to a rocketing, remote-guided paravane. It lined itself up and then glided right down into the cross hairs of SDF-3's main gun and the GMU's monster cannon, while ordnance from the VTs closed in.

The creatures so used to sleeping through the long night of Tirol in its transit behind Fantoma were stirred by the light. Something as bright and hot as a sun burned above, interrupting their hibernation.

But then the glare died, and the darkness took charge of the moonscape. The things that lived in Tiresian soil and water went back to their sleep, even though long, low-register sound waves shook them.

In the barely flightworthy framework of what had been the *Farrago*, which was attached to the big Karbarran vessel that was its largest single component, Bela wiped away the crimson seeping from the bloody nose Rick Hunter had gotten when he lost his footing.

She dabbed at it with the snow-white headband she had worn under her metal war helm. Rick looked through the blister, down at Tirol and the expanding ball of gas that had been the Pursuer, and the far-off spacecraft that had been parts of the Sentinels' battlewagon.

"When we saw through intercepted messages how soundly you Humans and your Zentraedi friends whipped the Invid on Tirol," she was telling him, "we thought you'd make good allies. But now we know for sure it's nice to meet you, friend."

She had his right hand in a kind of clasping grip, but a moment later she had his hand open, examining it, while Rick tried to make the compartment stop spinning.

"Not much callus," Bela observed. "How do you keep your sword from rubbing your skin raw?"

Rick shook his head, little neuron-firings making stars seem to orbit before his eyes, trying to figure out how to answer her.

Just then, there was an angry growl from Lron, who was overseeing the rejoining of the sundered parts of the Sentinels' ship. From what Rick could make out, it had something to do with a master junction that was located down near those impossible peat furnaces.

"Battle's over, so Crysta and Lron will be demoralized for a while," Bela said, releasing Rick's hand. "They're really quite dour, much of the time. Like all Karbarrans: morbid, always preoccupied with Fate and all of that . . ."

She snatched his hand back for a second, taking a longer look at his palm. "I don't think you're in for a very long or serene life, by the way, Admiral."

"No surprise there," he muttered, taking his hand back and frowning at it. Then he looked to Bela again. "Listen, this ship, you Sentinels—it's all so fantastic! How did you put together a fighting alliance like this? How did you assemble such a starship?"

They were on their feet once more and the other envoys had gathered round, except for Lron, who was still at the helm. "We *didn't*," Burak said. "The *Invid* did, by imprisoning us together."

When Rick asked, "But how'd you turn the tables?" everyone looked to Veidt. A moment or two elapsed while Veidt considered the question.

"I think you'd better come with us," Veidt said. "It will be more to the point to show you . . . certain things . . . than to talk about them."

A few minutes later, Rick stood at the barred cage that had once housed the ship's menagerie—Karbarrans in this case, if he was any judge of scent. But what lay moaning and clanking its shackles was nothing like any Karbarran, or any other Sentinel.

He spoke into a commo-patch mike the Sentinels had somehow crafted for him in their careless, make-do fashion. The microphone looked like some kind of jet-black motion-picture trophy, while the outlandish earphones were so big that he had to sort of drape them over his shoulders. The whole time, he was looking at the thing before him— the Sentinels' prisoner.

"Lisa, don't bother asking me to describe what they've

got here, please. Just get a couple of security platoons over to me on the double. And interpreters, recording equipment, a couple yards of anchor chain, some portable sensors—oh, babe, send the whole toyshop over here!"

He could hear a certain iciness in her voice. "Understood. Keep me posted, if you'll be so kind, Admiral."

One part of him berated itself for having hurt her feelings so; but most of Rick Hunter was simply staring, aghast, at what crouched in the cell.

CHAPTER

FIVE

> *It was almost as if I had called up something from the un-*
> *formed, the ultimate Potential, into existence. The appearance of*
> *the Sentinels was the answer to my every requirement, in the wake*
> *of the vast power I had secretly wrested from the Invid, power I*
> *was as yet unable to exercise.*
>
> *There are a few individuals in the timestream of this universe*
> *who have been granted the gift of sheer Will, to mold events ac-*
> *cording to their desire. I am one of them.*
>
> *Or perhaps, in a way, I am all of them.*
>
> General T. R. Edwards, personal journal

"NOT A MERE SCIENTIST," THE INVID CORRECTED
sharply, with a rattling of manacles that made some of the
guards put their hands to their pistol butts. "*I* am *Tesla*,
Master Scientist to the Invid Regent! Now, release me, you
pitiful lower life-forms!"

Tesla turned his huge wrists, testing the strength of the
forged-alloy shackles the Sentinels had put on him. His
grainy green skin rasped against the metal. He stretched the
three thick fingers of both hands and flexed the opposable
thumbs. "Release me, I say! Or you will feel the vengeance of the Invid!"

Tesla was a creature about ten feet tall, with a thick,

reasonably humanoid torso and limbs. But his head was a slender extension resembling a snail's snout, with two huge black liquid eyes set on either side. At the tip of the snout were two sensor antennae like glistening slugs that glowed whenever he spoke.

Rick found himself looking at those eyes, much as he tried to avoid it, while Lang and the others made their recordings and measurements. The eyes were as unemotional and unrevealing as a shark's, but they were set forward in the sluglike head. And conventional Darwinian reasoning said that the main purpose for such placement was *pursuit*—the Invid were predators.

Just like Humans.

Rick had yielded the floor to the astounded sci/tech squads from SDF-3 who had come in answer to his call, to evaluate Tesla and try to gain some kind of understanding of the bizarre turn the whole mission had taken.

Rick had a towel around his shoulders, wiping his forehead from time to time; he suddenly realized that Veidt was hovering near.

Wasn't he on the other side of the compartment a second ago? Oh, well. "Ah, Lord Veidt—"

"'Veidt' will suffice," the being corrected.

"Okay, okay, 'Veidt,' then: I guess we need to know first things first. You Sentinels aren't so much in a shooting war with the Invid as trying to put together an uprising, right?"

Veidt hesitated, and Rick threw the towel to the deck. Some of his blood was drying on it, scarlet going to rust-red. "Let's save fine distinctions for later! Am I right or am I wrong?"

"You are right," Veidt said as he and Rick and the Sentinels watched the Human sci/tech teams push and shove each other to get closer to Tesla. "Once, the Invid and the Zentraedi savaged this entire part of the galaxy, fighting their war. With the collapse of that struggle, contact with all the outlying stellar systems has been lost.

"Now, the war has boiled down to the few habitable planets in this close stellar group: Tirol, Optera, Haydon

IV, Geruda, and the rest. The ability—and perhaps the will—to venture out into the horrible aftermath of the great Invid-Zentraedi wars has been lost, Admiral.

"But, as I have said, you're right. The worlds unlucky enough to be here in the 'close stars'—accessible with non-Protoculture superluminal drives—are still under the Invid heel. Yet, time and history and the Shapings of the Proto-culture have their own rhythm, Admiral. And while the ...slavery!... we've suffered, the cruelty and mis-treatment, may not be high on your Earthly agenda, the war to free the Near Planets is the thing that unites the Sentinels in a blood oath."

Veidt was quivering like a tuning fork; Rick had thought him robotic and cold, but he now saw passion in his face. "We were in cages. Do you know what that's like, young Admiral? To be caged like an animal?

"Of course you don't! The Sentinels will accept you as allies, and enlist others who are willing to fight, but I'll tell you something, Admiral Hunter: none among us will ever feel quite the same bond with anyone who wasn't caged with us—trust them to fight, as we intend to, *until we win or until we die!*"

Rick thought for a moment about Earth history. Of monstrous freight trains and mass gas chambers. He picked the towel up off the deck, folding it carefully. "Fair enough." He looked to Veidt. "But we're going to help you. And if you want to know why, just look through our ship's history files."

Veidt nodded as if he already had. "We have all agreed to recrew this ship, if possible, and set course for Karbarra. Without delay."

"What? Wait a second!" There would have to be meet-ings; resolutions from the council, personnel allocations, resource diversion, interdivision liaison, staff meetings, marital counseling, maintenance checks...

"What d'ya *mean*, 'without delay'?"

"I mean that within twenty-four of your hours, we in-tend to depart," Veidt answered in a reasonable tone.

"Would ten days be better? Or ten months? You may multiply the beings who will die under Invid tyranny by the *minute*!"

"All right; you've made your point," Rick grunted in a sound like something Lron would make. "I guess it's doable." He was staring over at the people who seemed to be prepared to climb *into* the cage with Tesla to get good shots of him.

So that's the enemy. Or at least one form of him. "He was your, your zookeeper, right?" Rick asked Veidt.

"I think the words coincide," Veidt allowed. "Though I suppose Tesla had much more *unhappy* plans for us. Why?"

"How'd you beat him?" Rick pressed. "How'd you take the ship?"

"Ah. Well. Sarna and I were chained by the neck—no arms, of course—and fed by Invid functionaries, from beyond a line they'd drawn on the deck. But after some time we came up with a way to eradicate *their* line, and draw one of our own, a line much closer to us. The rest was even simpler than fooling the Invid."

So all this apparent limblessness didn't mean that Veidt and his kind couldn't knock some Invid out of commission, although they had perhaps used a method that had nothing to do with savate or tae kwon do. Rick filed the information in his memory, and was about to get on to matters at hand, when he heard a mighty roaring.

The Invid Master Scientist, Tesla, wasn't happy with Sentinel protocol. Praxian amazons harried him with electrified prods; Karbarran deck apes jostled him in rude fashion—preparing him for interrogation. Not a single Sentinel showed any excessive brutality, but not a single one showed the least kindness, either.

In that moment, long before his conversations with the Plenipotentiary Council or his consultations with his wife, Rick Hunter understood that the Sentinels would do just what they had pledged one another: win or die.

And he knew that he would go with them, even though

it might mean the death of his marriage. But the courage he admired in the Sentinels wasn't very much different from the courage he adored in Lisa.

The Sentinels were adamant about their departure schedule, despite the council's demand for time to mull it over. Then Miriya Sterling came up with a little salesmanship. She considered the problem with a soldier's insight, and whispered a suggestion into the ear of her husband, Max Sterling, Skull Leader. Max passed it on to Lisa.

Lisa Hayes Hunter still didn't know exactly what to feel about the Sentinels' appearance. Aside from the new crisis it had thrust upon the SDF-3, there was the striking change in Rick. But when she found herself hoping the council would vote *not* to extend aid to the revolutionaries, Lisa reminded herself of the lives being crushed and extinguished by the Invid.

So, she took Miriya's advice, and gave the Sentinel leaders a quick tour of some of the superdimensional fortress's armories in an aircar. The Karbarrans, in particular, showed their delight at the ranked mecha, howling and pounding the aircar's railing until they threatened to damage it. The pilot guided them slowly past Hovertanks and Logans, and second-generation Destroids along with armored ground vehicles and self-propelled artillery.

The women of Praxis, in particular, were loud in their praise of such wonderful war machines. Lisa felt fascinated and a little threatened by their bigger-than-life, bloodthirsty beauty. She looked to her husband from time to time; he seemed lost in thought. But she could tell, could almost hear, what he was thinking, and it made her feel empty inside.

"Amazing," Lang kept mumbling, skimming the preliminary reports from the sci/tech people and the intel teams that had gone aboard the Sentinels' flagship.

Justine Huxley, next to him at the council table, made an exasperated sound and leaned over to whisper into his ear. "Emil, please! This is crucial!"

He wanted to object, to tell her how much more fascinating his data was than more of the endless wrangling and political maneuvering the Sentinels' appearance had generated. But she was right; even the council sensed the urgency of the situation, and was moving with unaccustomed speed.

Still, there was a wealth of information the Sentinels had given the expedition teams! Take the drive of that incredible Karbarran vessel, for example. Hunter hadn't been hallucinating: it was powered by furnaces that consumed a substance analogous to peat or lignite. But the stuff seemed to be some sort of distant forerunner of the Flower of Life itself—an Ur-Flower! And then there was the half myth, half religion that surrounded the ancient being or entity known as Haydon . . .

He realized someone was addressing him. "Eh? What was that, Mr. Chairman?"

Senator Longchamps controlled his temper and began again. "I asked if, in your opinion, it would be feasible for the SDF-3 to accompany the Sentinels and lend her firepower in support of their mission."

Lang threw down his papers. "The entire idea is asinine, my dear sir! The damage we suffered is far from repaired, and it will be two years, at the very least, before our primary drive is repaired!

"But more to the point, the SDF-3 *must* remain here to insure that the mining of monopole ore goes on uninterrupted. Without Fantoma's ore, we have no way home. So you see, what the Sentinels proposed is the wisest course —the only sensible one open to us, in my opinion. We must detach what military forces we can to aid them in their cause and at the same time divert the Invid."

"I concur," Exedore said, and Justine Huxley nodded.

"You tell 'em," T. R. Edwards smirked from one side, having finished his testimony a short time before.

Edwards's sudden willingness to see SDF forces seconded to the Sentinels—his almost *eager* advocacy of the plan—perplexed and worried Exedore and some of the others. It wasn't like the man to feel compassion for non-Humans; in fact, his hatred of Zentraedi was well known, and his hostility toward Rem and Cabell was already evident.

But, Edwards saw the opportunity presented by the Sentinels' arrival as something of a miracle. The incredible secret to which he had been exposed during the first assault on Tirol had expanded his horizons until they spanned the galaxy.

With a little shrewd maneuvering, he could get rid of most or all of those who stood in his path to power. They would be out of the way for as long as the Sentinels' war lasted, and perhaps forever, given the vagaries of combat.

"We estimate that we can assign mixed forces totaling some thousand or so to the Sentinels' cause, along with mecha, equipment, and so forth, and still leave ourselves sufficient resources to defend the SDF-3, Tirol, and the mining operations on Fantoma," a G-3 operations staff officer was telling the council. "The Sentinels will need experienced senior commanders to help them plan strategy and arm, organize, and train the troops they mean to recruit as they go along."

He sat down; Justine Huxley spoke. "It comes down to this, ladies and gentlemen: shall we let these people fight for their freedom unaided? And shall we simply wait here, with the SDF-3 barely mobile, for the Invid to bring the battle to us?"

There wasn't much arguing after that; the motion was carried seven to three, with two abstentions. A G-1 personnel officer explained that records were being reviewed by computers, to pick the most appropriate people for the contingent to be assigned to the Sentinels.

"Along with the obvious criteria of combat performance and so forth," he went on, "will be such things as adaptability and mental/emotional profile—especially the capacity to work with non-Human life-forms."

Edwards hid his smile. His own aversion to aliens was

well known; there was little likelihood that he would be selected.

The meeting broke up quickly, with people hurrying off on assignments, burdened by a tremendous workload and a ridiculously close deadline. Only Edwards, shadowed by his aide, Major Benson, seemed to feel no urgency. But on his way out of the Royal Hall, he spied Colonel Wolff.

Wolff was trying to start a conversation with Lynn-Minmei, who in turn was doing her best to listen for news of what had happened at the meeting.

Edwards frowned at his rival. He murmured to himself, "Yes, Colonel. I think 'The Sentinels Need You!'"

Adams, his aide, heard, and said in a low voice, "But sir, what if Wolff doesn't volunteer?"

Edwards turned to the man, one arched brow going up, the other hidden behind his mirror-bright half mask. "Major, everyone in the SDF-3 is *already* a volunteer."

> *One of the Karbarran scientists was named Obu, and I posed
> to him some questions about the amazing Ur-Flower-powered
> starship they had arrived in. I asked him why the ursinoids had to
> actually handle the stuff for the process to work.*
>
> *His answer, even with help from a translating chip, was, "The
> Sekiton's [ ] likes our [ ] and then fondly yields up the conversion
> that permits the [ ] to take place and delights in energy being
> bestowed."*
>
> *Fortunately, scientists don't live or die according to their abil-
> ity to figure things out; they just want to try.*
>
> Exedore, *SDF-3 and Me*

TWENTY-FOUR HOURS WERE NOT ENOUGH, BUT THE
Sentinels would only push back their departure time on an
hour-by-hour basis.

Preparations for the Sentinels' campaign had people
working around the clock. The first lists of personnel assigned to the Sentinels appeared only two hours after the
end of the council meeting.

Anyone on the list had the option of applying for a de-
ferment; fewer then twenty percent did so.

Lang was one of those who *knew* his name wouldn't
appear on the list. Despite his vast curiosity about the

things that lay ahead for the liberators, he knew he could not go along.

At his request, Janice Em interrupted her labors as a computer operator and gofer for the Council Advisory Staff, and joined him in his office. He was alone, sipping tea, when she got there. She refused the offer of some orange mandarin, but accepted a chair.

Janice felt an undercurrent—not fear, but a reaction to Lang that she could never pin down. She knew he had been her friend for a long time, and that she trusted him implicitly. Still, she always felt things crowding on the edge of her consciousness, things she couldn't name, when he looked at her like this. After a little small talk Lang put down his cup and saucer and leaned very close to her. Janice wanted to move away, or tell Dr. Lang to, but found that she couldn't speak, and somehow hated the unfairness of it . . .

"Janice," he said evenly. "Retinal scan."

The part of her that was the conscious Janice Em slipped away, even as her eyes took on an inner glow that grew quite bright for a moment, then faded.

When it was gone, her eyes and face had lost all animation, and her skin its color and tautness. "ID confirmed, Dr. Lang. Your request."

Lang blinked a bit from the dazzle of her ID scan. "Janice, I have arranged for you to be selected to accompany the Sentinels' mission. You will accept the assignment."

"Yes, Doctor."

"Bring back all relevant data, with particular attention to Protoculture, the Flower of Life, Zor, the Invid Regis and Regent, and the nature and activities of the Robotech Masters."

"Of course, sir."

Lang rubbed his eyes. What else? "Oh yes: I am also *extremely* interested in matters pertaining to the life-form, being, or mythical figure known as 'Haydon.' Gather all pertinent data."

"I will, Dr. Lang."

"Good. Now hold still a moment . . ."

Lang reached behind her neck to remove the dermal plug concealed by her thick fall of pale lavender hair. He inserted a jack into the access port there, and began a high-speed transferral of information.

Janice was the most sophisticated android ever created, the crowning achievement of decades of work. She was programmed with a wealth of skills and abilities, but she was going forth now as part of a military expedition. Lang was giving her as much combat programming as he could, and he regretted that he would be forced to break up the formidable weapon of Janice and Minmei, and the tremendous effect of their harmonies.

But it couldn't be helped; Minmei simply wouldn't be permitted to go along on the liberation campaign, and Lang *had* to have an absolutely trustworthy agent on the scene.

He had detached the jack and replaced the dermal plug when there was a knock at his door. With a word, he transformed the android back into a woman. He was stroking her hair back into place when the door opened.

Apparently, it wasn't a Praxian custom to wait for permission to enter a private chamber. Bela stood there, with a large Terran book in her sinewy right hand. She was looking strangely at Lang and Janice, as Janice blinked and resumed coherent thought. Bela was wearing a two-handed short sword with a well-worn grip, and a basket-hilted knife with a foot-long blade.

"Is this some sexual rite?" she asked, her hawk eyes moving from one to the other, with no sign of embarrassment. "Should I leave?"

"No, no, er," Lang hastened to hand Janice a packet of notes he had prepared. "Miss Em was simply picking up some receipted documents for the Council Advisory Staff."

Janice seemed a little dazed, but recovered in moments. "Yes. I'll hand-deliver them and bring back your receipt, Doctor."

"That would be fine, my dear."

Bela's gull-wing brows furrowed, and when Janice had

left, she scrutinized Lang with a certain distant attention.

Lang considered her: a magnificent specimen, wasp-waisted, full-hipped and high-breasted, dressed, if that was what one would call it, in an ensemble of leather and metal that left her more naked than clothed.

So far, Rick Hunter had kept the Praxians separated from the SDF-3's self-appointed Romeos, but Lang assumed that some very interesting, and perhaps robust, social dynamics would come into play somewhere down the line on the Sentinel mission. Of course, Lang assured himself, he was above all that sort of thing. However, he couldn't help but admire Bela's amazing length of leg, her incredible abdominal definition . . .

He shook himself just a bit, blinking, just as Janice Em had only moments before. "How may I help you, er, Bela?"

She put her book down on one of his lab tables, handling it reverently. "I found this in one of your lore-houses. You know this creature?"

She had opened the mythology textbook to a series of photos and lithos of Pegasus, and similar winged horses. Bela tapped one photoplate with a spatulate fingernail that wasn't altogether clean. "You recognize this?"

Lang nodded. "But this is a . . . a creature that never truly existed. It's only a fairy tale."

Bela was nodding impatiently. "Yes, yes, that's been explained to me! But we Praxians have such creatures in our legendry, too. Or at least, near enough. They are icons of tremendous power, and their appearance signifies a time when every Praxian must do her utmost, a time of decision, and ultimate sacrifice."

Bela carefully closed the book, then looked at Lang. She wasn't sure what to think of this fey Earther, with his eyes that were all pupil, and the reek of Protoculture Shaping steaming off him. The image of the winged horse had taken hold of her, though.

"You and your teams have the power to shape new mecha. I've seen your SDF-3 production machines work wonders. Can they make me such a mecha, such a *winged* mecha? On Praxis, this creature would be worth a thousand rousing speeches, a million brave words!"

Lang pretended to be considering the proposal, but deep inside he had already been swayed. The Tokyo Center's teams had studied Robotech adaptations to quadruped models in great detail, and surely the equine data was in the SDF-3's memory banks. But winged horses weren't the optimal mecha for going up against Invid terror weapons and Enforcer skirmish ships. Especially sky-steeds ridden by wild women brandishing swords and lances.

However, if a Robotech Pegasus would have the kind of motivational impact Bela was claiming, it would be well worth the effort. Besides, the idea intrigued him, and he was pretty sure there were still some horse behavioral engrams lying around somewhere in the memory banks.

"Very well. Come back in, oh, say, forty-eight hours, and I'll have it ready for you."

Her eyes went very wide, but Bela had been told that Lang promised nothing that he couldn't deliver. She set her winged-owl helm down on the book, clapped her right hand to the sword on her left hip, and took Lang's right hand with her left, holding it to her heart.

"By the Eternal She and the Glory of Haydon, your enemies are mine, your debts are mine, your praise is mine to sing, and my life is yours."

Lang, so used to hearing false words from the council, and from most of the ship's aspiring politicians, heard the unaccustomed bell tone of truth then. It was like some half-forgotten song.

He was trying to get hold of himself, trying to pull his hand away from its sublime resting place without seeming to. He mumbled something about having to hold onto her helm for a day or two for the installation of control receptors.

The mind-boost of his long-ago exposure to raw Protoculture hadn't changed him from a man *that* much, and he was feeling certain inhibitions start to drop away.

Then Bela had let go of him. Lang's automatic, ironclad control reasserted itself—but for a moment he didn't know whether to be happy about that, or sad.

In one of the largest compartments of the SDF-3, a much-repaired and refurbished monolith of Zentraedi technology glowed and sent out deep, almost subsonic tones.

Exedore looked up at it worriedly. The Protoculture sizing chamber was perhaps the last that could still function, certainly the only one the Expeditionary Force had. Constructed for the Zentraedi fleet back when the miracles of Zor were commonplace, it was, like the Protoculture matrices, one of the few pieces of technology that combined Human-Zentraedi efforts could not duplicate.

Exedore held his breath. Monitoring indicators were already reading in the danger zone, but it was too late to stop the transformation now.

Returning Micronized Zentraedi to full, giant size, so that they could mine the monopole ore of Fantoma, had been a tricky business. The sizing chamber had already been pressed far beyond its rated limits. Without exception, the Zentraedi on the SDF-3 mission had volunteered —practically demanded—to be part of the mining operation. All were badly needed down on the giant world —all except one.

The rest had gone before, naturally; it was a commander's prerogative and honor to take on the greatest risk. And so Exedore, the one Zentraedi who must remain Micronized, waited and worried while the giant among giants underwent the trial of the sizing chamber.

Readings were all at maximum and some were beyond, yet the sizing chamber somehow held together. Then the semicylindrical door opened in an outrushing cloud of icy gas and billowing Protoculture brimstone.

Great Breetai stepped forth.

He was naked, of course, but turned to accept the clothing and skullpiece an aide brought to him. Exedore tried not to stare at the destroyed portion of the right side of his lord's face.

Sixty feet tall, Breetai squared his gargantuan shoulders and breathed so deeply that it seemed to lower the pressure of the compartment. He glanced around him as he fitted on the skullpiece. "So, Exedore! It worked!" He stretched, and his titanic muscles creaked like mill wheels; his joints cracked like cannon shots; the muscles of his back rose and spread like some bird of prey spreading its wings.

Breetai threw his head back and let forth a laugh that made the bulkheads quake. "Now we go back to where it all began, eh? Back to Fantoma! And Zarkopolis!"

Exedore nodded measuredly. "*You* do, my lord."

Breetai nodded, suddenly solemn. "But don't fear, my friend: when there's no more need for you on the SDF-3, you'll rejoin us at your true size!"

Exedore's first impulse was to shake his head and tell his friend and master the truth. The sizing chamber had *given up the ghost*, as the Humans would say. *That's all she wrote!* Why did human soldiers use that wording? Exedore had never investigated the matter. What's that other phrase? "*The last hurrah!*"

Hurrah!

But Breetai was in high spirits, and no amount of agonizing could change what Exedore read from his instruments. The sizing chamber would never work again.

The Zentraedi miners, Breetai, and Exedore would remain as they were forever.

Exedore, looking away from his lord to the huge panorama of Fantoma hanging there in the sky, hid his despair. He would never stand by his lord's shoulder again; he was forever Micronized, an insect by Zentraedi standards.

Exedore braced himself, smiled up at his lord, as brave as any samurai. "One or two things to attend to, my lord." He grinned. "And then, I shall be my true size."

Rick had just left the bridge and was signing off on an intel update when someone passing by in the other direction pressed a packet into the forearm-load of stuff Rick was holding, saying only, "Unit patches, sir."

It took him a few minutes before he could turn his attention to what he was holding. From the square red courier packet, he pulled a dozen insignia, holding them fanned out like a bridge hand.

They were all the same: rampant eagles face-to-face, with the legend SENTINELS at the bottom, and a crowned medieval jousting helmet at the top. The main part was a skull alongside a tip-uppermost sword that had a viper twined around it.

It didn't look at all like anything the Military Heraldry Institute would come up with. It looked more like the logo of some old time rock band. "Hey, who the hell approved . . ."

But he realized he was talking to himself; the companionway was empty. Everyone had gone off on their errands, and the mysterious patch deliverer was long gone.

Rick considered the patch again, giving particular attention to the skull. And the serpent.

What does all this mean?

Behind him, a hatch opened as a marine announced, "The admiral is off the bridge." Then there was the swift securing of the gas-tight hatch; Rick Hunter and Lisa Hayes Hunter were standing there looking at each other in the unflattering light of companionway glowtubes.

Lisa looked tired, looked *old*, it occurred to Rick—the same way he had looked after leading Skull Team in sustained combat.

"May I see?" she asked after a moment. He couldn't figure out what she meant for a second, until he realized that he was clutching the Sentinels' insignia. "I think they're sorta unofficial," he said, fumbling a bit, shifting burdens, then extending one toward her.

How do these things get decided? he wondered. Apparently the lower orders—the enlisted ranks, and perhaps a few NCOs—had made up their minds. So, the Military Heraldry Institute would have something quirky to fit into its grand scheme—provided anybody got back to Earth alive to tell about it.

Rick looked more closely at one of the patches, admiring the stitching—trying to avoid Lisa's eyes. Somebody had reprogrammed the automated garment manufacturing equipment in fine detail. The skull was a leering, bleached thing with sketchy ridge-lines, the sword sort of shiny in silver-white thread, the snake convincingly constrictor-looking, the eagles strikingly noble and angry.

Not bad. So, at least somebody had a little esprit de corps. Somebody way down in the ranks, maybe somebody who had befriended Lron or Veidt or the others.

And now this is our emblem, take it or leave it. He put down his various bundles and held the patch up against the breast of his uniform's torso harness, over his heart, where the duty patch went.

"Not bad," Lisa echoed his thought, reminding Rick she was there. She looked him in the eye, not so tired now that she was alone with him, and they shared a slow smile together. Rick suddenly remembered why they were in love.

Then she held the Sentinels' insignia over her own SDF-3 duty patch, studying his reaction. "How does it look?"

He drew a quick breath and then turned away from her for a split second, gathering himself and making sure he had heard correctly. His heart pounded; he had thought he was about to lose her. But she was telling him, in her own way, that she was coming along on *Farrago*.

What words were appropriate? None . . .

They took one another's hand and went to the Captain's quarters. There were not too many hours left until the Sentinels' flagship must leave.

They had some packing to do, but that could wait a while.

By order of the Plenipotentiary Council and in accordance with applicable military regulations, the following personnel are assigned detached duty with the XT Force designated "The Sentinels":

Baker, Jack R., Ensign
Grant, Vincent G., Lieutenant Commander
Grant, Jeanne W., Lieutenant Commander (Med)
Hunter, Lisa Hayes, Admiral
Hunter, Richard B., Rear Admiral
Penn, Karen L., Ensign
Sterling, Maximilian A., Commander
Sterling, Miriya P., Lieutenant Commander
Wolff, Jonathan B., Colonel

(Excerpted from seconding orders, mission "Sentinels," UEG starship SDF-3.)

YOU CAN HANDLE IT," LISA ASSURED COMMANDER —now Captain—Forsythe. She concentrated on tossing a few last possessions into a ditty bag. Her quarters—hers and Rick's—were so stark and cold now, stripped of decor and furnishings, ready for Captain Raul Forsythe, the new occupant.

Forsythe ran his hand over a forehead rubbed smooth of hair by decades of military-cap sweatbands. "I *know* I can handle it, Lisa; I'm just not so sure I can do it as well jumping in flat-footed like this. You know how many people alive have *ever* commanded a superdimensional fortress? Only one: you."

"Then, it's time there were two." She stopped, having come across something under the blotter on Rick's desk. It was a laminated snapshot of Lisa as a teenager, looking adorable, with a kitten perched precariously on her head. She had given it to him in a moment when she had thought it was all over between them; she felt a tremendous burst of love for him, discovering that he had kept it so close to him all this time.

Admiral Lisa Hayes drew a breath to keep from sniffling. "Um, Captain—*sir*, remember what you taught me at the academy? The first day, I think it was."

Forsythe allowed himself a chuckle. "That business about not 'consolidating knowledge or expertise in such fashion as to present a tactical disadvantage in event of death, disabling, or disappearance of senior personnel' *wasn't* supposed to apply to putting me in the hot seat, Admiral. Lisa."

Lisa ran her forefinger along the seam of her duffel bag, its microfield sealing up behind as if she had touched it with a magic wand. She hoisted the duffel, grunting a little, and Forsythe somehow restrained himself from the lèse-majesté of snatching luggage away from his admiral in macho assistance.

The bag landed next to Rick's: two remarkably small bundles of strictly personal possessions. Lisa looked back to Forsythe. "Captain, you've got more time in the service than I've got in *life*; we both know that. You'll do fine. If you have any questions, ask the bridge gang; enlisted ratings run that damn place anyway. Mr. Blake and I just let outsiders think otherwise." That notwithstanding, Blake was accompanying her on the *Farrago*.

Forsythe laughed a little, and then Lisa did, too. He remembered the terribly intense and *focused* cadet—daughter of another Admiral Hayes—who had come to the academy as a gawky, pale, set-jawed, frightened midshipman.

She put her hand on his shoulder. "It's time there were *two* SDF-qualified skippers." They saluted, then shook hands solemnly.

She leaned to him, kissed him on the cheek. Forsythe, eyes closed, inhaled the somehow exotic scent of her, and thought wistful thoughts that broke service regs, rationalizing it on the basis of the fact that she would be gone soon. No temptation or threat; just a memory.

Then Lisa was sniffling again, pulling one of those new-fangled totally-recyclable tissues from a dispenser, blowing her nose, and tossing it into the recycler. Forsythe busied himself with realigning the duffels by the quarters' hatch. The hatch slid open, and Rick Hunter was standing there.

"Admiral." Forsythe touched his cap's braided brim, and moved past, into the companionway, headed for the bridge. Time to take command.

Lucky dog! Forsythe thought of Rick Hunter as he went along.

Rick went to lock his hands around Lisa's waist, but she kept him at a distance for a moment. "My giving up this ship, dead in space as she is, useless for now as she is, means even more than your giving up Skull. You acknowledge, Skull Leader?"

He had been taken by surprise, but now he nodded. "I do, Lisa. But the Sentinels need me more than the SDF-3 does, and they need you more, too, and you *know* that."

She inclined her head, perhaps a little unwillingly. "And it works out so well, for you. No more situation rooms, Rick; no more sidelines. We're about to enter that Ur-Flower furnace that Lang keeps talking about. You'll be right out there on the edge, and so will Max and Miriya and the others."

Only, would that be enough? Or would he find out there was nothing short of flying combat that would satisfy him? She pretended to adjust her duffel's straps. Somehow, that puerile Minmei song, "My Boyfriend's a Pilot," started playing in her head and it took an act of will to exorcise it. Lisa closed a last side-pocket seam, and hoisted her bag up onto her shoulder. "Ready?"

Rick had been about to offer help, but knew her well enough to know she didn't want any. He wrestled his own bag onto his shoulder and wondered what he and his wife looked like: the willowy, overachieving-service-brat success story, new captain of the *Farrago*; and the shorter, maybe-muddled-looking guy at her side who suddenly found himself honcho of combat-operations coordination for the Sentinels.

"I love you," he said all at once. Not much of an apology, really, or a rationalization, but the only guidewire there was to his life.

Her duffel shouldered, she nudged his hip with hers. Lisa had to dip a bit to do it. "Mutual. You know that! But we *have* to understand each other."

She dumped the bag and put both hands on his shoulders, as Rick let his own duffel fall. "I know you were unhappy here. But I know, too, that if the war turns out that way, I'll be listening to your voice, out there in the Danger Zone, and I won't be able to do a single thing about it but hope and pray."

She could barely keep the resentment out of her voice. "You and I are married; we're mates for life," she said, taking him into her embrace and feeling his arms close behind her, the strong fingers locking with a kind of determination.

Suddenly the resentment was gone; whether it would reappear or not, she didn't know. Lisa brushed back the thick black hair over his ear. "Husband and wife," she whispered. She could see a tear fall from his cheek to her uniform's breast. Her own were streaming, too.

"It's a rifle!" Karen Penn hollered, having had about enough.

"A goddamn projectile weapon, but it's *not* a rifle!" Jack Baker screamed back at her, blood vessels standing out in his neck. He was wrestling the huge Karbarran musket around, about to shake it at her if he could get it off the deck.

Karen was pleased to see that she had gotten a rise out of him. Being stuck down in what was apparently the lowermost hold of the Sentinels' ship, inspecting alien weapons and recording evaluations for the G-2 staff, would ordinarily have been fascinating, but she was down there with J. Baker, the World's Most Obnoxious Ensign.

Now he tried to hold up the Karbarran firearm, its ornate, jewel-set buttplate still planted on the deck. All hand-polished wood and burnished metal fittings, it looked like some primitive work of art. Its wide leather sling was thick with embroidery, and its muzzle was decked with a rainbow of parrot-bright feathers.

Jack indicated the big, globular fixture just forward of the trigger guard. "Penn, we both agree that there's a lot of air in here, right? Under pressure, because the Karbarrans jack it in with this forestock lever, right? And it shoots bullets pneumatically, with the velocity of a primitive rifle, *Right?*"

She cringed involuntarily as he shrieked the last word. "So!" he concluded, "It . . . is . . . a . . . *gun!*"

Karen made a fist, her knuckles protruding, wishing she could punch him. She answered through clenched teeth, "Not by the G-2 guidelines, which specify propellant-ignition or energy. Now, d'you want to turn in a faulty report, or are we gonna list these pump-up blunderbusses properly?"

Perhaps, she thought, there was some sort of berserk sadist in the assignments office, and that was how she had been thrown in with Baker yet again. That would explain everything, but easy explanations were so often suspect . . .

Jack grumbled something she took as acquiescence, and they went back to work. They inventoried the strange-looking weapons of those Praxians—weirdly-conformed *naginata*, which looked like long halberds with a curved blade at one end and a spike at the other, and short, one-handed crossbows with their grips protected by boiled, shaped leather, and the rest. Swords, shields—the peculiar crystalline Spherian gadgets that looked like frozen lightning bolts—what were two ensigns to make of those, or of a Gerudan grapnel-shaped thing that didn't seem to come with instructions?

Jack made terse notes in the aud-vid recorder, wondering at the same time how a girl who was such a sweet armful at a dance could be such an awful pain in the neck on duty. He prided himself on keeping an open mind, but really, he was right and she was wrong, just about always, and some streak of perversion in Cadet Penn seemed to make it impossible for her to admit that.

Karen, for her part, was thinking of the Praxians and their maleless society. Dynamite! Where could she sign up?

Jack was inspecting a two-handed longsword that the Praxians used in fighting from chariots, a razor-sharp whip of steel. Suddenly, he lowered it and turned to her. "Look, Penn, I'm not trying to make life tough on you, y'know. It's just that I take my job very seriously."

She was weighing some kind of bulky slug pistol in one hand. "So do I, Baker."

Jack suddenly felt very confused. Her honey-blond hair smelled wonderful, and the strange, slightly sloe eyes that were fixed on him were exotically beautiful, as mysterious as any XT's. And now that he noticed it, her upper lip was longer and fuller than her lower, giving Karen a, well, kind of *sexy* look, really....

Except—why did she have to be so damn competitive? Why couldn't she just come right out and admire him, yield to his judgment, the way the girls back home used to do? "Okay," he answered her, wondering what in the world he meant. "Okay, then."

He held the aud-vid rig out toward her. "Let's do this right, agreed? You record, and I'll dictate notes and observations."

She put her fists on her hips. "Why don't *you* record, and *I'll* dictate notes and observations?"

He felt his lips pulling back to reveal his teeth. "For one thing, because I was the Academy First in military history, and I think I could bring a little extra insight to evaluation of XT weaponry."

"Oh, well, pardon me for consuming valuable oxygen! But it so happens *I* won a New Rhodes scholarship for a *thesis* in comparative military history, Mister!" Jack let go an exasperated growl and took a half step toward her; Karen raised a precisely folded fist, middle knuckle cocked forward. "And I have a first *dan* in *Uichi-ryu* karate. Want proof?"

He tried to calm down, then lost it. "You just offered the wrong thing to the wrong guy on the wrong day, *meathead*!" He began tearing at the fastenings of his torso harness. "I'll mail your dog tags to your daddy!"

"That does it!" she shrilled at him, kicking things out of the way for some fighting room. "Where d'you want your corpse shipped, *moron?*"

He couldn't think of a comeback, and so roared like Lron, fighting to get his tunic off. Karen was quartering the air with whistling hand cuts, taking practice snap kicks that reached higher than her head.

There was a sudden sound from the cargo hold's outsized hatch, the deliberate, diplomatic clearing of a throat.

"Admiral Hunter." Jack tried to figure out whether he should button back up first, salute, or get busy thinking up the least preposterous alibi he could, even while Karen was bracing to attention and stuttering, "T-T-Tensh-*hut!*"

"As you were," Rick said, wandering in and gazing curiously at the racked Sentinels' weapons, to give the two cadets a moment to pull themselves together. He sort of regretted intervening; it might have been educational to sit at ringside for a few rounds.

Now, who do they remind me of? Rick Hunter asked himself. A young hot-dogger VT ace and a pale, intense SDF-1 first officer, maybe? He suddenly felt old, but it wasn't such a bad feeling, in view of what youth had yet to go through. "Pardon the interruption, Ensigns, but G-1 just cut the orders, and as I was coming aboard anyway to settle in, I thought you'd want to know."

They were both a little rocky from the adrenaline of the would-be brawl, and from the surprise of his appearance. It took them several moments to realize that he had promotion orders in one hand and lieutenant jg bars in the other.

Rick took a secret pleasure in their shock. "Can't have ensigns assigned to the Sentinels; it muddles the chain of command. Congratulations, Lieutenant; congratulations, Lieutenant."

They shook his hand warily, as if afraid it were going to come off, and gazed down at the badges of rank he had put in their palms.

"Yes; well, carry on," Rick bade them when he saw that they were going to be flummoxed for a while. He returned their salutes crisply, and resolved not to listen at the hatch to find out what was going to happen next, even though he wanted to.

"Well? Let's do it," Jack Baker said. Tradition dictated a certain ceremony. Karen nodded.

They silently removed the ensign pips from each other's epaulets, and fastened the jg bars there. Then they braced at attention and saluted each other, and then shook hands slowly, all without a word.

"Congratulations, Lieutenant," Karen echoed Rick.

"Same to you, Lieutenant," Jack told her emphatically.

CHAPTER EIGHT

I felt that my place lay with the Sentinels—with observing and recording a unique event in Human history. But I was a little schizo about it, because I could feel that there were things shaping up at REF-Tirol that the Folks Back Home would need to know about, too. Heroes to be sung and villains to be fingered.

But one of the first things you learn when they hand you an aud/vid recording rig is that you can't be every place at the same time.

Or even two places.

Sue Graham, narration from a documentary *Protoculture's Privateers: SDF-3; Farrago, Ark Angel Sentinels, and the REF.*

JEANNE GRANT PAUSED AS SHE WAS ABOUT TO SE-cure the med-center diagnostic robot for transferral to the Sentinels' ship. As she had done intermittently through the morning, she glanced through the viewport at Tirol, and looming Fantoma.

"It sure isn't home," she muttered again, "but at least we know the dangers here."

She felt her husband's massive arm go round her shoulders. He brushed his lips against her cheek. She re-flected again on the oddness of it—how a man so big and incredibly strong could be so gentle.

"But we're not needed here," he pointed out. "Lang will

be years repairing the SDF-3, and in the meantime there are people suffering and dying."

And so the Ground Mobile Unit was being attached, figuratively and literally, as a new module of the *Farrago*, secured to the starship's underside. And Skull Team, now augmented to near-squadron size with Beta and Logan VTs, was now the main component of its assigned air group.

She clutched his hand. At least there was comfort in the fact that, with the GMU suddenly reallocated to the Sentinels' mission, Vince would be near her; she didn't know if she could have endured being parted from him as she had been before.

Jeanne took a determined breath to keep back tears, having made up her mind that there was no point to doing any more crying. Vince patted her shoulder. "I know, darling, I know. I miss Bowie, too. But I'm glad he's safe on Earth, he and Dana both. Rolf will take good care of them."

She sighed, leaning her head against his broad chest, wondering what their son was doing at that moment, on the other side of the galaxy.

On Fantoma, the first dropships began disgorging the mining equipment that the Zentraedi would use to wrest monopole ore from the heavy-g world.

Breetai stepped out onto the surface in his pressurized armor, stretching his arms and feeling his muscles work. Nearby, heavily shielded and powered mining vehicles were being off-loaded. They looked like high-tech dinosaurs, octopi, centipedes.

Breetai looked around him at the bleak planetscape, a scoured and blasted vista of grays and browns and black, with a typically high-g scarcity of prominent features; planets like Fantoma quickly pulled down mountains and hills.

It looked like a haunted world. And it *was* haunted, in fact: haunted by memories the Zentraedi had accumulated over generations as miners, only to have those memories wiped away by the Robotech Masters and replaced with false ones, implanted glories of the warrior race the Masters needed for their plan to conquer the universe.

Battlepods came off the dropships, too, to stand guard and serve as security for the operation. Breetai let his subordinates take care of the details, and paced here and there, looking around him.

Lang and the other Earth savants had expressed surprise that the Zentraedi had been conceived as colossal laborers for the Fantoman mining operation. "If anything, it would seem to me, very *small* organisms would be more appropriate," one Human had ventured.

But that was because they still didn't understand the exact nature of the sizing chamber, and how it altered Zentraedi physiology to meet the challenges of a gravity more than three times that of Terra.

Breetai stretched again, feeling energized and exultant, rather than tired, by Fantoma's pull.

It was the oddest thing, but—*memories* seemed to be coming back to Breetai. The first dropship landing had been centered on an open-pit area, and it seemed to Breetai that he recognized the landscape around him. Something drew him up a slope—twenty degrees, he estimated; a steep climb—until he reached the summit.

There was a bench there, a mere trestle of stone slabs, but how had he *known* he would find it at just that spot? Conversations from his past, or perhaps hallucinations, drifted in and out of his thoughts. He suddenly felt an impotent fury at having been deprived of his own past—at being unable to trust his own memory.

In that moment, an image of himself and Exedore came to him, sitting on the bench side by side, and Exedore saying something that Breetai was having trouble following.

I remember! The words were a thunderous rumbling in his chest.

"No; of course we won't remember this life, my friend," Exedore was saying, "but the Robotech Masters plan momentous things for us. We will become much like a force of nature—something that will sweep the galaxy— the universe—in glory and triumph!"

Breetai saw himself stop and ponder that; he was only a miner—though he was, aside from Dolza, the biggest and strongest Zentraedi ever created, the most durable and formidable of them all—and had difficulty understanding the interstellar *jihad* that Exedore was painting in words.

Now he recalled the peculiar stirrings in him when he had heard Exedore's exhortation. The thought of a life of battle and triumph had made him feel exalted. And he had had a preternaturally long lifetime of it, just as Exedore foresaw.

But where could these recollections be coming from? Surely the Masters had expunged all true memories. Breetai shook his head within the huge helmet, mystified and troubled.

"Lord Breetai?" He turned in surprise, both at the fact that someone was standing there, and at the realization that it was a Zentraedi *female*. "The construction gang is about to begin work on permanent housing," she said, "but they'd like you to make final approval of the site."

She was wearing Quadrono powered armor that had been retrofitted for labor and mining duty, he could see. One of Miriya Parino's spitfires, no doubt; Breetai had heard that the Quadronos had never quite forgiven their leader for undergoing Micronization, marrying Max Sterling, and having his child. Many of them had deserted to follow the mad Khyron and his, his *lover*, Azonia, but some had remained loyal to Breetai, and a few of those had survived the final battle against Dolza and the Malcontent Uprisings and the battle with the Inorganics.

Breetai looked at her uneasily. The Zentraedi had always been rigidly segregated by sex, and most of them found the thought of fraternization disquieting to the point where it had been known to make them physically ill. But the unusual circumstances here in the primitive Fantoman start-up effort had made it impossible to preserve the old ways altogether.

Breetai forced himself to look her over. Not easy to tell much about her in the bulky powered armor except that she was tall for a female, well over fifty feet. Through her tinted facebowl, he could see that she had prominent cheekbones and slightly oblique eyes, looking rather like what Lang or Hunter would call Slavic, and her purple hair was cropped masculinely short. But there was something else about her face . . .

He realized, stunned, that she was wearing cosmetics. The thought passed through him. *Great suns! Where did she get them? Surely a female of our race uses as much in one application as an Earth woman uses in a month!*

She had accentuated the fullness of her mouth, the length of her glittering lashes, the line of her long-arched brows. Breetai stared at her, openmouthed, as she saluted and began to about-face.

"Wait!" he said on sudden impulse. "What's your name?"

She turned back to him. "I am Kazianna Hesh, formerly of the Quadronos, my lord." She gave a slight smile, thumping the plastron of her armor with a gauntleted fist. "And now a Quadrono again, it seems. Some of our battle suits have been in storage all this time, and the hour is come when they're needed again."

"So it is." Breetai inspected Kazianna Hesh, not sure why he was doing so. It was one thing to interact with human females like Lisa Hayes, knowing there was no possibility of . . . of *relations* with them, at least not as far as he was concerned. It was quite another, and very unsettling, to have the smiling, rather alluring-looking Quadrono staring at him so boldly.

"And, if I may say so, sir, what with all the perils that Fantoma harbors, it is good to be serving in a danger zone under the command of my Lord Breetai once more."

She saluted again, precisely, but still with that odd half smile. Breetai responded, and Kazianna did a careful high-g march back down the little hillock. Breetai watched her go, studying her walk, wondering whether it was something about her armor—a malfunction, perhaps?—that put that nonregulation sway in her gait.

*   *   *

"I don't care what your platoon leader told you," General T. R. Edwards roared into the face of the cleanup-detail sergeant. "I'm telling you to stack those things in the catacombs for further study by my evaluation teams! And make goddamn sure you don't damage any!"

The sergeant chose the better part of valor, saluting Edwards, then shrugging to his men and reorganizing them. They had been using their powered equipment to move the inert forms of the Invid Inorganic fighting mecha up out of the catacombs so that the demolition crews could dispose of them for good.

The biped Inorganics, and the massive Inorganic feline automata called Hellcats, were immobilized once the huge brain controlling them was deactivated. But it still made the REF uneasy to have thousands of them lying all over Tiresia, as though they might wake up at any moment. Orders had come down to move them to an appropriate site and blow them all to smithereens.

Lang and Cabell and the other big IQs had taken a few of the things for study, but didn't seem otherwise inclined to countermand the council's orders. Be that as it might, all the lower ranks knew you didn't rub General Edwards the wrong way without risking some real grief. The heavy machinery began lugging the inert enemy mecha for careful storage in the catacombs under the Royal Hall.

Edwards took an aide, Major Benson, aside. "Get some of the Ghost Riders and keep an eye on things. Make sure the Invid mecha are all kept intact, understood?"

"Yes, sir." Benson recalled the bizarre events of the original capture of the Royal Hall: how Edwards had arranged to be first to break into the Invid command center deep beneath it.

Benson could only guess at what his general's plans were, but the aide made every attempt not to seem surprised or curious. Hitching your wagon to Edwards's star offered the chance of vast rewards somewhere down the line, but stars had a way of flaring up and destroying the things around them. Discretion was the indispensible tool for survival in Ghost Squadron.

"Wise-man, I'm told you wish to see me," Bela said, entering Lang's lab. She seemed cheerful with the prospect of having her heart's desire fulfilled, but she stopped dead, glaring, when she saw Cabell and Rem standing by Lang's side.

Gnea had been following close behind her warlord, and now collided with her back. The smaller, younger amazon had the same lithe grace as Bela, but she was more prone to show wide-eyed wonder at the things around her, and lacked that hair-trigger temper that was already gaining Bela fame in the REF.

Gnea's eyes were a gold-flecked green, her long, straight hair a sun-bleached white. Her helm was crested with a long-necked reptilian image that had a head like a horned lizard. Her battle costume was of a different design from Bela's, but had that same look of erotic glamour to it. Gnea wore sword and knife on her harness like Bela, but where the taller woman carried a crossbow, Gnea bore a Praxian *naginata* and a shield with a spiked boss in its center.

"What are *they* doing here?" Bela indicated Rem and Cabell with an angry gesture of her chin, fingering her bow as if she were ready to fire. Gnea seemed about to bring her halberd's curved blade into the ready position, glaring beneath feathery black brows.

"They have been helping me with my research," Lang answered, surprised. "They are allies of the REF now, just as you are."

"We Sentinels do not trust these spawn of the Robotech Masters," Bela spat, "any more than we do the Zentraedi who brought suffering like the Invid did!"

Gnea, eyes narrowed at Rem, added, "And you, you who so resemble Zor—we have reason to hate *Zor*, too, for the ruin his meddling brought down upon us."

"But he is not Zor," Cabell told her, stroking his long white beard with one mandarin-nailed hand. "Nor am I a

Robotech Master. Think of us, please, as two Tiresians who wish to help free all planets from the Invid."

Bela hissed at him in scorn and anger. Lang intervened. "Without their help, I couldn't have finished *this* for you in time."

He gestured, and a powered partition folded aside accordian style. Bela gasped, and Gnea cried aloud, seeing what waited there.

No one would ever mistake it for a live horse, even though it tossed its head, snorting, and dug its hoof at the deck in imitation of a real animal's movements. The two wings that sprouted from its back were articulated, and changed shape and position, but were more like something from an airplane or ornithopter than any bird.

Its leg structure widened somewhat down toward the hock, so that it seemed Lang's wonder horse was wearing bell-bottoms from which its shining hooves poked. The thing was a glittering silver with jet-black trim. Its noble mane and forelock and tail of hair-fine wire tossed and glittered as it stamped, waiting.

"She is magnificent," Bela breathed, forgetting her anger. "Superb." She went toward the mecha with one hand extended; the thing appeared to sniff at her. "Magical."

She appeared ready to vault astride, but Rem called out, "Wait!" As she whirled on him he held out her helm, showing her that the interior padding had been changed.

"Control receptors," Rem explained. "This is still a Robotech mecha, after all, and in order to control it, you'll need to do a certain amount of mental imaging—visualizing what you want it to do." She took the helm from him, settling it onto her head.

Bela held her hand out to the horse again. "I shall call you 'Halidarre,' girl—after the free sky-spirit of our great heroine.

"Halidarre I shall be," the horse-mecha answered, in a synthesized voice that sounded much like Bela's. Both women drew breath in surprise.

"There are other things you will learn about Halidarre,"

Cabell said, "as time passes. Things like this . . ."

He touched a control, and Halidarre's wings straightened, their area shrinking somewhat. From a niche in the mecha's back, a cylindrical reconnaissance module rose into the air, using the wings and its own lifting field. Cabell touched another control, and the module returned to its niche.

"Halidarre flies, too, just as promised," Lang put in. "But more by her antigrav apparatus and impellers than by using her wings; the aerodynamics of a *live* flying horse are quite impossible, of course."

"He is also compatible with some of the other REF mecha, like the Cyclone combat cycles—" Rem was adding, but Bela cut him off with a gesture and leapt astride the Robotech Pegasus.

"Halidarre, attached to a mere machine? Don't be absurd!" she snorted. "Gnea, come!" Gnea obediently took her hand and swung up behind, one arm around Bela's waist.

"Thanks for this gift, Dr. Lang; I salute you and pledge my fealty to you."

Her expression hardened. "But as for you, Zor-clone, and you, servant to the Robotech Masters, do not try my patience, and stay well clear of the women of Praxis!"

By way of underlining her warning, she turned and aligned her arm at the wooden leg of a lab table. She clenched her fist and made a sudden downward curling gesture with it, keeping the rest of her arm steady. A thin, gleaming object shot from the slightly bulky feature built into her forearm sheath.

The three men turned to spy it quivering in the wood: a slim, hiltless throwing dagger—fired by some sort of spring-loaded device in the sheath, Lang supposed.

Bela looked to Rem and Cabell again. "Be warned," she said.

CHAPTER
NINE

How I was torn when I saw that she wasn't going! Surely, the Sentinels are venturing forth on a mission far more likely to bring enlightenment than is the mere mining of Fantoma and rebuilding the SDF-3!

Just as certainly, along with the contemptible bloodshed that is war, there will be access to stupendous new horizons of knowledge and awareness. Perhaps keys to the Ultimate Truths that grow from the First Light, the birth pangs of the Universe!

Enough; Minmei will stay behind and that's only to be expected. Though the synergistic harmonies with Janice Em (and what of her? So many mysteries!) will be sundered, Lynn-Minmei seems to sense that the place for her and for her voice and her role in the Shapings— as Lang and Zand would have it—is here, with the REF.

And so it is my place too; I am content. She'll be here, away from Hunter, away from Wolff—here, near me. What feelings this stirs, I don't find myself able to put into words yet. I will allow myself some irony in this matter, and sign myself, when these writings turn to Minmei . . .

REF Service #666–60–937

FROM AN ENLISTED LOUNGE OF SDF-3, THERE WAS A great view of the Sentinels' flagship and the small escort flotilla from the dimensional fortress, preparing to get under weigh.

Drives flared in the night of Valivarre's umbra; the strange, orange-red fans of propulsive energy from *Farrago* stood out like a half-dozen immense, slitted searchlights—like no drives the REF had ever seen before, dwarfing those around the dreadnought. The Ur-Flower "peat" furnaces beamed incredible power out into space.

Off duty, Minmei sat at the lounge's piano by a big span

of viewport, not even realizing that she was picking absently at the keys. The Agitprop and Psych/Morale people had wanted her to sing a final farewell concert with Janice. Something to work everybody up into a liberationist fervor and prepare them for whatever lay ahead—either the backbreaking labor of putting SDF-3 in working order or the life-on-the-line campaign to dislodge the fearsome Invid hordes from the planets they had enslaved. The REF was already exhausted from the round-the-clock working shifts to get the Sentinels' mission ready.

But Minmei didn't feel like singing with Janice again. She refused to sing with the woman who had, in her opinion, betrayed her. For that matter, Minmei didn't feel like singing for the war effort. The whole Superstar-savior-voice-of-humanity act was behind her, couldn't they understand that? She was just another lowly recruit, and that was the way she wanted it.

"The voice that won the Robotech War," they had called her. But what had it ever brought her but a few glimmers of the spotlight, then pain and bitterness and loneliness? She considered the things she had been forced to endure in the wake of her triumphs, and decided that one more such victory would be her undoing.

The escort flotilla had fallen in around the Sentinels' flagship now, ready to guard it until it went superluminal. Then *Farrago* and the mismatched aliens and Earthers aboard would be on their own.

Minmei realized that she was hitting familiar keys, one at a time and very slowly. The tempo was different now, mournful, like some old torch song from one of the great blues singers.

She sang the words softly, letting her suffering come through, savoring the lyrics but filling them with irony.

Life is only what we choose to make it
Let us take it
Let us be free

Minmei chorded it unhurriedly, downbeat, so that the song sounded like it was time for the bartenders to be putting chairs upside down on the tables for closing. She felt her shoulders sag under a weight she simply wasn't strong enough to bear anymore.

There was a lamenting in each word. The famous voice caressed, rasped resentfully, then caressed again.

We can find the glory we all dream of
And with our love,
We can win . . .

But there was a strength in the melancholy, a strength the blues had owned from the beginning, something stronger than all the up-tempo marches put together.

The strength of survival—of going through the worst and coming out the other side saddened and chastened but alive and prepared to stay with the life that had done such unspeakable things to you, because there *was* no other life . . .

Her head was bent over the keyboard now, long raven wings of hair shrouding her face. Perhaps a few, nearby, would hear, but she didn't care. She looked again, briefly, to where the Sentinels' engines lit the night, and the conventional drives of its REF escorts grew brighter in anticipation of departure.

Minmei watched them as her fingers found unhurried chords that seemed predestined.

If we must fight or face defeat,
We must stand tall and not retreat

Unseen by anyone but their owner, hands manipulated the lounge sound system control panel: turning down the gain; adjusting the very fine room directionals; punching a ship's-intercom code that only certain selected commo personnel were supposed to know. Adjusting this; amplifying that—and it was all very practiced, very expert.

Minmei's song, low and intimate, was playing through the lounge softly, as if it were something a loud sound would shatter, amplified so discreetly that Minmei herself didn't realize the sound system was on.

It was channeled into the ship's commo, and Lang's head raised from his lab researches; Exedore's eyes took on a faraway look; Captain Forsythe and the bridge gang stopped what they were doing and listened; many in SDF-3 fought the tide of emotion as *the voice* swept through them. Breetai, confronting bleak Fantoma, heard it through a commo patch-in over which he had just wished Rick and Lisa Hunter good fortune.

Rem and Cabell wondered if any perfection of the Muse Triumvirate of the Robotech Masters could surpass the aching beauty of this song; they doubted it. Exedore heard it and thought, *This power she has—it's astonishing. No; it's humbling.*

Thousands of people froze, hearing Minmei, knowing her and her song, but never having heard either sound like this.

It's love's battle we must win . . .

The line rose and lingered; losing in personal battle was the epitome of the blues. Minmei was pure and high and luminous with pain at one moment, breathy with a return to the call of life the next. More in touch with her music than the gamine superstar version of herself had ever been.

We will win
We must win . . .

Minmei twisted the last note around with the wail of a suffering animal, then let it down gently with some chords that said *it's all right; life goes on. Lived through everything else. Not gonna die from this.*

She wavered a little on the piano bench, a bit dazed by the understated power of what she had just released—

something that hadn't been there, in her, before. She was unaware that so many others had heard it, unaware that the lounge was now utterly quiet.

The Sentinels' drive flared bright; the starship moved away, its escorts guarding the vessel, as Minmei thought of it, only so far as the end of the proverbial garden path, and then letting it set out into the long night alone.

"Nothing to report to me? Nothing to report? Is that all you can say?"

The Invid Regent stalked through his vast halls in the Invid Home Hive on Optera, and his closest aides, knowing his moods, trailed him dutifully but warily. He was capable of becoming violent without warning—feeding an unfortunate bystander to one of his huge, gem-collared Hellcats, or having them devolved in one of the Genesis Pits or simply lashing out with a physical blow.

And an enraged blow from the Regent was something few might hope to survive. Some twenty feet high, he was the tallest of his race, among whom an average height was some six or eight feet. His advisers, though, like Tesla, stood twice average height.

Unlike the underlings following him, the Regent was draped with an organic cape that grew around the back of his neck and resembled a manta ray, lined from front to back with tuberclelike sensors that resembled eyeballs. He often spread the strange structure like a cobra's mantle in times of fury, and the mantle was stirring restlessly, even now.

"No word from the reinforcements I sent to retake Tirol? No message on the whereabouts of Tesla? No answer from the Regis? Perhaps my servants need *motivation*."

He stopped to turn to them.

"Your troops have barely had time to reach Karbarra, to pick up forces from the garrison there for the attack on Tirol, much less reach Tirol itself," one of the lackeys managed to get out, trembling.

"A-and perhaps Tesla has paused to gather more varieties of the Fruit of the Flower of Life," another one ventured. "He has great hopes that a preparation made from
them will be of vast advantage to you, Mighty One!"

"And it may be that your communications have simply
not reached the Regis yet," the third pointed out. "She has
always responded to Your Magnificence's messages in the
past."

Yes. Usually with mockery and defiance. Repelled by
his de-evolutionary experiments, just as he was provoked
by her insistence on maintaining a form that was Tiresoid
—that was so like the females of the race of the hated
Zor—the Regis had abandoned him, followed by half their
species, like the dividing of some unimaginable insect col-
ony.

And with his resources of troops and vessels and Flower
essence so limited in the wake of the vast Invid–Robotech
Master war, he could scarcely afford to begin a civil conflict against his own mate and half his race. At least, not
yet.

The Regent was in no mood to listen to his underlings'
rationalizations, in no mood to be reminded of logistical
limits, or of Tesla's semimystical theories about the Fruit of
the Flower of Life. He stood now near the center of the
Home Hive, a stupendous network of domes and connect-
ing conduits that stretched far and wide across Optera like
an incandescent spiderweb. But, with its energy reduced
now and its population so depleted, it seemed to mock the
power that had once been his.

The feeler-sensors on his snout glowered angrily with
the words, "Yes: *motivation*."

He seized the adviser nearest him, not really caring
which one it was, and flung him across the chamber. The
underling sprawled and lay quaking. "Kill him," the Regent told the other two.

They didn't hesitate for a moment. Snatching weapons
from a pair of armored-trooper sentries, they turned the
guns on their former colleague and opened fire. Streams of

annihilation disks flew, flaring bright when they struck, enveloping the fallen Invid in a brief inferno. The stench of the charred body wafted through the Hive.

The Regent debated whether he should order the remaining two to shoot each other, or, perhaps more interestingly, themselves. But that would waste more time, since new lackeys would have to be trained from scratch.

His bloodlust had been sated a little. He contented himself with telling them, "Go now and do as I've commanded. And bring me no more news of failure."

Senep, the commander in charge of the Invid mission to send fresh troops to Tirol, was aware of the Regent's state of mind. He was at pains to do his duty well, but *quickly*.

Reports from Tirol were somewhat sketchy—word that Zentraedi and some apparently unknown Tiresoid race had attacked the planet in concert. Senep's hastily assembled task force, manned by troops borrowed from Karbarra's ample garrison, now moved out for deepspace, still preparing itself for the rather protracted voyage to its objective.

Senep was relieved that his plan to commandeer resources from Karbarra had been approved. To gather units in dribs and drabs from various other worlds, and from the forces patrolling the outer marches of the Invid's shrunken empire, would have cost him time that he could ill afford to waste.

But Senep had been able to make two telling arguments in favor of his idea. One was that Karbarra had more than sufficient Invid strength to perform its task, even with its garrison thus reduced. The second, and more important, was that the Karbarrans were most unlikely to become intractable or demonstrate any resistance or defiance.

No, the Karbarrans had a very *good* reason to obey their overlords' every whim without objection.

The Invid commander was still getting his ships into proper formation when a communications tech turned to him, its snout-sensors agleam with emotion as it spoke.

"Commander! Alien starship approaching from deepspace! It just went subluminal and appears to be on course for Karbarra!"

For Karbarra, and Senep's task force. "Identify."

"Impossible, sir. It does not match anything in our data banks."

Senep puzzled for a moment over the long-range sensor image of the Sentinels' ship. "I'm not going to ask questions. Battle stations. All units prepare to attack."

CHAPTER
TEN

> *It is a critical point that each new form of enemy in the Wars was a new problem in the use and application of Earth mecha. What would work against a Battlepod was suicide against Invid Inorganics; the vulnerable points, weaponry, and performance profiles were completely different.*
>
> *The Human fighters were lucky they had all those curious and experimenting monkeys in their ancestry; the REF in particular was a climate wherein only quick learners survived.*
>
> Selig Kahler, *The Tirolian Campaign*

THE VOYAGE FROM TIROL TO KARBARRA HAD BEEN filled with a schedule even more exhausting than the preparations for the Sentinels' departure. Rick, like all the others aboard, had been forced to take what little sleep he could get in catnaps.

They had had to familiarize the non-Human Sentinels with Robotech weapons, of course—as much as was feasible while under way. Some of them, like Burak and Kami, were more than willing to learn, while others—the Karbarran ursinoids and the Praxian amazons in particular—seemed unwilling to trust any small arms but their own. This, though the Karbarrans appeared inclined to try out mecha and Bela and Gnea could barely wait to ride that completely crazy winged horse of Lang's into battle.

Rick and his staff had racked their brains coming up with ways to try to integrate the wildly varied forces in battle and make everybody understand what they were supposed to do. Rick had moments of agonizing doubt that it had been accomplished, wondering if he was heading into one of the worst debacles in military history.

Then there had been the various misunderstandings and frictions to mediate. The Sentinels' resentment of Cabell and Rem; run-ins between the Humans and non-Humans as cultural difference led to clashes (well, the Hovertanker *did* have that fractured jaw coming to him for calling the Praxian woman a "brawny wench," even if it was meant jokingly); the constant insistence of Burak and the other Perytonians that their planet be given higher priority in the campaign—it was all beginning to give Rick migraines.

And there was the bewildering job of understanding the alien Sentinels themselves. As the ship drew closer and closer to Karbarra, Lron and Crysta and their people became more and more withdrawn and morose. Veidt was puzzled by it, too.

Normally, as Rick understood it, the gloomy Karbarrans—preoccupied with the tragedy of fate and the ultimate futility of things—made Earth's teutonic types look giddy by comparison; but the prospect of battle was one of the few things that made the big ursinoids cheerful. That wasn't true now, though, and none of them would explain why.

Rick tried to put it from his mind, along with things like this business about Haydon. Apparently, Haydon was some sort of extraordinarily important historical figure or deity or *something*, but beliefs and convictions varied among the Sentinels and led to sharp disputes. And so part of their pact had been to avoid all mention of Haydon. Lang was desperate for more information concerning the matter, but the Sentinels had clammed up about it.

Those were Rick's lesser problems. Bigger ones included trying to make things more efficient and organized, and constantly being stymied by explanations he couldn't quite grasp.

One of his first ideas had been to automate the feeding of the Ur-Flower peat—Sekiton, it was called—into the furnaces, freeing up the stoker gangs for other work. Lron and Crysta had given him a long explanation, which he didn't comprehend in the least.

They seemed to be saying that the Sekiton had to be *physically touched and handled by Karbarrans to be of any use*. If relegated to robotic handling, its affinity for Karbarran life-forms thus frustrated, Sekiton would have its feelings hurt or sulk or whatever, and refuse to yield up its energy properly.

It *had* to be a translation problem, Rick decided. Didn't it?

He just hoped that he had understood the Karbarrans' intelligence assessments properly. When they had left their homeworld, the Invid were maintaining a relatively small occupation force, and it sounded like something the Sentinels could cope with. Rick's plan was to use the production facilities on Karbarra—famous for their adaptability and output—to begin assembly lines to turn out mecha and ships with which to arm native recruits, increasing the Sentinels' strength perhaps tenfold.

Lron and his folk were disinclined to comment much about the idea, and apparently held the conviction that fate would bring what it would bring. That gave Rick reservations about the plan, and so he convinced the other Sentinel leaders to scout out the situation carefully before beginning any offensive.

To that end, the starship resumed sublight speed drive far out from the planet itself. Lisa, in her capacity as captain, gave the command to carry out the maneuver.

She had left behind the more formal REF uniform with its tailcoat and skirt. Now she wore the tight-fitting unisex bodysuit that seemed more appropriate for the Sentinels' rough-and-ready style, the group's insignia high on the left breast of her yokelike torso harness, just as it was on all the other Humans. The starship made its transition.

And found itself, all in an instant, practically in the lap of Senep's task force.

Lisa turned and yelled for battle stations.

As for Crysta and Lron, they had taken advantage of the preoccupation of most of the ship's company with the return to sublight speed to find their way to the hold in which Tesla was being kept.

The Praxians who were on guard were only too glad to let the Karbarrans relieve them long enough for the amazons to go get something to eat. Besides, it lay well within Lron's authority to conduct an interrogation.

When they were alone with him, the ursinoids went over to where the Invid scientist sat, shackled, behind bars. "You begged us to spare you," Crysta said in a growl. "You said you would be of use. Well, now you can be. Tell us what you know of the prison, and of its . . . its captives. How are they guarded? How may they be freed?"

Tesla had been watching her almost indifferently, Crysta thought, though it was difficult to tell any Invid mood by appearance. But when the scientist spoke, it was with an almost saintly kindness.

"Ah, Madam Crysta! If only I knew these things, I could tell them to you, and atone at least in some small part for the crimes I've committed against your race back when my will was enslaved by the Regent! But I know nothing of such military arrangements, you see."

His chains rattled as he struggled to his feet. "However, another idea occurs to me. Release me, that I may go down to the surface of Karbarra and negotiate for you at once. The Invid commander, without the Regent there to contradict, will listen to me."

Lron showed his teeth. "I told you asking this slime-thing was useless," he told his wife. And to Tesla, he added, "Now we try a different approach. Let us see how much you can remember with one of those antennae twisted off your snout!"

Tesla shrank back, even though he was the larger of the two. "Keep your distance! Your leadership circle said I was not to be tampered with. Have you forgotten so soon?"

"But the others aren't here now," Lron pointed out, putting one hand on the lock. "And I am."

Crysta, worried that this possible key to the Karbarran dilemma might not survive her mate's vigorous questioning, was just saying, "Lron, perhaps he's telling the truth—" Just then the alarms went off, exotic ululations and crystal gongs and warhorns and the various other calls to arms of the assorted Sentinel races.

Lron made sure the cage was secure, then he and Crysta pounded off for the bridge. As they rounded a corner in the passageway, they were unaware that they were being watched from the shadows.

Burak stayed back until the two were out of sight, then stared thoughtfully at the door to the compartment holding Tesla's cage. At last, the sounding of the alarms drew him slowly, unwillingly, off toward his battle station. Then he began to run, to run as if something were chasing him.

"They haven't fired on us out of hand; that's a piece of luck we didn't have coming," Lisa conceded. "Rick, I suggest we *not* scramble the VTs, at least not yet."

Rick met her gaze for a moment, then nodded.

There were far fewer of the enemy than the SDF-3 had confronted over Tirol. Four of the rust-colored Invid troopships, shaped like gigantic clams, were deploying around a much more modest version of the Invid command ship the Humans had glimpsed—the one Cabell had pronounced to be the royal flagship of the Regent himself. If the troop carriers were clams, this thing was an ominous starfish.

The Sentinel leadership was piling onto the bridge now, reacting or not according to the fashion of their species. "They've got the drop on us," Rick said softly.

Lisa shook her head. "I don't think so, or they would've

opened up right away; the Invid are the shoot-first type."
But I don't understand.

Aboard Senep's flagship, the task-force command finally got some results from the vessel's Living Computer. It seemed that most of the components of the unidentified craft matched with space vehicles from many Invid-controlled worlds, and the central structure to which they had been joined fit the profile of an outlandish craft that the scientist Tesla had had under construction.

Senep's antennae shone with anger. That blithering idiot! But—if it was Telsa, why hadn't he identified himself? Perhaps something was wrong.

Senep queried the Living Computer about the offensive capabilities of the newcomer. Of the weapons that could be identified from memory banks, none could match the range or power of the flagship.

It certainly didn't resemble anything the new foe—the Human-Zentraedi alliance—would conceivably field. And no ship of a subject race posed much threat to an Invid command ship.

"We'll close with it, then," Senep decided, "within range of our main guns, but out of Tesla's. Then we'll send our mecha to investigate."

Lisa refused to answer the enemy's query signals, of course; none of the Sentinels could imitate an Invid, and there wasn't even time to get Tesla up to the bridge, much less coerce him.

"But why are they approaching?" Veidt's eerie voice came.

Lron growled, "They know what our weapons can do; they know their flagship has us outgunned."

There were only seconds to act; Lisa turned to one of the gramophone mikes. "Patch me through to Commander Grant."

"Way to go," Rick whispered to his gutsy wife, realizing what she had in mind.

"I'm beginning to get unfamiliar Protoculture readings from that craft, Commander," the ship's Living Brain relayed.

"Launch mecha," Senep said, having taken up his position of advantage. "And at the first sign of resistance, open fire—"

It was as if he spoke into the ear of a listening deity. At that moment a tremendous bolt sprang from a peculiar design feature on the underside of the lone ship. It struck Senep's vessel almost dead-center, a star-hot stiletto of energy that pierced the command ship's shields and hull, stabbed it to its heart, and lit the vessels around it with its dying eruption.

But Senep had given a last order, and as the ball of superheated gas that had been the command ship expanded like a balloon, the troopships swung open like oysters about to yield pearls.

Invid mecha began boiling forth from them: bizarre, armored crab-shapes of assorted types riding powerful thrusters, diving for the Sentinels.

"Launch fighters!" Rick yelled. He could feel the ship shake as the Alphas and Betas of Skull Team roared from their launch tubes in the Ground Mobile Unit, and from the improvised bays in the rest of *Farrago* as well. "Vince, see if you can take out some of those other troop carriers!"

But before the command was out of Rick's mouth, the Sentinels' ship shuddered from a second firing of the GMU's monster cannon. Fastened to the underbelly of the ship as it was, the GMU wasn't in the best position for accurate volleys; but Vince's gunners and targetting equipment were unsurpassed. A second nova-beam went through a troop carrier like a leatherpunch through a bug. Less than half its mecha launched, the enemy craft vanished in outlashing starfire.

"Commence firing! All batteries, commence firing!" Lisa was saying loudly but calmly into a mike. In all the mismatched portions of the ship, turrets and launchers opened up. The GMU's secondary weapons began putting out the heaviest possible volume of fire. So did the non-transformable Destroid mecha that Vince Grant had moved into the ground unit's larger airlocks, using them as gun emplacements—just as Henry Gloval had on SDF-1 during the desperate battle with Khyron out in Earth's Pacific Ocean, so long ago.

In rushed the Invid Pincer Ships, the massive Enforcers and comparatively small Scouts, firing as they came, enraged though they had no individual emotions, with the single-minded fury of a swarm of hornets.

Out to meet them came the second-generation Alphas, sleekly lethal despite their deepspace augmentation pods; the burlier Betas, with their brute firepower and thrust; and the new Logans, with their rowboat-shaped noses, the latest word in Veritechs.

Leading Skull Team were Max and Miriya Sterling, as cool and alert as ever. To them, as to the rest of the veteran Skulls, heavier Invid numbers just meant there were that many more opportunities to make kills. The dying began at once. Skull Team's tactical net crackled with terse, grim exchanges, the pilots automatically maintaining an even strain, upholding the generations-old Yeager tradition of Cool In The Saddle.

"Y'got one on your six, Skull Niner."

"Roger on that, Skull Two. Kin ya scratch my back?"

"That's affirm. Scissor right, and I'll swat 'im for you."

The Beta that was Skull Nine drew the pursuing Invid Pincer Ship into Skull Two's line of fire. Brief, flaring bursts of free-electron laser cannonfire skeeted the bogey out of existence.

"Skull Leader," Lisa's voice came, "enemy element of six mecha has broken through your screen and is attacking the flagship."

"Skull Two, Skull Seven, go *transact* 'em," Max delegated, still concentrating on the Pincer that was trying to get into Miriya's six—the tail position, from which it could make the kill.

Two and Seven, leading their wingmates, headed off on a rescue at least as dangerous as the dogfighting; the Sentinels' AA fire was not as well coordinated as the REF fliers would have liked, and there was a very good chance the Skull two-ship elements would be flamed by friendly fire if the people on the bridge weren't completely on top of things.

On the other hand, that was what made combat more interesting to Max and his gang. They were the ultimate Robotech aces, living out on the edge where the juices flowed and death waved at you from every passing mecha.

"Skull One, Skull One, go to Battloid and hold 'em; we'll be right there," somebody was saying. Miriya pulled off an amazing maneuver, flipping her Alpha like a flapjack while the pursuing Pincer shot past her, its annihilation disks missing. Max's wife was suddenly in the six position.

Predator that she was, the onetime battle queen of the Quadronos lost no time in chopping away at the Pincer with short, highly controlled bursts of pumped-laser blasts. It trailed flame, debris, and outrushing gases for a moment, then became a drifting, brilliant cloudfront.

Max and Miriya came as one to a new vector, to engage three oncoming armored-trooper skirmish ships.

In my android state, I lack the appropriate Human referents to explain sufficiently what is transpiring here. I can only give factual synopses. But there is a Human phrase, employed in description of sporting events, that occurs to me, Dr. Lang: "playing over his-or-her head," which refers to achievement—due to psychological, emotional, and other factors that resist analyses—in excess of what one might logically expect under given circumstances.

Given that parameter, I think I can safely say that the Sentinels are playing over their heads. But the game has yet to reach its final score.

Janice Em (in android state) in a report to Dr. Emil Lang

RICK WAS TRYING TO FOLLOW THE BATTLE BOTH BY eyeball—through the huge inverted bowl of the bridge canopy—and via the Sentinels' still-unfamiliar tracking displays and tactical-readout screens. At the same time, he was doing his best to coordinate the Human and non-Human elements of the Sentinels, and make sure foe, not friend, was the target of *Farrago*'s gun turrets and missile tubes.

But always, in the background, there was that small voice prodding and eating at him. He wanted so much to be out there in a VT, doing the only thing he had ever really done well in his life—piloting. To be left out of the rat race and yet be so close, so intimately involved in it, was such heartbreaking torture that it seemed the universe must be against him—that Creation was malign, after all.

He was also keeping a nervous eye on that huge Sekiton-powered junction that held the ship together and made *Farrago* a functioning whole; if it failed, the Sentinels would be history.

The pair of two-ship Skull elements dispatched by Max tackled the flight of six armored Shock Troopers that had penetrated the Sentinels' defensive sphere. Far less maneuverable than the Pincers, the Shock Troopers mounted heavier firepower and had been no doubt sent in as kamikazes.

But the VTs were there first, two Alphas and a scratch element made up of a Beta and a Logan. The Alphas went to Guardian mode, in that process unique to Robotechnology that Lang had dubbed mechamorphosis.

The Beta reconfigured like some ultratech origami, thinning and extending as components flowed until it was in Battloid mode, a gleaming Herculean-looking Robotech body.

The Logan went to Battloid, too, mechamorphosing in response to its pilot's imaging. Where Alphas looked more Humaniform in Battloid, the Logan's boatlike radome made it seem like the upper half of a Robotech torso had been lifted away and some Egyptian icon-mask, the Spirit of the Twin-Thrustered Rocketcraft, had been lowered into its place.

But all the VTs were swinging and angling to confront the Invid. The Battloids clutched the repositioned cannon that had been integral weapons systems to the Beta and Logan but were now handheld infantry weapons, with barrels as wide as water mains, for the Robotech knights.

The attackers came in, and crewbeings on the bridge ducked involuntarily, as the darkness lit with crisscrossed beams of pure destruction and streams of annihilation disks.

The Shock Troopers looked like bipedal battleships, their clawed forearms bulging like ladybug carapaces. Their single sensor-eye clusters betrayed no emotion, and the twin cannon mounding at either shoulder made them appear invincible. But then the Battloids were there, and the mecha darted in and out of one another's line of fire; the enormous energy discharges lit the bridge crew below.

The hulking Logan stood in the teeth of withering fire from a Shock Trooper, the gun duel a simple question of who could get a telling hit first. In the meantime, a second Trooper was looping around for a pass from six o'clock, and nothing Rick could do in the bridge could get him a clear connection to that doomed pilot. Just about the time the oncoming Trooper broke up into fragments before the monstrous outpouring of the Beta-Battloid's gun, torso missile-rack covers flew back and a host of Swordfish air-to-airs corkscrewed at the Invid.

The armored Shock Trooper disappeared in a cloud of detonating warheads. The Beta changed its attitude of flight with a complex firing of its many steering thrusters, and opened up again with its handheld artillery in support of the Logan.

On the bridge, Lisa looked at Rick. No one could fault the job he was doing; despite the disadvantages of the Sentinels' slapdash organization and communications systems, he was keeping things sorted out—was, perhaps, an even more pivotal part of the battle than she. And yet she could see, in the moment's glance she could spare her husband, that he couldn't cope with the frustration of his job much longer; that he was actually *in pain* because he wasn't out there in the rat race.

Another concussion shook the flagship and a beam leapt out from the muzzle of the GMU's main gun. It was set for wider dispersal this time, since the clamshell troopships weren't a worthwhile target anymore. The stupendous cannonshot took out a few of the enemy mecha, like killing several flies with a howitzer. But this was no artillery duel; the mecha would decide the day.

The Alphas sent by Max Sterling mopped up the enemy machines that the Battloids hadn't stopped. The very last armored Shock Trooper tried a headfirst dive at the very bridge canopy, and most of the beings there dove for the deck, useless as that was, by sheer reflex.

The Beta got in its way, backpack thrusters flaring so hard that the wash of flame blew across the adamantine bridge canopy. Some systems overloaded and areas of the shields failed. There were explosions, sending flame and shrapnel flying, and everybody's ears popped as the ship began to lose atmosphere.

There were only a few Sentinels on their feet. Lron, at the wheel, held his place and let forth a challenging rumble. From where she stood, hands at the small of her back, Lisa looked every inch the captain—near the helm. She saw Rick still at his place; he turned, with a frantic look on his face, a look that was haunted and bereft—yet it held so much fear, wildness . . .

But at that moment, he saw that Lisa was all right, and he burst into a grin and gave her the thumbs-up, then turned back to his coordinating duties. Lisa understood that the panic in his eyes was that she might have been hurt, or killed. It had been a sudden vacancy—an immobility, really. True fear, and Lisa recognized it because she had seen it before, and felt it herself. *Terror* that he had lost her; it had debilitated him for a moment.

She thrust the thought aside. A few hundred yards above the long blister of the bridge, the damaged Logan had actually *bulldogged* an incoming armored Shock Trooper, interposing itself and going hand-to-hand with one of the enemy's most feared mecha.

The bridge crew couldn't hear the creaking of metal, the hiss of compromised seals, the parting of welds and seams. They watched the silent wrestling match as the bigger, stronger Beta rushed in to lend support. But the Beta was too far away.

The armored Shock Trooper grappled the Logan around into a certain mecha-infighting position, spread-eagling it, and bent it backward across one knee. There were the puffs of escaping atmosphere and the electrical arcing of destroyed systemry.

The Beta blindsided the Shock Trooper, rebounding to hit thrusters again and lock with it in mortal combat. Despite everything the Shock Trooper could do, the Beta Battloid forced its arms back and back—and worked a wholly Human wrestling hold, freeing one arm to grip the monolithic turret-head, seize, strain, apply torque with everything it had.

Rick was ordering the Beta clear; the flagship had been maneuvered so that the GMU's cannon had been brought to bear. But the Beta wouldn't relinquish its death grip on its foe. The Shock Troopers' pincers scraped deep furrows in the Beta's armor; its oval forearms levered in moves conceived to let it break free.

To no avail. The Beta bent the Shock Trooper's arm up around behind it, and Rick understood in that moment that where matters of Robotechnology stood even, a deciding factor emerged. That factor had to do with things that were *the exact opposite* of mechanical processes. Emotion and belief, a passion for victory that was fueled by hatred of the outrages the Invid had perpetrated; in place of the unquestioned instructions the Invid got from their Hive, the Beta was animated by a reasoned mind's drive to win.

The Beta got its free elbow under the Shock Trooper's chin and pressed up and back, and back. All this, while VTs and enemy mecha swirled and fought, while the kill scores climbed, while *Farrago*'s gun emplacements hammered.

There was a slight outventing, then seals gave and atmosphere rushed from the Invid, along with what appeared to be a green liquid that became weightless beads and globules and vapor as soon as it hit vacuum. The Invid came apart with explosive separations of its joints. The Beta braced one bulky foot against the dead carcass of it, and pushed free.

The Beta sailed like some lumpy puppet toward the dead Logan. "No life readings," somebody relayed the readout to Lisa; the Logan was so mangled that it came as no surprise.

Rick looked up from his apparently primitive but surprisingly sophisticated scopes. His features were closed of expression; self-contained. "Those are the Valdezes."

Everyone knew them, brother and sister VT hotdoggers, top-of-the-roster aces. Henry had flown the Logan; his sister had just avenged his death in the mighty Beta.

The repeated attacks of the Invid had only turned the battle into a turkey shoot; what the REF mecha didn't bag, the Sentinels' guns had managed to find. Lisa heard from her commo analysts that the instant destruction of the task force's command ship had kept word from going out to Optera, *or even Karbarra*, of the presence of the Sentinels. Something groundside might have detected the weapons discharges in space, but the Invid garrison must have been at a loss as to what they meant. Karbarra had a thick planetary ring, and the Invid below might think that was the cause of the commo breakdown. It didn't make much difference to the Sentinels now; Human and XT alike, they had gone to war—and in this Robotech era that meant something they were all used to: win or die.

The energy salvos and counter-salvos sent narrow beams of blindingly bright light and streams of angry red-orange annihilation disks skewing through the blackness. The mecha whirled and pounced like craft maneuvering in atmosphere, though that was prodigiously wasteful of power; such were the peculiarities of Robotech, the pilots' Earth-honed flying instincts channeled to action by the thinking caps.

It was the thickest of the rat race, the centerpoint of the fighter pilot's life, the Heart of Unreason—the terrible venue of the dogfight.

Barrages of missiles *whooshed* and energy blasts of such power were exchanged that they seemed almost *material*. Holed and damaged machines tumbled and spun, leaking atmosphere and flame, and dying. The Invid fought with the unanimity of the group mind, but it became manifest that the REF, too, had learned to wage war with total concentration. Neither side lacked for ferocity.

But the tide turned in the Sentinels' favor; in a mass Robotech rat race like that, the shift didn't take long to make itself apparent.

Max and Miriya flew through it like gods, dealing death when they saw an opponent and, by their intervention, granting life to beset VT fliers. Max felt like he had an extra edge, with Rick behind on the bridge.

Once Max's boss as Skull Leader, Rick had been away from combat flying too long to be jumping into a VT seat, no matter *how* restless he might feel. Max had already saved Rick's life once, at considerable risk to his own, since Rick had begun chafing at the restrictions of flag-rank life.

Max had to endure no such distractions now; with the enormously augmented power the pods and other enhancements of their Alphas gave them, Max and Miriya, wingmates and soulmates, flew where they willed. Mighty Enforcers and evasive Pincers were their prey, like prey for tigers. The Invid quarry stalked the VTs, too, with fire that could kill them, but that only made the hunt more worthwhile.

Computer and sensor constructs of the battle in various tactical-analysis thinkpools showed a moving nimbus of death and destruction—Max and Miriya Sterling, in an almost superhuman performance of cunning and aero-combat excellence.

The tide turned quickly and surely against the survivors of the late Senep's task force. In seconds, the scale had dipped unmistakably; the Invid were trying to disengage, to run for troop carriers that weren't there anymore, as the volcanic cannonshots of Vince Grant's GMU found their mark again and again.

The Invid's turning tail tripped some essential instinct of pursuit in the VTs, and they rushed in, crowding one another, for the kill. A whole field of retreating Invid mecha were suddenly in a shooting gallery like nothing seen in any Robotech scrap so far. Some turned to fight, others ran and dodged; the Skull fliers went after them all, merciless because they had seen what the Invid did to captive worlds, and hungry for kills. Wolves flying at the fold were no more voracious.

Screened from Karbarra by its planetary ring and by the

jamming efforts of the ECM techs, the Sentinels had managed to win their first battle with a sort of unintended stealth. But the first of their main events waited below.

The last of the killing was still going on, the mopping-up of the Invid mecha being carried out by the men and women of the Skull squadron, but that was already a fait accompli. Rick Hunter wanted to stay where he was until the last of the VTs was back, safe, or at least accounted for. But he knew he couldn't; the strike at Karbarra must be launched *now*, within the hour, because the Sentinels' presence might already have been discovered.

Rick had a sudden vision of Henry Gloval, and knew what had been trying to bow the old man's shoulders as he stood there on the deck of SDF-1 in the old days. Rick thought of Lisa with a vast burst of love, and wondered whether any of the Sentinels would be alive in a few hours.

"We hit them now; take them by surprise, and the whole of Karbarra is ours!" Kami, the foxlike Gerudan, said from behind his breathing mask.

The rest of the Sentinels agreed with that and Rick Hunter slammed the flat of his hand down on the U-shaped table, making everybody, even the stolid Lron and Crysta, start a little.

"I lost eight good people in the fight just now, and eight mecha *we couldn't afford to lose*; I won't lose more if I can help it! The quicker we jump the planetary garrison, the fewer our losses and the quicker we win major mecha-producing facilities."

Lron suddenly reared up, there beneath the bridge dome where a trestle table had been set out atop empty Karbarran beer barrels. "And I say we, we . . ."

He seemed to be drifting in thought, and many of the Sentinels looked at one another, especially the Humans. But nobody appeared to have an explanation. Still, the deaths of REF-assigned fighter pilots were Rick's direct responsibility, so he found himself pressing his own view.

"We *must* exploit our current tactical advantage to the

fullest, to minimize our losses, by attacking at once! Intel-computers and sensors and the G-3 ops staff have already pinpointed the primary and secondary Invid targets on Karbarra. Our VTs are being refueled and rearmed at this moment; we can strike in something under an hour. Fellow Sentinels, let's free Karbarra."

Lisa was looking at Rick in a new light. Granted, he hated his desk job, but he had shouldered the responsibility that had been given him and was undergoing that torment, that near-schizophrenia, that any decent commanding officer knew in combat: the need to carry out the mission weighed against the lives of his or her command. She wouldn't have wished it on him, but she saw now that he had come into his full growth, as Captain Gloval had always put it.

Rick, for his part, looked over at his wife and saw that she understood the forces vying to rip him apart—understood, too, more vividly than he ever had, the forces that had pressed Lisa so agonizingly when she was SDF-1's first officer, and later SDF-3's captain.

Rick had something of a revelation. *I'd rather be in a cockpit, responsible for one VT and my own life, because it's* easier! *Let this cup pass . . .*

But it didn't. Nonetheless, Rick saw that Lisa fully understood, and that gave him a strength that surprised him. He also felt a measure of shame; how often had *she* been in this kind of dilemma, when he couldn't see beyond his own Skull Leader problems?

Every time he thought he had run out of reasons to love her, a new one appeared.

Except it didn't help him with his Karbarran problem. Lron, till now, the Papa-bear stalwart, swung a fist the size of a Thanksgiving turkey, and took a considerable portion off the lip of the table nearest him.

"No!"

■ ■ ■ ■ ■ ■ ■ ■ ■ ■ ■ ■ ■ ■ ■ ■

CHAPTER
TWELVE

Here's where you get back
Some of your own;
Here's where we visit
Part of the horror upon its author

From an Augury chant of the Karbarrans

NOBODY WAS ABOUT TO TELL LRON HE COULDN'T have his say, or to try to stifle Crysta, who had risen up next to her mate.

Their goggles were pushed down around their thick, furry necks; The armor and accoutrements they wore only made them seem that much more like captive and danger-ous wild animals.

"We cannot attack yet," Lron roared, and Lisa began to consider the tactical problems of having half-ton ursinoids turning mean on the bridge. Stun guns might not even faze them, given the thick pelts and subcutaneous fat. It was either shoot to kill, or listen. And given how much

Humans still had to learn about their allies, she followed the example of Veidt and the other Sentinels, and listened.

Rick saw her decision clearly by the lines of her face; he backed off, too, and for one moment they shared a brief, small smile—but it was something that warmed them both out of all proportion to the moment.

"We cannot attack," Lron was grunt-howling, "because the [here he made an ursine noise that didn't translate into the lingua franca the Sentinels used] is not correct! You are outsiders, and blind to the ways of Karbarra, and yet I tell you: if you go against the [that same word again], then there is nothing but total disaster awaiting you."

It took considerable time to sort out, during which Rick fidgeted. Long-horned Burak and the crystal-bright Baldan spoke in defense of Lron's past accomplishments. Rick felt like pulling a fistful of hair out of his head.

But it seemed that Karbarrans had a certain sense of fate, and Rick got the impression that it was depressingly downbeat and debilitating. And the fate of the bears was that there be no all-out attack on Karbarra at this time. What Lron and Crysta wanted was a very small recon group, a handful, to go down and scout things out.

"That's crazy!" Rick yelled. "We *know* where the Inorganics and the rest of our targets are! Let's *paste* 'em, then go in and save the Karbarrans! My *god*, is there anybody here who doesn't understand what we're talking about? The Invid aren't going to spare your people, no matter what concessions you make! There'll be another demand, and another!"

Crysta came out of her big chair with a growl, showing her snow-white peglike canines. Rick stood his ground— arguably the bravest thing he had ever done; Lisa's hand was clawing for a pistol that wasn't at her belt.

"The Shapings of the Protoculture do not dictate . . . that," Crysta said slowly, as if in a dream. She lowered her head as though she had come at bay. "Do not necessarily say that."

Rick shook his head, unable to understand what it was they were getting at. "What's wrong with you? We hit 'em high, then hit 'em low, and Karbarra's *yours* again! Your planet's *yours* again!"

Lron spun on him, one paw raised high, its claws standing out from the splayed hand, looming over Rick. There was almost a debate in the slow orbiting of it, and Rick Hunter knew death hovered close.

"We . . . won't . . . hit . . . them . . . at . . . *all*, yet!" Lron bellowed, at such volume that the others winced.

Lisa Hayes Hunter was the first one to raise her head again and look Lron in the eye. Rick tried to pull her back down, and wished he had thought to bring a firearm. Something in the elephant-gun category.

Lisa looked Lron in the eye. She said, "In case you've forgotten, we didn't come here to be frightened away. Now, do we attack with your help, or without it?"

Lisa had put herself on the other side of the argument without qualification. And Rick was bracing himself to fight, because he was pretty sure the bears were going to charge his wife in a second or so.

But instead, Lron and Crystal subsided, making gnawing sounds but not objecting. Lisa went on. "It's clear that we have the Invid at a disadvantage, since it is highly probable that the ground forces aren't aware that their task force has been wiped out. Computer projections and G-3 evaluations are unanimous: we have a window of advantage at this moment and it won't last long. On the behalf of the Human Sentinels, I say that we should take our shot."

Other Sentinels pounded the table and cried their support. Rick looked at his wife and felt a powerful pulse of love mixed with a certain envy; but when he thought about it, the envy was separated out into equal parts of desire and admiration. Both of those were good for a love affair, better yet for a marriage.

But the Karbarrans were up, like grizzlies on their back haunches, to rebut. "You do not understand the————"

For that, they made a sound incomprehensible to the Sentinels, something the translation computers had to labor at, at last rendering up a marked and qualified interpretation: "the Shaping of Things."

Rick looked to his left, to Kami, the foxlike Gerudan who sat there in his breathing mask that was fed from the tank on his back. "What in the world are they talking about?"

Kami made an exasperated sound that somehow penetrated the mask. Rick leaned his way. "I don't know what to think. Crysta and Lron aren't behaving as they did when we formed our alliance," Kami said.

"We could *sock* into that garrison before they knew what'd hit them, then mop up the remains," Rick pointed out.

Kami nodded. "But something seems to be holding the Karbarrans back," he pointed out.

"Are you gonna let that hold *you* back?"

Kami regarded him with a long look. "I would give some benefit of the doubt to you or the Praxians or any of the others. There are many things we don't understand about one anothers' species, and so we must proceed with caution. Am I wrong-thinking?"

Rick didn't quite know what to say. "What we must do is make a reconnaissance of the situation below," Lron announced. "Crysta and I and a half dozen of our people—"

"No." Lisa was shaking her head. She wasn't sure what the ursinoids were being so secretive about, but she was wholly opposed to letting them go off on their own. She wanted very much to trust them—had come, in fact, to like Crysta and Lron—but couldn't shake the feeling that they were concealing something.

Everyone had something to say, of course. The Sentinels' alliance was put to its first real test, and for some moments it seemed that the need that bound them together wouldn't hold. Unexpectedly, Cabell was one of those who put things back on track. "Have you all forgotten the horrors the Invid inflicted on my planet? We must work together—compromise! The life and death of whole worlds are at stake!"

In the end, it was agreed that recon would be carried out by living beings rather than by remotes or drones. Veidt, acting as chairman, finally decreed that the unit would be composed of Lron, Kami, Rick, Gnea, and Bela, along with Jack Baker and Karen Penn. Those last names surprised Rick, but then he supposed Veidt had come to know the two lieutenants.

Lisa wanted to object, wanted to be included, but knew that Veidt's selection was right; her place was on the bridge of the starship, especially now. But one last name was added to the roster: at both Cabell's request and his own, Rem was included.

For the insertion, they would take a Karbarran shuttlecraft; with its Sekiton drive, it was much less likely to be detected by the Invid Protoculture instruments. This was no job for a VT or a Hovertank, as even Rick had to concede.

The recon party moved through the ship's armory, gathering handguns and rifles, along with rocket launchers and grenades. Meanwhile, human techs were checking out the assorted survival gear the team would need. Rick noticed that while the women from Praxis had no objection to buckling gunbelts around their waists or slinging Wolverine assault rifles over their shoulders—indeed, they seemed to understand firearms quite well—they still insisted on bringing sword, crossbow, and Gnea's *naginata*-like halberd.

He shrugged; to each his own. Besides, silent weapons might come in quite handy. Lron seemed set on bringing his pneumatic musket, too, and his huge, cleaverlike knife, but Kami was apparently more than happy to carry Human weapons with their greater firepower.

The equipment and the shuttle were checked while sensors and intel staff people and computers debated over optimal landing sites. There was still no sign that the Invid garrison below had any inkling of the Sentinels' presence in the planetary ring; at least the recon group had that advantage.

Rick had found time to snatch a few hours' sleep before the final briefing was to commence. He had hoped for a moment or two along with Lisa, but she had been preoccupied with preparations—and with trying to figure out contingency plans for dealing with whatever the scouting mission might run across.

Now, though, she entered their quarters as he settled his web gear and ran yet another check of his equipment. Medpack, spare ammo, emergency ration concentrates, inertial tracker—

"Happy, Rick?"

"Lisa, we can't have this same argument again! Veidt picked me; I didn't even volunteer."

"You didn't have to. You've made your preferences known."

"I took an oath to serve in a military outfit, not sit on the sidelines!"

"Well, you got your wish, hmm?" But she couldn't stay mad at him, not with his departure so near. "Oh, just make sure you come back safe and sound, get me?"

He took her in his arms. "Quit worrying; I'm not looking for any medals. Rick 'Cautious' Hunter, that's me."

They kissed, then she pushed him away. "And no flirting with those Praxian lady wrestlers, or we're going to be short one admiral around here."

"No, ma'am. Yes, ma'am."

At the shuttle lock, Jack Baker was making final adjustments on his thinking cap. While the team wasn't bringing any large transformable mecha, there were still a couple of Cyclone combat cycles and Hoverbikes. Besides, Jack didn't favor climbing onto anything fast-moving, or, for that matter, being in a combat zone without all the protection he could get. He wished Lang's researchers had given the Sentinels some prototypes of the bodyarmor they were working on, full armor that was supposed to integrate with the Cyclones somehow.

Anyway, the helmet would be necessary for communications, with its built-in commo gear. Apparently Gnea and Bela were going to stick with their showy Praxian helms as reengineered by Lang; sometimes Jack found their blending of the old and new rather illogical.

"Well, well, so they're sending the scrub team along to see how *real* soliders get the job done, hmm?"

Karen Penn had a way of making even a combat suit look good. She was shrugging into her web gear, resettling her burdens, giving Jack a mocking smile.

"*Somebody*'s got to be there to chafe your wrist after you faint, Penn." They were about to get into another row when Jack became aware of a sound that made him turn with his mouth hanging open.

They're not serious!

It was Bela, mounted on the Robotsteed, Halidarre, with Gnea riding pillion behind. Halidarre's hooves rang against the deckplates. It took him a few seconds to get out any sound. "What d'you think you're doing? This is a recon mission, not a carnival!"

The towering Bela's brows knit ominously as she glared down at him. "Halidarre is my steed; with her, we'll cover more ground and be able to rest assured that triumph in battle shall inevitably be ours!" Bela slapped the sword on her thigh, but Jack noticed that she carried a Wolverine assault rifle in a saddle scabbard too, and had a heavy energy pistol in a shoulder holster.

Gnea was carrying her halberd and her shield, although she was adorned with grenades and firearms. Jack could see now that the inner rim of the shield was lined with a row of throwing knives held in place by clips, convenient to her hand. Gnea slid to the deck, then Bela did, taking Halidarre's bridle and leading her toward the shuttle's open freight hatch.

The Karbarran spacers and the others standing around were too stunned to interfere, and in a moment the amazons were easing the mecha horse into place in the cargo area. Totally unskittish, Halidarre looked like she went through this kind of thing every day.

"The admiral's not going to like this," Jack muttered.

Karen shrugged. "Oh, well, at least she didn't decided to bring along that four-winged miniature gunship that she—"

Just then Bela turned and uttered a piercing whistle, adding, "Hagane. To me!"

Jack and Karen, like the rest of the ship's complement, had learned to duck when Bela gave that whistle. Something small and fast, moving and darting like a hummingbird, came blurring through the air on a whirring of multiple wings, buzzing the two lieutenants just for the fun of it. Jack felt like taking a swipe at Hagane, but decided it wasn't worth the risk of having a finger nipped off by a beak as keen as a pair of tin snips.

Hagane was what Bela called a malthi, as much a royal bird to the Praxians as the falcon was to the pharaohs. It settled on the heavy sheath on her forearm now, a creature no bigger than a sparrow-hawk, ruffling its double sets of wings and gazing around suspiciously. Her eyes bulged strangely, savage and unreadable, and Hagane let out the *birring* hunting sound that seemed to go right through one's eardrums.

"*God*, I hate when she does that," Jack frowned. "Horses and birds! Why don't we take along some clowns and a tightrope walker while we're at it?"

"You don't approve of the TO&E, Lieutenant?"

Jack spun. "Oh, Admiral! The Table of Organization and Equipment's just fine with me, sir! I, uh—that is, I was just surprised, that's all."

Rick was, too, but decided not to let it show. Actually, he was curious about how useful the Robotech horse and the Praxian hunting bird would be. Certainly, they wouldn't exactly be inconspicuous if Bela insisted on tearing all over the sky—but on the other hand, they were nothing that the Invid would connect with an expedition from Tirol.

He sighed, not looking forward to getting Bela to see reason and use her pets with restraint. Maybe Lisa was right, and this outing wasn't such a great idea after all.

But it was too late for that. Lron showed up, and Rem, and Kami. They boarded the shuttle and belted in, as Lisa began her careful approach swing through the planetary ring.

CHAPTER
THIRTEEN

The pivotal point, unanswered as yet, is what success the Regent felt he was achieving in his "devolution," and how he chose his course. That he still felt an unshakable desire—perhaps love, perhaps obsession—for the Regis is obvious.

But this doesn't jibe with "de-evolution" as Humans would picture it; surely his self-remolding should have taken him away from such feelings. Did he refuse to give up those feelings, or was de-evolution something completely different from what we might surmise?

Lemuel Thicka, *Temple of Flames: A History of the Invid Regent*

ONCE AGAIN, CRYSTA STOOD BEFORE TESLA'S CAGE. "I ask you yet again, Invid: what can you tell me of the situation on Karbarra?"

Tesla spread his hands with infinite sadness. "Only what you yourself know. Yet, I say to you once more: release me and let me go down to your planet and do my best on behalf of peace and the opening up of new dialogues."

Crysta made an impatient sound. "If I discover that you're lying, I'll throw you out an airlock." She turned to go.

"Wait," he blurted. "Why haven't you told the others of—this matter?" As a scientist, he had discovered interesting things about the ursinoids' belief system. He had expected Lron and Crysta would have explained their quandary to the Sentinels long ago; though it was perhaps some slight advantage to him that they hadn't, he found it puzzling.

Crysta made an irritated sound. "You understand nothing, Invid! The knowledge that comes from our Seeing is fragile. Revealing it can change the Seeing and the Shaping to something else, something even worse. If you hadn't already known about—about our dilemma, I would never have mentioned it."

Tesla nodded to himself. So. It might be that there was hope for him yet, if he could manipulate things. Certainly, he hadn't much else going for him. He, above all, had reason to hope that the Karbarrans' vision of the future came out well; otherwise, Tesla would be among the first to feel their wrath, and he knew how terrible their vengeance could be.

The entry was more of a free-fall, really, Lron's piloting veering between the suicidally reckless and the professionally competent. He peeled part of the ablative layer off the shuttle but got them down without registering, as far as they could tell, on any Invid instruments.

Jack Baker found himself pressed into his seat, eyeballs in, slipping into and out of a red-out. He just hoped Lron had a greater tolerance of g-forces, because this felt like it might be an embarrassing moment to have the pilot take a snooze.

Karbarra was a barren, windswept place, pockmarked and wormholed as a result of their generations of intensive mining. Lron pulled out of his bone-jarring entry and gave the ship some thrust, leveling off at virtual landing altitude, searching. He quickly had his bearings, and closed in on the landing site he had selected.

All the Sentinels were alert, manning weapons stations and ready to open fire. But the spot selected by Lron, an abandoned operation where a major vein of iron ore had given out, was deserted. The Sentinels had been counting on decreased surveillance and patrolling, what with the Invid occupation forces presumably cut to minimal strength. It seemed they had won the bet—so far—but that still left an awful lot of the enemy.

Lron set the shuttle down gently through a huge gaping hole in an enormous cracked dome at the center of the processing area. It was a location already noted by the Karbarran resistance, he explained. It was as safe a base of operations as the team was likely to find, at least for now.

Rick began getting things organized even before they unbelted. Bela was anxious to get Halidarre up for a look around and to feel the freedom of the sky; it took some strong talk to make her see that a ground sweep and sensor scan of the immediate area would be necessary first, to make sure the Sentinels weren't spotted by somebody before they could do the spotting themselves.

Karen Penn felt some foreboding, seeing the young admiral standing up to the imposing amazon and camly telling her it was about time she started learning to take orders. Her hand went to her sword again. "Orders? You dare tell me I lack discipline? And who are you to give *me* orders?"

His mouth had become a flat line. "I'm one of the people you Sentinels came to for help, remember? I'm part of the force that's giving you a fighting chance at winning back your planet. Now, when our joint council makes a decision, we stick by it; that was the bargain. And the decision in this case was for a recon mission with me in command and Lron in second place. So let's see if you can take orders as well as you give them."

Bela suddenly grinned, throwing her head back. "I keep forgetting that you males can be just as hard-nosed as a woman! All right, Admiral, we'll do it your way—but, mind: when I'm put in charge of an operation, I'll expect the same from you."

"Fair enough." Privately, Rick decided that he didn't

want anything to do with an operation run by the impulsive
warrior-woman.

His every footfall in the vast, echoing halls of the Invid
Home Hive seemed to be mocking the Regent.

There was still no word of the task force he had sent to
Tirol, no answer from the Regis. It was all too troubling
for him to even take pleasure in punishing subordinates. He
paced along now with his elite bodyguard marching a dis-
creet distance behind, their armored steps resounding.

And he cursed again the tactical misfortunes that had
made it necessary to abandon the Living Computer, the
newest and by far the best of the giant Invid vat-grown
brains, under the Royal Hall. It was inactive, and could fall
prey to harm, could atrophy—could even be damaged by
the upstart mongrel species who had somehow routed his
legions.

He had been obliged to recall more troops from the
outer marches of his crumbling realm to insure that nearby
worlds under his dominion remained that way. The Regent
rasped angrily at the thought that perhaps his task force had
met with some reversal. At the worst possible time!

And then there was the thought that chilled him as much
as any. What if the Robotech Masters should return to
wage bloody war, and catch him in this disorganized state?
He rumbled with displeasure, kicking out at a pillar that
resembled a neural axon.

He cursed his mate again, for taking half his race from
him. What could she need them for? She wasn't even engaged in conquest! Wasn't even pretending to help him
maintain sway over the realm. It wasn't fair; this was all
her fault.

Something had to be done.

The Regent paused, turned, started off in another direction. When he got to the vast egg chamber, he was pleased
to find that nothing was amiss, and the Special Children of
the Regis were all there, unmoving and unaware in their
gelatinous suspension. Row by row, rank on rank.

"Special Children." Typical of her, she hadn't even deigned to tell him what the phrase *meant*. The Regis had merely made it clear that these were to be some ultimate manifestation of the Invid genetic heritage, and that theirs would be some higher destiny.

"Indeed?" the Regent snorted to himself. When the empire was crumbling and the enemies of the Invid might be at the very Home Hive soon? What higher destiny could such Special Children have than to defend their Regent and conquer, conquer for the glory of the Invid?

Yet—he must proceed carefully. He wasn't even sure what he was dealing with. It wouldn't do to unleash some new and even worse danger—perhaps a generation of Invid who would know no loyalty to him, or even be infected with aspirations of their *own*.

No, best to go cautiously. In the interim, he could reassign his forces, maintain the status quo for the time being. He had already managed to scrape up some frontier troops and dispatch them to reinforce the depleted Karbarran garrison. Perhaps he could even use the Special Children as a bargaining chip—get the Regis to trade him the loyal fighters he required in return for these quiescent eggs.

And Tesla! With his mystical talk about the Fruit of the Flower and his promises to bring a menagerie of defeated enemies for the Regent's entertainment! What of him?

Seething, the Regent went off to dispatch another message to Haydon IV and demand immediate word of Tesla, on pain of horrible punishment to those all along the line who might fail to provide it.

"I simply have a feeling she'll listen to you," Vince Grant told his wife. "You just have that way with people, darling."

She put down the medical report she had been filling out, preliminary evaluations of the vast array of salves, preparations, pills, and powders from every Sentinel's homeworld; she was trying to understand them and the physiologies of the patients she would be expected to minister to.

"Vince, why don't *you* talk to Crysta. I mean, you're more her size."

That got a grudging chuckle out of him. "I don't think this has anything to do with size. I'm just a jumped-up engineer who got a commission 'cause he knows what makes the GMU tick. But you understand people, and Crysta's just big furry people. Besides, you're a mother."

Jean looked him over. "What's that got to do with it?"

"I'm not sure. I was showing her around the GMU and, you know, there's that picture of Bowie on my desk. When I explained about him, it made her clam up, and she cut the tour short."

Jean felt a mixture of curiosity and professional obligation now; he had seen her get interested in a case, just like this, so many times before. "We really don't know much about the Karabarran children, do we? Oh, the reproductive cycle's right there in the data banks, nothing unusual —especially when you compare them to those Spherians! But I mean, what's happening to them right this second?"

"That occurred to me, too," Vince said soberly.

She rose and kissed her husband, standing on tiptoe to do it. "You're pretty smart for a jumped-up engineer, y'know that?"

He gave her a half smile. "Smart enough to come to you when I run into a *real* problem."

The sensors and detectors indicated that they had made their landing without being spotted. Sweeps by Rick, Jack, and Karen on hovercycles, and, inevitably, a surveillance flight by Bela and Gnea on their flying horse, just confirmed the fact.

Then it was Rem who got stubborn, as Rick assigned him, along with Gnea, to guard the shuttle and man the commo-relay equipment, so that the recon team would be sure of getting a direct link to *Farrago* if and when it was needed.

"This whole mission is pointless if we can't report back what we find here," Rick fumed at him. "Now, I don't want any more arguments from anybody!"

Rem subsided, and the team began loading up with weapons and gear. Lron casually weighted himself down with twice as much paraphernalia as any of the others and didn't seem to feel the burden a bit. Something was making him most untalkative, though.

As it was, Rick was more concerned with trying to get the right mix of equipment and weapons distributed among his team. Lron had revealed that the network of natural caverns and abandoned mines constituted a virtual underground roadway, and that the unit could make most of the distance to its objective that way.

That meant spare handheld spots, night-sight gear, and so forth. Rick let Bela keep her Wolverine rifle, but assigned Kami to a much more powerful but short-range Owens Mark IX mob gun, in case of close fighting down below. Rick took a Wolverine for himself. Karen was assigned an elaborately scoped sniper rifle, her marksmanship scores being the best of any of them.

Lron lugged the magazine-fed rocket launcher and an assortment of ammunition; Jack was given a solid-projectile submachine gun that fired explosive pellets. Rick made sure they were all wearing "bat-ears," in case there was any subsurface fighting. The bat-ears amplified soft sounds, left normal ones unchanged, but dampened loud ones—so the scouts wouldn't be deafened in an underground firefight.

Bela didn't put up the expected argument about leaving Halidarre behind; even she could see how impractical it would be to drag the horse through the tight spots the team could expect to hit down below. She put aside most of her Praxian weapons, taking only her long knife.

Lron led the way to a mine elevator that smelled of must and stale air. He fiddled with a power connection that looked dead, and made the elevator's motor hum with readiness. The group boarded, turning on helmet lights. Rem and Gnea watched them descend into the darkness.

Veidt, Cabell, and the others were mystified by what they saw—or, rather, didn't see. Long-range readings on the surface of Karbarra indicated that there had been little or no battle damage on the planet below. Their main city, Tracialle, was still shining and whole under its crystalline dome.

"This isn't logical," Veidt said. "The Karbarrans are fierce haters of the Invid, and we assumed the fighting had been furious."

But instruments definitely indicated heavy Invid military activity below, although there was no sign of combat. With some few exceptions, the industrial and technical infrastructure seemed to be intact and functioning to a modest degree, the buildings still standing for the most part, the social systems operating normally.

"Perhaps this is all some ruse?" Sarna wondered, turning to her husband. "Can it be that the Karbarrans went through all this to lure us into a trap?—but no. Surely they could have diverted the ship here on one pretext or another as soon as we staged our mutiny?"

"And it makes no sense for them to have risked their lives against the Pursuer, or again in combat against the task force we surprised," Cabell pointed out. "Then there's this business of the reconnaissance. Some piece of the puzzle is still missing."

They were interrupted by the ship's mismatched alarms again, and Lisa's voice came over a PA speaker that resembled a cornucopia.

"Battle stations, battle stations! An enemy force has left hyperspace for approach to Karbarra. They have detected us and are maneuvering for attack. Skull Squadron and Wolff Pack, prepare for launch. All weapons stations prepare to fire on my command!"

For Jonathan Wolff, it was a relief to be called to the cockpit of his Hovertank. He had been driving his Wolff Pack all through the voyage, trying to wrench his mind away from the thoughts that tormented him, with preparation and drill, maintenance checks, and intense briefing and training sessions.

It hadn't helped. There was still the guilt that he had left his wife and son far behind so that he could share in the REF glory, and now it would be years before he saw them again.

But an even worse guilt, grinding his conscience raw and then grating at the bloody wound, was the undeniable image of Minmei, Minmei. The sound of her voice, the aroma of her hair, the face and eyes, her coltish charm. The recollection of how it had felt to put his arms around her in the garden at the New Year's Eve party on Tiresia. Her kiss, which had made him as light-headed as some school kid.

The ship was shuddering at the launching of the Skull VTs. Wolff snapped rapid commands, and his own Hovertanks went to Battloid mode, sealed for combat in vacuum, following him in a dash for the designated cargo lock. The Destroids assigned to the GMU would be going to their firing positions, Wolff knew, and the Ground Mobile Unit itself would be warming up its weapons.

But there would be no question of an ambush this time; today both sides were forewarned. Wolff had felt disappointed at not being included in the recon team, but that had proved premature. Now, the Wolff Pack looked like it was going to get all the action it could handle.

And as for Hunter and the rest, trapped below? Wolff felt briefly sorry for them, then got his mind back on running his little corner of the war.

CHAPTER
FOURTEEN

Of course I heard all those cracks about "aliens," and to her great credit, my wife let them pass, knowing what it was like for people fighting a war.

I'd hoped the Human race had learned, in meeting the Sentinels, to be a little less indiscriminately prejudiced. But few aside from the Skulls were.

Miriya overlooked all that, and fought like a tiger on behalf of the Human race and the Sentinels. And you're telling me that's alien? Then so am I.

Max Sterling, from *Wingmates: The Story of Max and Miriya Sterling by Theresa Duvall*

 ORM UP ON ME, SKULL TEAM, AND STICK WITH your wingmates," Max Sterling recited automatically, his attention devoted to the tactical displays in his Alpha cockpit. He knew his wife, comrade and wingmate, would keep an eye on the team for him.

Max found a moment in which to be concerned for Rick. At least Rick wasn't out here trying to fly combat in a VT; he was a good flyer, a natural, and once he had ranked only behind Max in proficiency. But Rick was years out of practice, and that had been obvious the last time he had gone into space combat with Skull. If Rick and his gang just kept their heads down, they would be all right—perhaps a lot better than the Sentinels' main force was going to be, unless Skull got on the stick and took care of business.

Luckily, this new enemy contingent wasn't as numerous as the task force the Sentinels had handled when they arrived: two saucer troopships, and no command vessel at all. On the other hand, the Sentinels weren't going to get in any surprise Sunday punches today. Even now, the clamlike troop carriers yawned open and Pincer ships poured forth, interspersed with some Shock Troopers and even a few of the fearsome, armored Shock Troopers.

The Veritechs leapt to meet them in a mass duel. It was a mad, swirling combat wherein friend and foe were so intermingled that it was often dangerous to risk a shot. But those Invid who got through found that the Sentinels' flagship was throwing out an almost impenetrable net of fire, augmented by Wolff's tanks and the GMU's firepower.

Novas lit the night as mecha erupted in fireballs; tremendous streams of destructive energy were hosed this way and that, and clouds of missiles flew. Jamming and counterjamming made guidance systems erratic and put both sides in almost as much danger from their own ordnance as from their opponents'.

A small group of Pincers, led by an Armored Officer mecha, got to the upper hull of the Sentinels' ship after suffering heavy casualties. But as they were about to attack the craft at close range—and get aboard to wreak havoc if possible—they were met by Wolff and a squad of his Battloids. Most of the fighting was too close even for hand weapons, and the conflict came down to REF alloy fist against metallic Invid claw—mecha feet and elbows and knees came into play.

A Pack member wrenched off a Pincer's arm and flung it away; the Pincer's power systems overloaded and blew it apart from within. The enemy Armored Officer unit and two Pincers seized a Battloid from behind and began pulling it to pieces.

But the Invid were outnumbered, being beaten or kicked or torn to bits. Just then more Hovertanks showed up, in

Gladiator mode: stumpy, two-legged walking artillery pieces the size of a house. Their tremendously powerful blasts nailed the last of the interlopers; then all the tanks went to Gladiator to repulse any further attempts to land on the starship.

The GMU's massive main gun had sent out its inferno shots again and again, but all the enemy mecha had dispersed, the clam-ships unimportant for the moment. Vince Grant ceased fire and diverted power to the secondary gun emplacements, to conserve energy for the battle.

An Invid suicide attack got through the Sentinels' net of AA fire toward the stern, and Vince dispatched Destroid war machines across the outer deck to join a pair of Hovertanks in trying to maintain cover back there. He had his exec double-check with Jean to make sure the sick bay would be ready for casualties, and got back an answer that rattled him.

"Sick bay standing by, sir, but Lieutenant Commander Grant isn't there and hasn't reported in yet. Her whereabouts are unknown at this time."

Far below, on Karbarra, the Invid noted the military action being fought high above.

In accordance with standing orders, certain specialized units were mobilized and moved out en masse, weapons primed. Karbarrans in the street, frozen with dread and hollow-eyed with fear, watched them go. But the big ursinoids could only stand rooted to the spot, and pray.

Even with the inertial trackers, it was tough to figure out where Lron was leading them.

Lron, however, didn't seem to have any doubts. Down abandoned mineshafts, along connections that had been made to drain underground watercourses, and through cavern systems, they made their way, the spotlights stabbing through the utter blackness. Rick had had them moving combat-style at first, wary of attack despite Lron's reassurance that the Invid were unaware of this underground travel system. But infantry tactics slowed the recon party down considerably, especially since the alien Sentinels were unfamiliar with REF procedures.

So in time Rick settled on modified procedures, with Lron on point and Jack and Karen taking turns on rear guard, the rest of the group together or spread out somewhat as circumstances dictated. The team moved faster than combat-zone precautions would ordinarily have dictated.

At one point they passed through a mined-out, shored-up space where an ore seam had been, a place not quite four feet high, though it was fifty yards wide and went on for over two miles. It was backbreaking travel, especially hard on Lron. Their shuffling progress raised a fine dust that had them all black-faced in no time.

Kami, with his Gerudan breathing mask, was relatively comfortable, and after a while the REF members closed their flight helmets. Lron improvised a face mask from strips of fabric.

At another point, though, the group rode two ore cars that they powered with energy cells Lron had brought. It was a welcome relief, even with the weight of a planet hanging overhead, and they made good time along the railway.

Lron and Crysta had explained that the apparently limitless tunnel system had grown up over the years before the coming of the Invid and the Robotech Masters, when Karbarra, a center of industry and trade, had had its assorted rivals and enemies. War production under the planet was seldom slowed down as a result of attack from space, but nowadays much of the system had fallen into disuse and disrepair.

Sometime later, after a short break to eat and rest, Lron led them into a cavern system of unutterable phosphorescent beauty, and they paced along the brink of an underground lake in which strange, blind, parasollike, glowing things could be seen to swim and drift. The cavern ceiling was like a dome mosaic with jewels of every conceivable color. There were plants that looked like coral formations made out of tiny crystalline needles.

During the journey, the scouts maintained contact with

Rem and Gnea, taking turns raising the shuttle guards at thirty-minute intervals for a commo check. Slightly more than eleven hours after they had started out, Rick formed them up into as good a security perimeter as he could achieve in the confines of the cave, and took Lron aside.

"All right; you said we'd reach the first checkpoint two hours ago, but I don't see it around here yet. And don't give me any more of this 'it's just ahead' stuff, I'm warning you." Every muscle ached, and sheer fatigue was making him edgy and paranoid, fearing a trap or a terrible screwup that the big XT was afraid to admit.

Lron rumbled, "If we'd moved as quickly as Karbarrans are used to, we *would* have been there long since, Admiral. But never mind; a hundred paces or so—*my* paces!—along that way over there will bring us to the beginning of our ascent. If you can keep up with me for another hour—two at the most, if we go slowly—we will sleep tonight in a cave overlooking one of the Invid outposts in the Hardargh Rift.

"And in the meantime, do you realize what we've passed under? Inorganics; flying Scout patrols; prowling packs of those murderous Hellcats; formations of Enforcers in their skirmish ships; Terror Weapons drifting along on their surveillance routes; and more! Save your breath on this final climb, little Human; you'll need it to do some gasping when you realize how far we've come."

Now it was Rick's turn to grunt. *Talk's cheap; let's see you prove it!* But he kept the remark to himself, trying to avoid more friction. Instead, he turned and whistled; then, with voice and hand signals, formed up his tiny command to move out again.

They had barely reached the beginning of the long ascent when Rem contacted them with word of the new battle.

When things go wrong around here, they really do it in rows, Lisa thought, but there wasn't much time for regret. Reports coming in to the bridge indicated that the Skulls had repulsed the enemy attack, inflicting extremely heavy losses; the few Invid survivors were limping for Karbarra, their saucer troopships having been blown to particles by the GMU's big gun.

There had been losses in all Sentinel combat elements and the ship had suffered damage. Skull had lost two Betas, an Alpha, and a Logan, and several other VTs were badly damaged. Rick's group was standing pat in a relatively safe position, apparently, but a pickup was impossible, and it looked like the whole recon would be a failure. Lisa refused to think about what would happen if the Invid garrison's heightened state of alert on Karbarra meant that the shuttle was permanently pinned down in its present location.

And perhaps most shocking of all, Jean Grant had been absent from her post in time of combat. Lisa still didn't have all the details, but it involved Crysta and the Invid scientist, Tesla. Whatever it was, it had old Cabell about ready to throw a fit.

"Report," Lisa snapped. Subordinates reassured her that things were being seen to. Damage-control parties were already at work, casualties being attended to by various Sentinel healers and the medical staff. Skull was refueling and rearming in case of another hot scramble, but that didn't seem likely for the moment; apparently the Karbarran garrison had been stripped of its spacecraft, or else didn't care to launch a counterstrike quite yet.

Not after the way we've bloodied their snouts twice running, she thought with a small glimmer of satisfaction. Lisa issued orders that the flagship be held in orbit, and added, "I'll be down in medical."

Her first thoughts upon entering the big compartment where Jean Grant's medical labs abutted the hole set aside for Cabell's equipment and research was, *This must be a violation of the Geneva Accords!*

Even though the Zentraedi had shown no impulse to obey the Rules of War, and the Robotech Masters and the Invid were no better, the Human race had made it a point of honor not to sink into unnecessary cruelty. And that was most definitely what this appeared to be.

How else could you explain Tesla's being suspended inside an enormous glass beaker of greenish fluid, only the end of his snout sticking up into the air, and all sorts of electrodes and sensor pads connected to various parts of him, particularly his head?

"Admiral, please do not jump to conclusions," Cabell hastened. "The Invid isn't being hurt, and what we're finding out here may change the course of the war." Veidt and Sarna, looking on, nodded agreement.

Tesla objected loudly, "Not hurt? They torment me with their probings! They strip me of my dignity and take the vilest liberties with my person! They seek to slay me through sheer fright, so that they may dissect me. Save me!"

He thrashed a little in the cylinder. Jean Grant looked up from reading her instruments and rapped, "Be still. Or do you want me to hand you over to the Karbarrans? I bet *they* could get some information out of you, if I told them you've been holding out on them all this time!"

The thought of that made Tesla suddenly quiet down and float, trembling. Jean turned to Lisa. "I'm coming up with a sort of lie detector for Invid. At least I think I am. About all I can tell so far is that he's got high concentrations of Protoculture-active substances in various parts of his body, especially his skull. And their composition and signature varies quite profoundly. It's like some weird variation on a lymphatic system—and hormones, endocrines—but bizarre alien analogues, of course."

Lisa put aside the list of questions *she'd* like to put to Tesla. "But why are you doing this *now*, Doctor?"

Jean gestured to a corner, where Crysta slumped against a bulkhead. "I finally got Crysta to tell me why the Karbarrans have been acting so strangely. Lisa, the Invid have their children in a concentration camp. At the first wrong move from the populace down below, or in the event a defeat of the garrison becomes imminent, the Invid will kill every cub on the planet."

Lisa spun on Crysta. *"Why didn't you tell us before?"*

Crysta was actually wringing her pawlike hands. "The

Invid had been an occupation force, had made us work for them, but they'd never forced us to fight for them, never made actual slaves of us. They knew we could not stand for that.

"But we didn't understand how truly evil they were. They'd been preparing their plan for a long time; in a single afternoon, they swooped down to take up thousands of our young, and that immobilized us. You don't know how precious our cubs are to us, now that our population has dwindled so!

"And so we were helpless, as the Hellcats and the Inorganics rooted out most of the rest of our children—only some few managed to remain in hiding. My people held a great Convocation, chanting and seeking a Unified glimpse of the Shaping . . ."

Lisa had been briefed on it, a sort of religious ceremony that could go on for days, as the Karbarrans sought contact with the Infinite. "The Shaping was that we must not defy the Invid, but that *neither could we tell any outsider of our plight*! That part of the Shaping was very clear."

No wonder the Karbarrans had been against the Sentinels' simply leaping into the attack with both feet and a roundhouse swing! Their children were hostage, and the big ursinoids had to simply let the crisis carry them along, with nothing but a forlorn hope that circumstances would change—or that they could *be* changed.

"That's why Lron wanted the recon party," Lisa suddenly saw. "That way, you wouldn't have *told* us; we'd've seen for *ourselves*."

Crysta nodded miserably. "But now I have transgressed."

Jean disagreed. "No, you didn't. I had a pretty fair idea what was wrong—it was Vince who gave me a clue—and I wormed the rest out of you, Crysta. But don't worry; the Sentinels didn't come all this way just to let a generation of children die."

She turned back to Tesla. "Okay now, Slimy: Cabell and

Veidt are going to ask you one or two questions. If my instruments say you're lying, I'm gonna zap a coupla thousand volts through that bath you're in, get me?"

She turned a knob, and a nearby generator hummed louder. Tesla thrashed a bit. "I—I hear and will comply."

Veidt stepped closer to the vat. "There must be a Living Computer controlling the Inorganics below—coordinating and animating them. That much we know. But is it like the Great Brain that was sent on the expedition to Tirol, or is it one of the lesser sort?"

Tesla bobbed for a moment, studying Jean Grant's hand on the control. She looked straight back at him. "It is one of the first, one of the most primitive and smallest," Tesla said, "placed there when one of the earliest Inorganic garrison was assigned to duty on Karbarra."

Jean looked at her instruments and turned up the control knob, so that a hum filled the compartment. Tesla churned the green fluid around him and cried, "Stop, *aii*! I am slain!"

Jean turned off the apparatus. "Looks like he's telling the truth." To Tesla she added, "Oh, shut up! That was just some low-frequency sound and a volt or two."

Veidt told Lisa, "That being the case, my wife and I have a plan that may serve ideally."

Lisa was giving instructions at once. "Get the rest of the leadership together for a briefing, ASAP. And have the intel people get all the information they can from the Karbarrans aboard ship; now that the cat's out of the bag, they ought to be willing to talk. And *somebody get that recon party on the horn and tell them what we're up against!*"

In the abandoned mining camp, Rem frowned as he listened to the word from the Sentinels' flagship. "But how can—I don't understand why—"

"You're not required to understand, soldier," a commo officer barked at him. "Just relay the message, word for word, exactly as I gave it to you. At once, do you understand?"

"I understand," Rem replied sullenly. "Ground-relay base, out."

He broke contact, grousing to himself about the high-handed tone these Human military types took with each other and everyone around them. As Cabell's pupil and companion and sometimes protector, he wasn't used to being treated like a lesser intellect or an unimportant cog.

He was switching over to the recon party's freq when he realized he felt a stirring of air, and it came to him that Gnea hadn't spoken or made a sound in some minutes. The shuttle hatch was open.

Stay buttoned up, had been Admiral Hunter's order, *and no wandering around!* Confinement and inactivity had chafed on the free-spirited amazon more than it had on Rem, who had been forced to sit out most of the terrible Invid onslaught on Tirol in a bunker.

He went to the hatch and peered around, then let out a yell. Overhead, Gnea guided Hiladarre through slow banks and turns, getting used to guiding her. "Is she not beautiful?" Gnea called down, plainly pleased with herself.

"Come down!" Rem shouted. "You know our orders! We're to stay hidden, and not attract attention!"

She sniffed, "Mere males do not give orders to the warriors of Praxis! Besides, I'm *tired* of sitting in that machine-reeking ship. And who is there to see us, so far from any settlement or outpost? Go back in, if you're afraid."

Rem had a mind to close the hatch and leave her outside, too. And there was the urgent need to relay the awful, bewildering message about the Karbarran children. But he knew that Hunter had experience with war, and that extreme caution was always advisable when one was dealing with the Invid.

He took a few steps further into the open, craning his neck to look up at her. "If you're through with your little games, you can act like a solider, and—"

He was stopped by a voice-processed growl, a feline hunting cry as uttered by a terrifying machine. A Hellcat had come around the shuttle's bow, moving to cut him off from the hatch. A second appeared at the stern, and let out a scream of pure catlike anger.

> Consider the sentient "Tiresiod" brain—Praxian, Terran, Karbarran or what have you. Roughly one hundred billion-plus neurons. The potential number of connections these neurons can make with one another, according to some calculations, exceeds the total number of atoms in the Universe.
>
> One sets mere machinery against such a creation only at some risk of unlooked-for results.
>
> Cabell, *A Pedagogue Abroad: Notes on the
> Sentinels' Campaign*

BELA SAW THE HELLCATS, TOO. REM WONDERED why their presence hadn't registered on the much-touted sensors of the winged horse. Perhaps Gnea's flying lessons had distracted it.

The Hellcats, their slitted eyes glowing like coals, stalked closer. They were a form of four-legged Inorganic mecha, so jet black that they shone with blue highlights, and much bigger than the biggest saber-tooth that ever lived. The Hellcats were armed with razor-sharp claws, sword-edged shoulder horns and tail, and gleaming fangs.

Rem had kept an Owens Mark IX mob gun nearby in case of trouble, but not near enough; the short, heavy two-handed weapon and its shoulder-strap-equipped power pack were lying near the inner side of the hatch beyond reach as the two Inorganics moved toward him.

That left only the pistols he and Gnea were wearing—and from what Rem had seen on Tirol, it took more stopping power than the heavy handguns had to put down a 'Cat. Rem backed up slowly, step by step, the Hellcats padding after; they were gaining a little each second but savoring the moment, not quite ready to pounce.

Then he recalled the saddle scabbard Bela had mounted on Halidarre, with its Wolverine rifle. "Gnea, do you have—"

Somehow, his voice triggered the Robotech beasts, and they both slunk forward, segmented tails lashing, preparing to spring. Rem tugged at his pistol, doubting he had time to get a single shot off, doubting that Gnea could take accurate aim from a banking winged horse even if she *did* have the Wolverine.

The Hellcats sprang just as something brushed past him and he felt himself struck from above and behind. Or at least, that was what he thought. The next thing he knew, he was being hoisted aloft, held against Halidarre's saddle, by the Robohorse's lifting fields and beating wings, and by Gnea's firm grip on his torso harness.

The lead 'Cat almost got him, its wicked claws sliding along Halidarre's flank but leaving no mark. The horse banked, eluding the second 'Cat's aim, and gained altitude. A sizzling bolt from Gnea's pistol missed both felines.

"Your jostling spoiled my aim!" she scolded Rem, as he kicked and grabbed wildly for purchase. Then, between her hauling and his struggling, she had him up and draped over the saddle bow, belly-down.

Rem thought the horse's power of flight would save them from the surface-bound Hellcats, but he could see he was wrong. One was already leaping up a small hill of discarded equipment and stacked crates with astonishing speed, giving chase. His field of vision was severely limited by Halidarre's neck, body, and wing, and by Gnea; he couldn't see where the second 'Cat had gotten to.

He called a warning to Gnea, but she had already seen it. Halidarre changed course abruptly. With its fantastic quickness and strength, and in the confines of the dome, the Invid mecha came close to nailing them. Halidarre almost bucked Rem into the air, filling with her wings and cutting in her impeller fields. Gnea herself only kept her seat by a determined gripping with her long, strong legs.

But the Hellcat missed, landing on a lower ledge of the heap and turning to surge up its side again for another try, missing its footing twice in the shifting debris. Gnea turned the winged horse for the opening in the dome, to reach temporary safety.

"No!" Rem yelled. "I left the shuttle hatch open! We can't let them get inside!" It was very likely their only hope of escape, now that the flagship was engaged in battle, and probably the only way of linking up with the recon team again in time to get them offworld.

To his horror, as he looked down dizzily, he saw the second 'Cat's tail disappear through the hatch.

Rem spied the Wolverine rifle in its scabbard and somehow managed to get it out without dropping it. But by that time Gnea had banked around a mountain of decrepit machinery off at the far side of the dome, and he had no clear shot. She picked a spot that looked stable and landed, high above the floor of the dome.

He slid down off the saddle and Gnea leapt down after. Off in the distance they could hear growling and the shifting of junk that meant the first Hellcat was still stalking them.

"There's no time to waste," Rem decided. "I have to go after the one that got into the ship. Can you handle this one?"

She pulled her own sidearm from its shoulder holster and took his from his belt as well, balancing them in hands bigger than his. "It seems I must, doesn't it? And so I will, somehow."

Halidarre snorted and reared a bit, wings deploying and

beating a little faster, half lifting her into the air. A sudden thought occurred to Rem. "We'll have to split up and take on both Hellcats at once. Gnea, how good is your control over the horse? How fine is your touch?"

She smiled grimly. "Try me, Tiresian!"

A few moments later, the feline mecha bounded up among the peaks and sinkholes of discarded industrial rubble and came around the corner to behold Bela standing, waiting, with both pistols leveled. There was no sign of the male Tiresiod, but the sound of jumping and occasional slipping told it that he was in all probability making his way down toward his ship.

The Inorganic ignored the sound of Rem's frantic escape; its huntmate would take care of him. And, more to the point, once a Hellcat was zeroed in on a particular quarry, it pursued that quarry to the exclusion of all else.

The limitations of the early-model Living Computer in Karbarra's capital meant that the central brain could spare no attention for the 'Cat's report of the encounter, what with the outbreak of battle above the planet and the immediate need to prepare for defense. The Hellcats would simply return with slain enemies, to show what they had found and eliminated.

Surprise wasn't a mental trait of any great importance to the Invid mecha; when it saw that the tactical situation had changed only slightly, it simply began an even more straightforward attack, dodging Gnea's inexpert shots by jumping behind a mound of debris. Then it began working its way in her direction. There was no sign of the winged-quadruped mecha, but the 'Cat kept eyes and ears and other sensors alert for possible air attack.

It watched from concealment as Gnea crouched in the inadequate shelter of a smelting processor, and the Hellcat began gathering itself for the final rush, choosing a route around a convenient bit of broken machinery.

The 'Cat rushed, and knew that it would have her before she could so much as bring the handguns around, much less get off a volume of fire sufficient to stop or damage it.

But just as it skittered around the debris to cover the final few yards, the debris came alive.

Armor-hard, scalpel-sharp rear hooves lashed out with the power of twin battering rams, scoring on the Hellcat's jaw and side; the Invid machine was thrown off-balance, leaking power from damaged systemry in its shattered jaw and crushed "rib cage." It went tottering off the ledge of the junk mountain with a yowl.

Gnea rushed to the brink, imaging a call to Halidarre. The winged horse disengaged itself from the splayed pose it had taken, pretending to be part of the ruined jumble of a millwork multirobot—the debris the 'Cat had seen. Halidarre was wingless now.

Gnea looked down to where the Hellcat lay squirming and partially broken, but took no chances; she held out the pistols side by side, pouring down bolt after bolt until it stopped moving, and internal disruptions sent flames shooting from its seams. It gave a last great howl and lay inert, smoking and molten.

Gnea was up on Halidarre's back at once; surely the second Hellcat was warned, and Rem had gone after it alone.

The second 'Cat was indeed aware, and waiting. It had no fear, but it did have cunning and a total commitment to slay the enemy and carry out its mission; since the 'Cat's destruction would prohibit that, such destruction and defeat were to be avoided.

Now it crouched within the shuttle, making low sounds to itself. It had scanned and recorded the nature and construction of the ship for later analysis by the Living Computer on Karbarra, then began demolishing the shuttle, only to be given pause by the death sounds of its huntmate.

Its first impulse was to go out and meet its enemies, then it decided to do as much damage as it could in the ship—perhaps drawing *them* to *it*, the better to avoid its enemies' ambush. It swiped at another bank of intrumentation; shattered pieces and shredded console housing fell to the deck. The 'Cat watched the hatch avidly, certain that it could defeat either of the Tiresiods or the bulky winged-quadruped mecha in the limited interior space of the shuttle, before they could make any effective moves.

But what came zipping through the hatch was neither the Tiresiods nor their odd machine; it was something small and fast, darting about the cabin at great speed, spoiling the Hellcat's savage calculations and provoking it to launch itself for the kill before it had really planned to.

The Invid mecha landed on the far side of the main cabin, snapping the copilot's chair off its mount. The flying thing made an audacious dive, smacking the 'Cat rudely on the head, then zooming for the hatch again. The furious Hellcat catapulted after it, and out the hatch.

Rem, kneeling against the outer hull by the hatch and sweating profusely, saw the flying remote-reconnaissance module that fit in the niche on Halidarre's back come flashing out of the shuttle. He braced himself, feeling his hands slick with perspiration on the Wolverine rifle.

The Hellcat came through the hatch like a dark comet. Its powerful pseudo-muscles gathered and it launched itself into the air, but the quick-moving remote module had changed course with the agility of a dragonfly, and eluded it. When the 'Cat came down, Rem was ready, holding down the Wolverine's trigger and spraying a steady stream of white-hot devastation at it.

The 'Cat reacted with amazing dexterity, almost somersaulting out of the line of fire. Rem stood his ground and he slewed the beam back and forth in an effort to get a sustained hit. He was unaware of Gnea's ululating war cry as she guided Halidarre down from the junk hills, heedless of the peril to herself, rushing to help even though it might mean a fatal fall . . . even though she knew she was too far away.

Rem held the trigger down still, in spite of what his Human instructors had cautioned. The explosion of an overloaded power pack was preferable to being rent and savaged by a Hellcat.

Then the 'Cat seemed to stagger, howling, as he had it in his sights for a second and more, washing the Wolverine's raving blast across it. But a moment later, the Wolverine's beam quit, its systemry burned out. The assault rifle was so hot that he dropped it rather than have the flesh scorched from his palms.

The 'Cat, mortally wounded, lurched and limped toward him, still agile enough in its dying moments that Rem saw that he could never outrun it. One eye was cold and dead; the other was all the brighter with hatred. It cut him off from the hatch he would surely have headed for.

He scuttled backward and sprawled. The Inorganic was about to throw itself upon him when it wavered, its systemry fluxing. At that moment something swooped into view, flying erratically. The remote module from Halidarre could barely stay aloft, bearing as it did a burden it wasn't designed for. Like a butterfly delivering a key chain, it did a snap roll and slipped the strap it had managed to catch with its wing, dumping its cargo into Rem's lap.

The 'Cat shook off its momentary malaise and looked back at its prey. Rem activated the power pack and fumbled at the thick olive-drab cable that connected it to the blunt, heavy Owens gun, opening fire. The Owens was built for just the kind of sustained close-range annihilation that had burned out the Wolverine; the Hellcat threw up a terrible screech and seemed to collapse in on itself.

Rem didn't take his finger off the trigger until the 'Cat looked like a lava runoff. Gnea was standing by; the module had already returned to its place in Halidarre's back, and Halidarre was stretching her wings once again, making a sound-processed whinney.

Gnea offered her hand to help Rem to his feet. He pushed the Owens and its power pack aside wearily and accepted. Gnea, who had followed Bela's lead in showing hostility to Rem, now thumped him on the shoulder.

"We'll make a woman of you yet," she told him with vast approval.

Rem was happy for a split second, until he remembered

that the second Hellcat had been in the shuttle. With a cry, he leapt past her for the hatch.

The scene within made him slump against the hatch-frame. From what he could discern from the damage the huge 'Cat mecha had done, the shuttle could lift off again, and the uplink to the Sentinels' flagship might still work. But the recon-relay rig was in fragments, and the scouting party was out of touch, maybe for good.

CHAPTER
SIXTEEN

Here's a peculiar thing: I wasn't the only one at the Academy with something to prove or disprove; I never asked, but it seems to me now that there were a lot of 'em like me, pushing the envelopes of their own lives the way the test pilots were pushing the envelopes with their aerospacecraft.

My father's Doctor Penn, naturally, and everybody calls him the leading brain on Earth after Emil Lang. I like my father, but I think he has the conviction that because I didn't accept that New Rhodes scholarship, and went into the Academy instead, I'm some sort of intellectual failure. Since I'm enjoined to tell you about all the things that pertain, I'll say that my father still holds the death of my mother, in childbirth, against me—unconsciously, of course.

I forgive him—he's a brilliant man. But I don't want him running my life. I have my own agenda.

From REF-selection diagnostic session, cadet-graduate
Penn, Karen

RICK'S GROUP KNEW THAT SOMETHING WAS WRONG almost at once; when one of their thirty-minute-interval commo checks failed to draw any response after repeated efforts, Rick called a halt to consider what to do.

The equipment the team was carrying couldn't punch a signal through to the Sentinels' flagship, certainly not without giving the group's position away. Only the more sophisticated system aboard the shuttle could do that, and Rem and Gnea weren't answering.

There wasn't much dissention; the recon party had become closer through shared hardship, and Rick's position as leader had solidified. "We can't stop so close to our objective," he told them. "Maybe Rem will reestablish contact. But even if he doesn't, reaching our objective and carrying out our scouting mission before we turn back won't cost us that much more time."

Nobody seemed inclined to object, least of all Lron. But it was Bela who came up with an interim solution. She approached Rick with what he now thought of as "that goddamn canard-winged pest"—her malthi—resting with its many claws dug into her forearm sheath. "Hagane can serve as our messenger," she said.

Rick and the others looked at the woman and the little hawk. "You mean she can find her way to Rem?" Rick asked slowly. "What if she gets lost?"

Bela gave him an indignant look. "Hagane does not *get* lost." She was already taking banding and writing materials from a fancy tooled pouch at her belt, nodding. "Any route she has passed over, she can retrace, even one underground."

Bela looked to Lron. "And *much* faster than any Karbarran. If the shuttle is gone or the others are dead, my Hagane will simply return without a message."

And it seemed unlikely the creature would have any trouble with the winged things the team had spotted in the caves; Hagane's few exploratory flights had shown that the cave's inhabitants were only too eager to stay clear of the diamond-clawed, knife-beaked whirlwind that was Bela's pet.

Rick's head was swimming, but he made a few decisions then and there. "We'll send Hagane on her flight from the observation point, so that she'll know her route all the way back to us and—and won't, uh, have to track us." He had a vision of the avian thing whizzing through the caves, and tried to figure out how fast Hagane could make the trip. Hell; it would be a quick commute.

Bela nodded at Rick's wisdom, and he returned the courtesy. They pressed on and, as Lron had promised, soon found themselves looking out over a huge expanse of weather-tormented Karbarran landscape. The cave's irregular opening might have been any one of hundreds honeycombing the wind- and sand-scoured landscape of cliffs, but it was the only one that connected directly to the Karbarrans' secret underground maze. Natural phosphorescence gave the place a dim blue-green glow, so that they didn't need their vision devices to see one another. They shed the bat-ears, too.

The Praxian had settled down to work. "Now, the message must be short, so what will it say? Bear in mind, Gnea can send an answer back to me here, but that reply must be concise, too."

The message Bela laboriously wrote, her tongue in one corner of her mouth, was in cramped glyphics, the whole-concept code symbols of the Praxians, using a pen with a point as narrow as a syringe. She tucked the tissue-fine bit of paper into a tiny metal capsule and bound it to Hagane's leg. Hagane sat still, though her menacing beak opened in objection to this liberty, even taken by her beloved mistress.

Bela kissed the lambent-eyed Hagane's feathers and Hagane nuzzled her. The amazon released the creature from her hands. Hagane dove down the cave, retracing her route. "How long will it take, do you think?" Kami asked, voice muffled by his mask.

Bela considered. "To get there and back? Perhaps there will have to be consultation with the flagship. Let us say, two hours."

"Then, we'll get what rest we can," Rick decided. Everybody was bushed, and the call to move fast and hard again might be no further away than Hagane's return. He saw no reason to set up double guards, or anything more than short lookout watches, so that everybody could get some rest. There wasn't likely to be anything to observe or analyze for military intelligence purposes under the Karbarran night sky in the next few hours. The guard on watch would also make periodic commo calls in an effort to reestablish contact with the shuttle.

Karen Penn volunteered for the first half-hour shift. No one objected. Lron, who felt no need of blanket or bedroll, curled up by the mouth of the cave, and looked off into the night. The rest of them took swigs of water or went off into a private alcove to attend to personal business, and then composed themselves for sleep.

Karen Penn, muscles still cramped from the grueling traverse of the Karbarran underground, moved to a rock surface off to one side and silently began a t'ai chi routine, moving with precision and a flowing grace that wasn't occidental. Jack, curled in his mummy bag with only one eye showing, followed her every move but said nothing.

"What is that you do?" asked Bela suddenly, her voice unexpectedly soft, while the others began nodding off.

Karen spoke softly, too, without stopping. "This is an exercise/combat system that was devised long ago on my world. It gives a person focus and intimate awareness of the body and of nature."

She stopped and assumed another pose. "We have more vigorous, forceful systems as well." She went through a brief *kata* at full speed, snapping punches and kicks, demonstrating rotary blocks and stiff-fingered blows with much less grace but as precisely as a machine.

When Karen was done, Bela regarded her for a moment, then said, "These are beautiful and effective-looking fighting forms, and you seem adept. You are not so foolish as I thought, Karen Penn." She began pulling her campaign cloak, the only cover she appeared to need, around her.

Karen blinked. "Foolish?" *Listen, honey, as big as you are, I'll—*

"Foolish for placing such importance on a mere male," Bela said, and closed her predatory eyes, turning away to sleep. Karen stared at Bela, thinking about what she had said. Luckily for Jack, he had covered his face completely before Karen glanced his way, immersed in confused thoughts and crosswired impulses.

The fourth watch was Kami's; Rick woke him, then retired to his own ultralight but warm and comfortable mummy bag. He was asleep in seconds.

Kami went off into a small cul-de-sac so as not to dis-

turb anyone and tried another commo call to Rem and
Gnea, without success. Putting the apparatus aside, he realized he was feeling a certain oddness in his perceptions, a
lack of depth and a flatness of feature. It occurred to him
that he had lowered the flow from his inhalant tank, to
economize during sleep.

The tank wasn't his sole source of air, of course; such a
supply would have been too bulky to carry. Instead, his
mask frugally mixed his homeworld's atmosphere with that
of the local surroundings at any given time.

He increased the flow, and in moments felt the Higher
Reality come into sharp focus again, with its enhanced perceptions and expanded awareness. The winds rustling the
sands whispered their secrets to him, and the stars overhead
twinkled messages from the moment of their birth. Ghostly
—but unfortunately, minor—Sendings made themselves
known in the form of images or disembodied voices. But still
he couldn't perceive the greater Truths of this war.

Lron, his snore surprisingly soft, had rolled away from
his watching place at the cave's mouth. Kami stepped to
the very edge to gaze out into the night. A glow lit the
horizon, and he knew that somewhere over there was the
great domed capital city, Tracialle, the single major population center of Karbarra.

Kami and his people diplomatically refrained from ridi-
culing the Karbarrans and their days-long chanting rituals
and dramatic, sometimes painful rites and grandiose reen-
actments, all performed in the name of some Foresight the
ursinoids claimed to achieve. The Higher World was nothing one could contact that way; the Karbarrans were simply
indulging themselves in mass delusions.

The Higher World spoke to the Gerudans through their
every sense, thanks to their strange ecosystem, and showed
them routes and possibilities. Thus, they were allowed to
listen in on the constant monologue put forth by *every single extant thing*, by dint of its very existence, and—sometimes—to comprehend what was being said.

Kami saw a vision and didn't hesitate. Noiselessly gathering his equipment, he scampered down the narrow ledge leading from the cave mouth to the foot of the cliff.

It was as his vision had shown him. Kami raced light-footed across the sands toward the glow on the horizon. He followed the lay of the land, as sure in his skills as any wild animal.

Yet, somehow his vision hadn't shown him a swift flight of Enforcer skirmish ships that, flying high above, picked him up on infrared heat detectors. Nor had it shown him the troll-like Inorganic Scrim and Odeon mecha that appeared without warning in the darkness and surrounded him.

Kami turned to run, but they were everywhere, as big as any Battloid, reaching for him with their multiple appendages—metallic claws and segmented tentacles and waldolike Robotech hands. He groped for the Owens gun, but it was ripped from his back.

There was no time to use his commo link with the rest of the scouting party; he tore his breathing mask away to howl a single mournful, echoing cry into the desert night.

The cry woke Lron at once, and Bela leapt up, throwing back her cloak. The Humans were a little slower, but not much.

They didn't dare show a light, but donned their night-sight equipment. Between Lron's sense of smell and Bela's eye for tracks, the two reconstructed what had happened.

"Another Gerudan follows his mirages to a bad end," *wuffed* Lron.

"He came here to help your people, just like the rest of us," Jack sneered back, "so quit mocking 'im." Bela nodded in agreement, and Karen, standing to one side, studied Jack anew.

"As you *were*, Lieutenant!" Rick snapped.

The question was, what to do now? As many as three of the original eight on his team might be dead, and the remainder—himself included—were quite possibly stranded in the midst of an aroused Invid stronghold. All of a sudden, the Tactical Information Center back in SDF-3 didn't seem like such a bad tour of duty.

Rick was prepared to believe that Kami was in the hands of the biped Inorganic grotesques of the Invid. But was he supposed to lead his remaining scouts out for a desperate rescue mission, like the Fellowship of the Ring off on their marathon jog across the plains of Rohan?

Damn it, this operation was in a very tight spot, and he couldn't sacrifice more people for the sake of a vanished team member who was possibly hallucinating and quite probably dead.

"We'll stay put right here and give Hagane a chance to get back," he went on. "Everybody make ready to leave on a moment's notice. Baker, Penn: warm up some rations over in the cul-de-sac, where the Invid won't pick up the heat readings. And try another commo call to the shuttle while you're at it.

"Bela, stand watch at the cave mouth. Are your night-sight goggles working? Good. Lron, come here and help me orient my map readouts on the local topo features."

The rest of them got busy, and suddenly they were a unit again. They were so intent on their tasks that Hagane's sudden, screeching return came as a shock that made them raise weapons' muzzles, wide-eyed.

This time, Bela's pet wore a capsule on each leg. As she read through the delicate papers, Bela frowned. In a few terse Zentraedi lingua franca phrases, she told the rest of them what she read. Rem and Gnea had resumed contact with the Sentinels' ship, and the shuttle was spaceworthy, but the special commo rig for reaching the scouting team was permanently out of commission.

Then Bela went on to reveal the secret of the children of Karbarra. As she did, Lron's shoulders slumped more and more, until they began heaving, outlined against the growing light of day. It took the rest of them a moment to realize that the poor old fellow, as strong as an oak, was weeping.

In the end, he told them the same story Jean Grant and the rest had heard up above. They also had hope, because

Lisa and the other leaders had put a plan together. Bela's brows knit as she puzzled over the symbols. When she caught on, she threw her head back and roared, and smote Lron on the back.

Jack Baker cussed under his breath, and Karen's features drew taut with resolve. Rick stood up from the rock he had been sitting on. "It looks like we get the desert tour after all. Bela, do you think the Invid will be able to sweat any information out of Kami?"

She was caressing Hagane's Alpha-sleek head. "If you think that, you don't know Kami. They could dismember him, and he would regard it as a learning experience granted him by the Universe."

Rick nodded. He did some calculating and realized that there was no time to retrace the whole journey from the shuttle's landing place.

"Send Hagane back to the shuttle to let them know that we acknowledge the plan and will stand ready at our present position. Mention Kami's capture, too." He wanted to send some special word to Lisa, but that would take unfair advantage of his rank. He rubbed the bridge of his nose between thumb and forefinger.

As Bela bent to her task, mumbling something about being regarded as a "lowly scribe, instead of a war leader," Rick turned to Jack and Karen.

"Double-check all gear, especially the weapons. Lron, check the route Kami took down the cliff. Do it carefully, to make sure there are no tracks to lead the Invid back to us."

"The toughest duty of all, now, eh, sir?" Karen said.

Rick nodded ruefully. "Yeah: waiting."

They say the dying part's not so bad; but then, we haven't got much firsthand testimony.

CHAPTER
SEVENTEEN

This book won't tell you how to cheat, because when you fail to deal with reality, you only cheat yourself. What I mean to do is turn you into a shrewd player who wins whenever possible.

Kermit Busganglion, *The Hand You're Dealt*

TESLA ALMOST FELT LIKE HIS OLD SELF AGAIN, BATHED and arrayed in fine raiments—robes far above the station of most mere Scientists, more appropriate, in fact, to the Regent himself—and ushered along by numerous attendants.

But the attendants were wary Sentinels armed with an alarming variety of weapons, and he was still a captive. A large hold had been converted into a commo studio, and techs were warming up equipment for contact with the Invid-occupied Karbarran capital.

Ah, if only this illusion were the truth! thought Tesla.

Before him some of his worst enemies stood chained,

disheveled and bedraggled-looking, thanks to makeup and wardrobe. Learna, Kami's mate, was there, and Crysta, her paw-hands restless in their confinement. Between them stood Lisa Hayes Hunter, who wasn't about to be left out of this grand swipe at the vaunted Invid group intellect.

Glimmering Baldan, froward Burak, and one of Bela's lieutenants, a Junoesque brunette, were fastened in place, too—all looking like they had been dragged in the mud and given a taste of the energy lash. At either end of the slave coffle, like living bookends, were the Haydonites, Veidt and Sarna, hovering some few inches off the deck-plates. Their robes were torn and faces smudged, and their necks were encircled by riveted collars, since they had no wrists to cuff.

Janice Em watched from the sidelines, ostensibly a guard but more of a media adviser—and more of an ob-server than anyone there knew. Sue Graham, the young camerawoman, was production coordinator for the project. She had signed on the Sentinels' mission because it offered her more freedom to do her job her own way.

"You know that this can never work." Tesla tried, one last time, to get them to understand. "We Invid are a per-ceptive and wary race, our intellect boundless! Are we to be fooled by this naive bit of play-acting?"

"We'll worry about that," Lisa said to him. "Just do as we've told you. Oh, and by the way..."

She motioned, and two Spherians came forward with a gorgeous jeweled collar, a kind of regal gorget. They fas-tened it around Tesla's thick neck, and it clicked shut with a strange finality. He could see that it had been fashioned from some of the dragon's-hoard of gemstones, collected from many planets, that he had planned to take back to the Regent, before the Sentinels staged their inconvenient and patently unfair uprising.

Still, he thought, admiring himself in the reflective metal of a nearby power panel, it looked quite striking on him. Something he would one day gloat over, when he had his revenge.

"Thirty seconds," Sue Graham called out.

The ersatz slaves moved to their place in the background. Out of vid-pickup range, guards on either side trained their weapons on Tesla. As the time counted down, Lisa stepped forward a bit, her chains ringing, a sardonic look on her face. "And, Tesla? One more thing: you'd better play your part exactly right."

"Is that a threat, female?"

"It's a fact," Lisa told him evenly. "That collar's locked on you now, and it's got fourteen ounces of shaped Tango-Seven explosive charges built into it. If you *disappoint us*, I'll blow your head off in front of all your friends down there."

"Surely, in this lower-lifeform gender business, the females are the worst of a bad lot!" Tesla nearly wept. But then a tech was silencing them. A moment later, the image of an Invid officer unit—the heavy cannon mounted on its shoulders making it look like Robotech Siamese triplets— peered out of the screen at them.

It seemed to recoil a bit in a gesture of surprise. "Tesla!" it said in the strange, single-sideband sound of a mecha drone.

"Yes, of course it's me!" Tesla broke in. The lights around him felt disturbingly hot, and he wondered if they might set off the explosives around his tender throat. The Sentinels couldn't be *that* deranged, could they? On the other hand . . .

"Let me speak to the Living Computer!" Tesla burst out. "I arrived just in the nick of time to drive our enemies from this star system, but I have important news!"

The officer appeared to hesitate, but Tesla screamed, "Do as you are ordered!"

Used to obeying, it complied. In another moment, a Living Computer appeared before Tesla on the screen. It was far smaller than the one captured on Tirol, and seemed to have less peripheral equipment and fewer convolutions.

We're inside their system! Lisa exulted, trying to look defeated and numbed from beatings. *Here goes.*

Tesla began his spiel again: how he had returned to Karbarra in time to repulse the Sentinel raid, and how he needed landing clearance, to repair damage and hold urgent consultation with the Living Computer.

What the Computer didn't see, what Tesla himself barely felt (and dared not register), were lines of mental energy reaching out from Veidt and Sarna. The Haydonites —bracketing Tesla from either side in a kind of mental crossfire—meshed their wills and thoughts with his, guiding and reinforcing, sending a steady current of emphasis and believability along the link Tesla had established with the Invid brain.

Invisible to all, Veidt and Sarna manipulated Tesla and, through him, the brain, though their powers were very weak here, so far from Haydon IV. But it didn't take a vast, brute effort of mental force to accomplish what the Sentinels needed; it only took a slight touch here, a psychic stroke there, to create a conducive atmosphere. It only took a convincing patina of truth.

The Living Computer went so far as to call off its red alert—even more than the Sentinels were hoping for—and granted immediate landing clearance.

"And, incidentally," it added. "The Inorganics have captured an alien, a Gerudan, out in the wastes. He's being brought here now. I shall begin the torture slowly, so that you may enjoy the finale."

"No, no, er . . ." Tesla didn't know exactly what to say, but knew his captors wouldn't take kindly to having one of their number subjected to Invid inquisition.

There was no time to consult with the Sentinels, so the scientist improvised. "I wish to examine him whilst he is still intact. Therefore, have him imprisoned with the other hostages for now."

"Very good, Tesla," the brain responded. "When do you expect to make planetfall?"

"Um, my vessel has suffered damage in the heroic fight to drive away those insurrectionists, and so I will make one decelerating orbit before making my landing."

"As you wish." When the brain signed off, Tesla's knees buckled. He moaned weakly, begging for his captors to remove the resplendent collar. Lisa turned and shouted orders for the bridge. The helmswoman, a Karbarran nearly Lron's size, brought the enormous wooden wheel over. The *Farrago* left orbit, to edge out of the planetary ring for a Karbarran approach.

Down in the bays and holds and hangar decks, the mecha came to full alert, systems at high pitch. Logans, Alphas, Betas, Hovertanks; drum-armed Spartans with their giant, cylindrical missile launchers; long-barreled MAC IIs that were walking hydras of cannon tubes; quad-muzzle Raider X self-contained artillery batteries; and ground-shaking Excalibers bristling with a half-dozen diverse heavy-weapons systems—the Godzillas of the second-generation Destroids.

Scuttlebutt about the Karbarran children and the concentration camp had filtered its way through all ranks in no time, though nobody had made any official announcements.

So, they think they're gonna gun down a buncha kids, huh?

The mecha formed up and waited, their crews avid for the word to go.

"That's it," Rem said. "That's as much as I can get working. *Farrago* says turn-to, and that means there's no time left."

Gnea nodded, taking a place behind him in the communications officer's chair since there had been no time to repair the copilot's. She took one last look in the aft hold, to make sure that Halidarre was well secured. Then she said, "Prepared."

Rem smiled, punching up the ridiculous mission the shuttle would have to fly. Admiral Hunter's book said he should let the computers do the flying, but the computers had been used as a scratching pole by a very *big* polecat. Besides, Rem had invented new computer designs and he didn't trust them as much as people who knew less about them.

The shuttle's engines shrilled, coming up to power.

"Not long now," Rem told Gnea.

The *Farrago* began its long approach orbit on a course chosen by the Sentinels because it led through the least-well-monitored portions of the enemy detection skynet.

This time, Tesla's face filled the communication screen. His would-be slaves couldn't be exhibited because they were all otherwise involved in getting *Farrago* and its fighting forces ready to hit Karbarra like a sledgehammer.

"Er, Karbarra Control," Tesla said delicately. He still wore that dismaying, priceless bib; moreover, there were unsmiling Sentinels surrounding him, just out of camera range, with an appalling collection of energy devices and even cruder things—pointed, glittering implements with unpleasant implications.

"Some of these pesky ablative surfaces and hull features on the captive ships I've incorporated into mine have begun to break up under the stress of entry. Inferior technology, you know. I'm sure they'll burn up upon hitting the deeper atmosphere, but you might, um, alert your sensor techs not to pay any attention to the little cloud of objects coming down with me."

The Haydonites' spell was still in effect. "Of course," said the Living Computer, "of course. Your landing area is at coordinates 12−53−58 relative; we will roll back a segment of the Tracialle city dome to permit your entrance."

Tesla tried to sound enthusiastic and grateful, expecially since one of those horrid, overmuscled Praxian harridans stood ready to stick a halberd into his side if he made a mistake.

"Oh! How very kind! I will speak to the Regent of your cooperation and efficiency."

"Thank you, Tesla." The brain signed off.

*   *   *

"We've got a tentative location on that concentration camp," Vince relayed up to Lisa, "but it's still not dead certain. It's obvious that they're not in the camp Lron mentioned, because that's been torn down. But we're ninety percent sure we've got the new one spotted."

"We'll go in with a wide deployment of the attack forces," she decided. "I want everything we've got in the air."

"All set," he answered.

"Then, begin launch operations."

The composite ship began seeding the sky with air-combat elements. The VTs and the Logans went first; then the Skulls dropped and deployed, beginning a slow approach toward Tracialle, skimming the ground. Max and Miriya got the Skulls in proper array. Down almost at the surface, Jonathan Wolff's tankers made their drop and took up least-conspicuous routes, minimizing the chances of being spotted and riding low on their surface-effect cushions.

Farther along, the flagship moving even slower, Lisa ordered the dropping of the scouting force. Fighters on Tiresian airbikes, one-passenger Gerudan flitters and Perytonian skycars, and even Veidt and Sarna in their bubble-topped Haydonite flier—shaped like a Robotech ice-cream cone—dispersed. They took up an immediate search formation, preparing to move closer to the city in order to pinpoint the location of the Karbarran children.

Rick and the others heard the roar, were ready for it. With a wash of sand and superheated air, the shuttle set down at the foot of the cliffs. The star Yirrbisst was just rising, bringing daylight to Karbarra's barren landscape.

Rick and the others dashed aboard while the ship was still hovering, the engines barely lowering in pitch. "Move it! Move it!" Rick was yelling, even before they reached their seats.

Rem complied, the shuttle leaping away only a yard or two above the flat desert. Rick had started for the copilot's seat, to take over, when he saw with some shock that it wasn't there. Rem had neglected to mention that particular piece of damage. Rick knew Rem was a pretty fair pilot; he would just have to trust the youngster to handle the mission, because there was no time to land and change places. Rick buckled into an acceleration seat and hung on.

Rem cut the shuttle in the direction of the concentration camp as Lron had spotted it on the map. They saw no Invid patrols; Rem said that Invid occupation forces had pulled back most of their mecha in anticipation of Tesla's arrival, to render military honors.

Rick checked the screens and could see, far to the west, the approach of the *Farrago*. The Skulls and the Wolff Pack could reach the objective faster than the shuttle; Rick just hoped they hurried.

"Patch me through to Captain Hunter," he told Gnea, who was sitting at the commo officer's station, but she shook her head.

"Can't, sir. We had some system burnout when we applied power to lift off. No commo with the flagship at all."

We're on our own, Rick realized. What else was new? He hoped the timetable didn't change, because if it did, he was living his last few moments then and there.

"No!" Tesla wailed. "I refuse! Put me back in irons; torture me! I will not go down that gangway to be roasted like an insect!"

Lisa Hunter showed him a control unit. "If you do as I tell you, you'll be all right; if you don't, your head's going bye-bye, snail-face."

She tried to sound as ruthless as she could, but she doubted she could actually do it in cold blood. It was against the REF rules of war, and went against what she believed in. On the other hand, she was counting on Tesla to evaluate things in terms of what *he* would do if the situation were reversed.

*   *   *

A minute or so later the *Farrago* drifted at a near-hover through the opening in the Tracialle city dome. It settled down on an acres-wide landing area near the heart of the capital, amid the blunt, functional buildings typical of Karbarran architecture.

The city stood on a mesa surrounded by chasms thousands of feet deep; the glassy hemisphere over it and the upper portion of the city itself rested on an immense cylinder reinforced by hydraulic shock absorbers something like a cross between an insect's leg and a flying buttress. It reminded her of a titanic mushroom sprouting limbs.

The ship's forward ramp opened and Tesla stepped out. Arrayed below him in rank upon rank were the biped Inorganics—Scrim and Crann and Odeon. Few Hellcats were present; they were difficult to control among dense populations. Other troops were keeping the crowds of curious but silent Karbarrans back beyond the far periphery of the landing site.

"Hail, Tesla!" cried the local commander, in his eerie, artificial voice. "And welcome to the Regent's loyal and contented dominion of Karbarra!" That brought an angry rumbling from the crowd, but no outbursts.

Tesla, trembling a little, replied over a loudspeaker, "A-and hail to the stalwart Invid garrison! To add to our glory, I bring you captives lately taken in my . . . my momentous clash with the Sentinels!"

At that, cargo ramps extended from the various independent modules that made up the flagship, including the GMU. The Destroids marched down them, mostly single file or at most two abreast, due to their size.

"Prisoners of war!" Tesla was haranguing. "New slaves to fight for the honor and increase of our Regent!"

The garrison commander hesitated, surprised, conversing with the Living Computer for a moment before saying, "Well done. To serve the Regent is the only reason for living."

The first of the Destroids had reached the landing-zone surface, and began forming up in single ranks. Still more emerged from the flagship. "But, perhaps these examples will suffice for now," the commander added.

"They are all completely under my sway," Tesla vouched, voice cracking a bit, as he edged toward the hatch.

"That may be," the commander replied, "but such creatures are lower life-forms, wild animals, unpredictable." He turned to his Inorganics. "Deactivate those mecha and remove their occupants from them!"

As the first ranks of Inorganics moved at once to obey, Tesla turned and dove headlong through the hatch. Lisa, watching from the bridge, thought, *Dammit*! She had hoped all the Destroids could emerge and get to more advantageous positions before the crunch came.

"Fire at will!" she yelled.

CHAPTER
EIGHTEEN

The 'Gaia' model was by then so thoroughly entombed, we had to blow the dust off it and study up in a hurry once we met the Gerudans. The theory of a planetary ecology as, in essence, a single interactive metaorganism? Too absurd to accept, right?
You wouldn't last long in the Great Beyond, Citizen.

Jack Baker, *Upwardly Mobile*

LIVING WELL ISN'T THE BEST REVENGE. GENERAL T. R. Edwards thought, lounging in his luxurious chair. *Revenge is the best revenge*!

But better yet to have both: comfort, and the blood of an enemy flowing.

And surely the blood of his enemies was flowing even now. Despite the spottiness of interstellar communications, the *Farrago* had gotten through a message that the Sentinels had suffered casualties in one battle and were now launching themselves against an Invid stronghold in another. There were those on the Plenipotentiary Council who had talked vaguely of sending reinforcements, but Edwards had managed to nip that one right away.

Now he gazed out over Tiresia with vast satisfaction. For the most part, the city had been cleared of rubble, its unsalvagable debris and structures removed, and was quickly being rebuilt. Not much of a miracle, really, given Robotechnology. And REF Base Tirol was well on its way to completion; in fact, Edwards was looking down from his office on the top floor of the headquarters building.

It stood like the lower half of some early ICBM missile, a vaned cylinder at the center of great ribbon loops of elevated roadway. There had been some nonsense about putting the council up here, but with pressure tactics and backstage maneuvering, Edwards had gotten his way. That was becoming more and more the case.

Edwards wasn't altogether satisfied that some resources were being diverted into urban renewal, rather than into building the fleet of starships he meant to commandeer for his own designs, but some things couldn't be helped. At least it was making the Tiresians more tractable and grateful, and they, too, would have their uses, not far down the line.

Of course, Lang, and the sprawling research complex he was setting up with Exedore, were necessary inconveniences. He had to be kept pacified and working on the SDF-3 and the fleet above all.

A buzz from his aide announced that Lynn-Minmei was waiting to see General Edwards. He acknowledged, then flicked the control in his chair's arm, spinning back to look across a gleaming, polished desk as big as a landing field.

Lynn-Minmei? Now what in—

It was a bit of a shock when she stepped through the door in a cadet uniform, halted before his desk, and saluted smartly. He still didn't think of her as military. "Cadet Lynn, requesting permission to speak to the general, sir."

He returned the salute slowly. "Permission granted. Stand at ease."

She only relaxed a little. "General, I know something about people, and while everybody's been working like dogs to accomplish our mission here, time's been passing and, well . . ."

"I haven't got all day, Cadet," Edwards grated. "Spit it out!"

He was pleased to see he had made her flinch. "People need something to keep them going," she burst out. "I *know*! I saw it in SDF-1! They're sort of coming up with what recreation they can now, of course, but that's very makeshift and haphazard.

"What we need is an organized program of entertainment, and some kind of center where people could go to unwind, no matter what shift they're working or who they are. So they could forget their troubles and have their spirits lifted. A place where they could remember—remember why we all came here in the first place."

She said that last softly, she who hadn't been invited on the REF mission in the first place.

Edward's own voice took on a softness, a dangerous tone from him. "Let me be clear on this. Knowing your past, do I assume you're suggesting we open up a *cabaret*?"

"No, a service club!" she corrected. "People need their morale kept up, sir!"

"And you're just the one to organize it, hmm?"

She couldn't meet his gaze for a moment. She knew that all her arguments were true, but Edwards had seen right through her. When she had sung that last good-bye aboard the superdimensional fortress when the *Farrago* left, she had sworn she wouldn't sing in public again.

But bit by bit, her resolve had crumbled. She missed it too much. She missed the good things her songs did for people, the happiness they brought. But she had to admit that she missed the spotlight, too, the applause and adulation and attention. They were in her blood. She *needed* them.

The REF's situation was so much like Macross's in the old SDF-1 that it was as if her life were a Möbius strip. And so she found herself following old forms, feeling old longings and dreaming dreams she had told herself to bury.

"I'm more knowledgeable about show business than anybody else we've got, sir," she pressed on. "I'll do it on my off-duty time! But I was hoping you'd speak to the council, General."

It all sounded like something out of one of those twentieth-century films for which he had such utter contempt. *Hey, I've got it, we'll put on the show in the barn! Yeah, you can make the costumes! Swell; they can build the sets!*

He almost ridiculed her out loud, would have enjoyed it, but at the last second held back. There *was* something about her presence, her gamine appeal and wide-eyed winsomeness. Where other men might have felt attracted to her, and suddenly protective toward her, Edwards began to feel possessive.

He knew she had been courted by hundreds of lovestruck admirers, worshipped by thousands, perhaps millions, of fans. And none had had her, none had really touched her, save only two. One of those, Lynn Kyle, her distant cousin, was long since missing and presumed dead back on Earth.

Edwards also knew that Minmei had once been Hunter's passion. He was aware, too, through his spies, that that fool Wolff had a hopeless crush on her.

Minmei wasn't sure what reactions or thoughts she was seeing cross Edwards's face; the gleaming half cowl and scintillating lens-eye made it difficult to tell.

Edwards steepled his hands before him and tilted his chair back. "This idea may have some merit, Cadet. We'll discuss it further over dinner."

In Edwards's mind, she was already his, body and soul.

Kami realized blearily that he was being borne along to the clanking of mecha. Reviving a little, he saw to his horror that he was in the grip of a Crann Inorganic.

The memory of being jumped, mixed with his Vision, began to sort out as he struggled like a wild thing to no effect. The dreadful recollections of being caged by Tesla made him look about for a way to take his own life. The Inorganic's armor and grotesque design screamed mindless hatefulness; the sky was screeching a death song at him.

But he was held fast and couldn't squirm free. That changed in a few moments, though, as he was dropped without ceremony. He landed in a heap on hard, gritty soil, dazed, the Vision almost clouding over into unconsciousness. He could hear the Invid marching away, and could make no sense of it.

Something prodded him. Kami rolled over with a sharp yip of alarm, to find himself looking up at a ring of furry faces. "What are you?" one of them said. "Are you an Invid, then?"

One of the others made an exasperated sound and jabbed the first with an elbow. "Stupid! How could he be an Invid?"

"Well, he's no Karbarran!" the first shot back, and they seemed about to scuffle.

"I'm a Gerudan," Kami said tiredly. "Don't they teach you whelps anything in school?"

He could see he had found the Karbarran children, even if he had arrived in somewhat ignominious fashion.

They started to babble, and a few of them worked up the courage to actually give him a hand getting to his feet. The Karbarran children were roly-poly versions of their elders, some of them nearly as tall as Kami himself; but unlike their parents, the cubs wore no goggles. Their eyes were round, dark, and moist.

He groaned, trying to bring things into focus. One of the cubs tried to touch his mask and he gave the paw a little slap; it was withdrawn. Kami couldn't understand why the Invid had taken his weapons and gear and yet left him his mask and tank. Perhaps they knew that they wouldn't have a sane prisoner for very long—or a live one—if they took the breather from him.

There were some hundred or so miniature Karbarrans around him, and many, many more walking around an extensive barracks area. From the size of the place, he was prepared to believe that just about every cub of the planet's reduced population was there. Most of them seemed listless though, not caring that something was going on.

Kami squinted a bit in the early light of Yirrbisst, glancing around to orient himself to the landmarks he had seen on the map and get his bearings. It wasn't long after sunrise; the raiders would be here soon and he must prepare the cubs as best he could. But the three-in-a-row spike crags weren't there; the broken butte was nowhere in view, the foothills covered with scrub growth couldn't be seen.

His blood suddenly went cold. *The Invid have moved them! This isn't the place on the map!*

"Where are we?" he asked the first cub who had spoken to him, a tubby little male with streaked highlights in his pelt.

"The old Sekiton works," the cub said. "They moved us here from the prison compound near the city so they could guard us easier." The young Karbarran pointed vaguely toward the rising greenish primary, Karbarra's star. "You can barely even see Tracialle from the tallest tower here."

The raid on the old prison had provided for searching possible alternative sites near the city, but not this far out. Kami looked off the way the cub had pointed, feeling waves of defeat flow over him.

"Sir? Sir?" the little one was saying. "Who are you?"

He shook off his despair as he would have shaken off water, fur ruffling and standing out, tail fluffing. He held out his hand to them for silence.

Somehow the valve of his breather had been turned down. He increased the flow a bit, looking at the sky, inhaling.

Lron had been unfair, and wrong, in accusing the Gerudans of using hallucinogens. The fact was that the Gerudans' mental processes were symbiotically linked with an astounding range of microorganisms and a wide variety of complex trace molecules found in their planet's ecosystem.

Their brain activity was a result of interaction with these factors in their environment. It reacted to and was influenced by those stimuli on a subcellular and even atomic level, in ways that left Human molecular psychologists shaking their heads and talking to themselves.

Gerudan life was a partnership with their world; their neurological systems were a vital part of the reproductive cycle of the microscopic life-forms that were indispensible to the Gerudans' perception and very ability to think.

Kami inhaled and thought. Certain perceptions began to shift and intensify. The sky sang a dirge and the windblown sand took on strange shapes. Then he realized something was chanting, in a register so low he could barely hear it. He knelt and put his ear to the ground; the cubs looked at one another dubiously.

Kami listened to the dull thrumming.

Sekiton. Sekiton. Sekiton.

Of course. He spun to the cub who had spoken to him. "My name is Kami. Who are you?"

The cub drew himself up proudly. "I'm Dardo, son of Lron and Crysta, leaders among our people. The children needed a leader, too, and so I got them organized. My parents—"

So apparently this was the action committee, the ones who hadn't succumbed to hopelessness.

"I know them. Listen, all of you! We haven't much time. There's still Sekiton around here, is there not?"

"Over in the warehouse." Dardo pointed to a low bunker. "There's not much use for it now that the Invid stopped us from spacefaring."

But between the prisoners and the Sekiton was an imprisoning Invid energy wall, a ghostly curtain of angry red power a hundred feet high, generated by pylons spaced every hundred yards around the prison compound. Kami knew that it meant a searing burn and unconsciousness to get too close to one, and immolation to try to pass through.

"So Sekiton's not much good to us anymore," Dardo said. "Worse luck, because there's still plenty of it around here everywhere."

He scuffed the sand aside with his foot, digging down a

depth of several inches. Pushing aside thicker, grittier soil, Dardo dug stubby fingers in and came up with a fistful of darkish Sekiton mixed with sand. "See?"

"Yes; I've seen the stuff, thank you," Kami said offhandedly. Yirrbisst was getting higher, and there wasn't much time left. With the first air strikes or the attack of the Destroids, the order would go out for the killing to begin at the concentration camp.

Dardo shrugged, formed the clot into a dirtball, and heaved it. The dirtball went up in a blaze as it hit the energy wall. Another cub took some and heaved it for an even bigger fireworks effect. From the gouges here and there around the compound, Kami could see that they had done it quite often to pass the time.

Sekiton. Sekiton. Sekiton. The ground thumped it into his feet like the vibration of some huge pile driver, but the message was lost on him. Kami picked up a clot of the stuff, too, made a ball of it, and heaved it disgustedly at the wall.

The dirtball passed through unharmed, to land and break up several yards beyond.

"It—it didn't burn up," Dardo blinked.

"That's because . . . *it wasn't handled by a Karbarran!*" Kami fairly howled through his breather. He didn't understand any better than anyone else what the weird Karbarran affinity for Sekiton was, but he had seen for himself that the stuff was stubbornly inert if a Karbarran didn't come in actual physical contact with it at some point.

"Quick, get sticks or boards from the buildings, or anything else you can dig with, and start uncovering more, but *don't touch it directly*! And fetch me water, lots of water!"

A short time later the cubs stood in a crowded circle shielding him from view, although the Invid had shown little interest in keeping the prisoners under close surveillance, trusting their energy wall. Kami packed the thick mud onto himself. It was gratifyingly adhesive.

"I'm going to need a weapon. Did anyone see what the Inorganics did with my equipment?"

One of the taller cubs, a female with a dark tinge to her fur, pointed at a blockhouse. "I saw them set some things down over there just before they brought you here."

Kami was slapping mud onto himself frantically, trying to be thorough, because any missed spot would probably get him fried, but trying to be quick, too, because time had just about run out. "All right! *If* I get my gun, and *if* I can blow out one of these pylons, all of you run as fast as you can for the Sekiton storage bunker! If the rest come along, fine, but don't wait for them, because I'm going to need you over there! Do you understand?"

They said they did. He was about as covered as he would ever be, except for his eyes. He had layered over his breather mask, and would have to get by on pure Gerudan air from his tank.

"But—what are we going to do then, sir?" Dardo inquired.

"Send a message," Kami told him. He made his way stiffly and cautiously toward the energy wall, until he could feel the heat of it on his exposed eyes. He made a last application to the bottoms of his feet from the armload of mud he carried and slapped more over his eyes until they were covered. He took a deep breath and stepped in the direction in which, he hoped, the wall waited and glowed.

And promptly lost his footing, falling.

He expected to be burned to ash, but he was still alive after he thumped to the ground. But he had lost his bearings completely and didn't dare remove the blinding mud.

Hoping for the best, Kami rolled and rolled in what he thought was the right direction.

CHAPTER
NINETEEN

I'm runnin' away an' joinin' th' Robotechs! Then *you'll be sorry!*

Popular threat among Earth children during the period of preparation for the SDF-3 Mission

AT LISA'S COMMAND, THE DESTROIDS OPENED UP with all weapons. The first terrible barrage of pumped lasers, particle beams, and missiles struck the nearest organics at virtual point-blank range, like a tidal wave rolling over a shore.

Inorganics went up like roman candles or simply vanished from sight. The Destroids trained their weapons on the next target and the next, exploiting the element of surprise for all it was worth, because the odds were still badly against them. Those on the ramps were firing, too, and marching down, heavy-footed, to join their fellows.

The assorted weapons of the *Farrago* opened up, show-ering down fire like burning hail, careful to keep their aim in close to the ship where the Invid were, to avoid hitting the Karbarran crowds.

Invid were blown to smithereens, or holed through by star-hot lances of energy. They were confused and indecisive for those first few seconds, and in that time dozens of them were wiped out. Lisa watched a monitor, as a Crann under the flagship's bow was hit dead center by a laser cannon round, like a white-hot needle going through a beetle. The Crann's characteristic snout tentacle, or flagellum, or whatever it was, was still snapping like an angry whip as the thing flew apart in all directions.

The Inorganic bipeds seemed to be the last word in the strangely perverse Invid design preferences, misshapen and wrongly articulated to Earthly eyes. The low-hanging arms and malformed bodies—stick-thin here, bloated there— made them appear as if the Invid had set out to make them as repulsive as possible.

Not that the Sentinels needed that added incentive to fight; *Farrago* and all her personnel were committed now and the only way out was victory. Inorganics flew into the air like burning, bursting marionettes, or were blown back into the ones behind them, to explode.

But the Invid were firing back now, their annihilation disks and beams ranging in among the Destroids. With the last of the Destroids down on the landing surface, the big Earth mecha stood shoulder to shoulder and put out a stupendous volume of fire, a walking barrage that reaped rank after rank of the troops who had been drawn up for Tesla's review.

But with each enemy down, another moved up to take its place, firing dispassionately. And Enforcer skirmish ships darted in overhead now, to fire on the flagship. Many of the upper hull batteries had to turn from ground support to AA fire. Lisa was just glad the task force drawn from Karbarra had taken away its Pincers and Scouts and Shock Troopers; that left a lot fewer flying mecha to contend with, a critical point in this battle plan.

The biped Inorganics were doing their best to contain the Destroids' advance, as the Earth machines began a slow march, traversing their fire here and there, pounding away at the enemy in an inferno of skewing cannon beams and boiling missile trails.

A cluster of Scrim made a stand, and concentrated their fire. A Spartan, busy emptying its racks at another target, was riddled; it lurched and then flew apart in flame.

The Karbarrans had all fled for their lives, ducking into the first shelter they could find. The Destroids suffered another loss, a Raidar X, and a skirmish flier got a shot through a weak point in the upper hull shields, disabling a powered twin-Gatling gun mount on the Gerudan module of the ship.

Nonetheless, the Destroids had driven the Inorganics back from the landing area. Damage reports were pouring in, but the ship was still spaceworthy. But, it was a sure bet that the Invid were moving up more reinforcements. Lisa gave the order for the Destroids to move out and secure the area—dig in and hold. Then she gave Vince Grant the go-ahead, and the GMU began to uncouple from the *Farrago*.

The enormous Mobile Ground Unit rolled out on its eight balloon tires, tires some hundred feet or so in diameter. Once out from under the flagship, it could add its own upper-hull missile and gun batteries to the antiaircraft defenses.

Lisa wasn't too worried about the skirmish ships; there were fewer of them than there had been a while ago, and she was sure the Sentinels could handle the rest. Nor did the Invid seem to have any supercannon—anything in the GMU's class, anything big enough to take out the flagship with a single round—in Tracialle.

No, this would be a battle of ground mecha, Destroid and Inorganic. It was already beginning to the east, where a quartet of Odeons had arrived to try to dislodge some MAC IIs, and they were slugging it out almost toe-to-toe, the hastily-abandoned buildings collapsing around them. But the MACs' multiple barrels, firing beams and solids both, were beginning to tell.

There were requests for reinforcements from another sector, and reports that the Invid were bringing up more troops and even some Hellcats from a third.

Lisa did her best to look calm. *Max, Miriya—Rick! Hurry!*

In the sanctum of the Living Computer, the Invid brain seethed with something very much like wrath. Far above it, the sounds of battle sent vibrations through the entire colossal concrete-and-glass mushroom that was the capital city.

"The Karbarrans have somehow betrayed us!" it said. "Give the order! Slay the children; exterminate them all!"

The Hovercycles and airbikes and the rest had checked out all nearby outposts and seen nothing; the VTs and Hovertanks closed their pincer movement and swept in from every point of the compass, converging on the objective.

The mecha swept down with half of each unit in Battloid form, the better to sweep through the compound, while the rest supported them in Guardian or Gladiator mode, or flew cover in Veritech.

Battloids needed no special forced entry tools; they simply ripped the buildings open and peered inside, being careful because they didn't want to hurt the hostages. They ran from building to building, pulling doors off or prying up roofs, calling in amplified voices.

It didn't take long for the report to be relayed back to the appalled Max Sterling. "Results negative, sir. They're not here. We hit the wrong place!"

"Come onto course 115," Lron roared to Rem.

"But—the locator says—"

"Do it!" Lron shook the bulkhead with his anger. "I see a Sekiton fire over there, where the old processing plant is. The Invid don't build infernos like that, and the Karbarrans have little cause to, but the Gerudans love signal bonfires. Do it, I tell you!"

"Take 'er in, Rem," Rick said. "All of you, get set."

"Sensors are picking up a lot of heavy Protoculture activity over in the direction of the city, Admiral," Jack told Rick. "Looks like the party started without us."

"Rem, *floor it!*"

Rem wasn't sure exactly what Rick meant, but he made a screaming approach, handling the shuttle with quiet skill. In seconds, they were retroing in over the camp, looking down on a scene that made them all gasp.

An eerie blaze had been started in a processing pit, flaring in the indescribable colors of Sekiton, being fed by a chain of what looked like Karbarrans. But Inorganic bipeds were headed that way, and still more were approaching from the far distance along with the sinewy forms of Hellcats moving at top speed.

Most of the Crann, Scrims, and Odeon, though, were ranging around an area marked off by what the Sentinels had come to recognize as energy-wall pylons. But the energy wall was gone. Apparently the enemy mecha were intent on keeping the rest of their prisoners from escaping, and hadn't been given the command to execute them—yet. The bipeds were firing short bursts into the ground, driving the vast majority of the Karbarran children back toward the barracks area.

One tiny figure, crouched behind a building, jumped out to let a Scrim have it with a fierce wash of brilliant blast. The Invid was rocked and its fellows halted. Their counterfire smashed and consumed the corner of the building, but by then the sniper had fallen back. Only he had no place else to hide; he had his back to the flames.

"Hard-nosed little runt, that Kami," Jack said admiringly.

"Karen ..." Rick called to her. She was seated at the main fire-control station.

"I've got 'im, sir," she said with vast composure. With one shot from the shuttle's pumped-laser tube, Karen took out the Scrim Kami had hit, and traversed the stream of brilliant energy to the next, bisecting it.

As the shuttle zoomed past, the third Scrim turned to

fire at it, but Rem's evasive piloting frustrated it. Kami took the opportunity to duck past it and around the building, headed for the blockhouse. He would have cheered at the shuttle's arrival, but he didn't have time and couldn't spare the breath.

Kami hadn't had to shoot up the pylons of the energy wall because he had discovered a power-system junction, over by the blockhouse where he had found his Owens gun and power pack. Shutting down the barrier was simply a matter of wrestling down a Karbarran-scale knife switch.

But now the Inorganics were closing in on the masses of cubs who hadn't or couldn't make a break when Dardo and his pals did. Kami had to do something fast, or the slaughter would begin in seconds. He knelt in the shelter of the blockhouse doorway, calculated his timing carefully, got his shoulders under the massive porcelain handle of the knife switch, and heaved it back up again to close the circuit.

The energy wall sprang back into existence, a red curtain of death—and there were two Odeons standing in its field. Both appeared to writhe in agony. An instant later, they vanished in twin flares of blinding discharge.

Kami saw that he had been in time; the rest of the Inorganics were outside their own wall, cut off from the hostages. That might not last more than a few seconds, but every second was infinitely important now.

He gathered up his gun and turned, racing back to the fire pit.

"Are you sure we can't raise Max and Wolff?" Rick asked without turning to Jack; Rick was busy assuming control of the missile racks, retracting their covers and adjusting his targeting scope.

Jack frowned at his commo board. "Negative, sir. Maybe if we got up high enough and tried one of the helmet radios in an outer hatch—"

"No time!" Rick cut him off, and he was right. Even as he spoke, a Hellcat leapt into view and covered the ground between itself and Kami with frighteningly long leaps. But

Rem had already snapped the shuttle through a turn and was beginning another run.

The guy's a natural, Rick concluded—how else to explain Rem's facility with a Karbarran vessel? He might be a scholar's apprentice, but he had great reflexes and coordination.

Rick got the Hellcat in his sights even while Karen was zeroing in on another Inorganic, an Odeon that had been circling toward the children by the fire pit. Karen hit her mark with a sustained beam; it stood its ground and shot back with everything it had.

They felt the shuttle jar from a partial hit and Rem started assessing the damage, wondering if he could keep the vessel in the air. Karen's long burst cut the Odeon in two at the waist and it fell apart in a cluster of secondary explosions. Rick's first two missiles missed the Hellcat completely, their warheads fountaining flame and dirt and rock to either side of it.

But even though the shuttle's flight was becoming more and more erratic, Lron—who had taken over the stern gun pods—got a stream of autocannon rounds into the 'Cat. Its hindquarters began dragging, crippled, and Kami was increasing his lead on it.

Rick thought it was unlikely that the shuttle could get high enough to attempt contact with the Skulls even if it could break away from the battle when he heard a hatch open. He turned and saw Bela disappearing into the aft hold.

"Hey! Get back here!" But she was gone, though the hatch stood open. Rick didn't know what she was up to, but he wasn't sure the amazons really knew how advanced technology worked. "Baker, make sure she doesn't wreck us!"

He looked at Gnea, who had looked up from her weapons position. "You stay at your post!" He didn't need two of these overdeveloped Valkyries wandering around in the middle of a fight. Gnea looked as if she might give him some lip, then went back to manning the upper-hull ball-turret mount via remote.

Jack lurched aft, grateful that the shuttle wasn't doing

—couldn't do—any sudden manuevering that would mash him against the hull. When he got through the hatch he found Bela crouching by the emergency ejection hatch. Apparently, she had fired the escape capsule that was there and, when the outer hatch reclosed, had somehow gotten Halidarre to sort of crouch with legs folded and wings pulled in.

She looked up at him. "It's the only way to get a signal through," she said, tapping the mike Lang had installed on her battle helm. "And I could use a gunner, Jack Baker."

No time to go ask permission. *Personal initiative, Baker!* he told himself. But the thought of the Inorganics closing in on the defenseless cubs made it even easier to decide.

"How d'you stay on one a' these things?" He said it as he jumped to a rack of weapons, unclipped a magazine-fed rocket launcher—about all the extra weight he could safely handle, he figured—and staggered over to her while the shuttle jarred.

"Mount behind me," she said, "and fasten yourself in with the belt there." He did, finding a retractable safety belt built into the rear of the cantle. Bela was already secured with the saddle's belt. Jack managed to both hang onto the launcher and close his flight helmet. Activating his commo unit, he heard Rick Hunter ranting.

"—the hell are you two doing back there? Get up here, that's an order!"

"Sorry, Rick Hunter," Bela said calmly. "But I'll give your regards to Max Sterling. By the way, Baker here is braver than he looks."

Or maybe dumber, Jack thought.

She punched a button on the inner hull and pulled her hand back quickly. The ejection-port cover rolled shut and there was a feeling like being shot from a cannon. Jack glimpsed the ground, spinning up at him.

FILE #28364-4758
BAKER, JACK R.
Subject was orphaned of all close family members during the Robotech War, his last relatives having been killed during Khyron's final onslaught.

This young man has erected defenses against close emotional ties, although, bafflingly, he manifests none of the hostility or self-destructiveness that traditional theory would predict. He demonstrates far-above-average intelligence, dexterity, and, in cases where it is not threatening to him, compassion—particularly toward individuals who have been victimized.

He simply seems to have turned off his pain by not investing anyone with the considerable affection of which he seems capable.

While there is no valid justification for denying this youth Academy entrance, particularly in light of his scores, it should be remembered by military authorities that this client shows a certain hostility toward discipline and may be unsuited to military service.

Caseworker 594382, Global Care Authority

"I'M SORRY, LISA; THEY'RE JUST NOT HERE. WE'RE widening the search pattern," Max Sterling said, sounding a little helpless. He had a child himself, back on Earth.

The Skulls and Wolff Pack and all the scouts were unable to locate the Karbarran children, and more and more Invid reinforcements were arriving at the capital city. Three more mecha had been lost: a Spartan, a Raidar, and, tellingly, an Excaliber that had virtually disappeared under a mass of flailing Scrim and Crann and Hellcats.

The Destroids were holding their own in some places. But in others they were pushed back inexorably, in furious, point-blank, sometimes hand-to-hand exchanges, by Invid who didn't seem to care how heavy their losses were. The GMU had deployed to a point on the other side of the landing site, bringing all but its heaviest weapon to bear; but given the nature of the street-fighting, neither it nor *Farrago* could give much fire support without the risk of hitting friendlies or civilians.

Lisa had hoped the general populace might pitch in, if only to create diversions. But the Karbarrans were staying out of it, no doubt hoping against logic that their children might still be spared.

A report came in that the perimeter to the south was collapsing; the Invid had somehow brought down an entire row of high rises on the MAC IIs and Spartans there, literally pinning them down, and had waded in to dismember them.

Lisa was reluctantly coming to the conclusion that the mission was a failure. She looked out from the bridge at the flaming city, and prepared to give the Destroids and the GMU the command to fall back in orderly fashion to the ship to withdraw from the city.

If we can just get through that dome, she reminded herself.

The order was on her lips when a strange sound came over the command net. It was a kind of—of singing. Three notes like a hunting bird's scream made into music. Then a voice said, "This is Bela, of Praxis! We've found the children! Home in on my beacon! Sentinels, *come join the fight!*"

Jack Baker struggled to steady the launcher over Bela's shoulder, the skirmish ship in and out of his sights, as Halidarre banked and evaded and the Enforcer peppered shots at the wonder horse and its riders.

Jack fired, but the rocket went wide as the skirmish ship rolled and got ready for another pass. "Can't you hold this nag still?"

"Yes, Jack Baker," Bela said, almost laughing. "Still enough so that slug cannot miss. Would you like that?"

She would be just crazy enough to do it, too. Her wild laughter in battle, her bravado and amazing skill at handling Halidarre—they were a little tough to top. What do you say to a woman who rides through the air on a winged Robosteed, firing a pistol with one hand and waving a *sword*, for god's sake, with the other?

I'll tell you what old Jack Baker says, he thought angrily. "Yeah!" he said, before he could think about it twice. "Yeah, hold still for a second, if it's all the same to you. Looks like the only way I'm ever gonna hit anything today."

So she did. Halidarre hovered on her impeller fields, wings beating at half speed to steady her, as Jack wrestled the launcher around. He hadn't hit anything yet; three rockets were gone and only two remained in the magazine.

The Enforcer was on a new attack run, firing at long range. Bela was as good as her word, holding Halidarre in a dead hover, laughing that wild laugh again, brandishing her sword. Jack lined up his shot with the tube resting on Bela's shoulder and let both rockets go. "Let's get outta here!"

Halidarre rose abruptly just as a line of annihilation disks shrilled through the spot where she had been a moment before. The Enforcer, intent on its aim, tried to bank away from the rockets a bit too late. It blew apart and began raining down in tiny, burning scraps.

Bela gave a howl like a Hellcat. "That's my lad!" Then she spied something and put Halidarre into a dive that nearly sent Jack's breakfast up into his throat.

The Invid had shut down the energy wall again. They were closing in ominously on the barracks where most of the Karbarran cubs had taken refuge. The bipeds began firing at long range, setting the buildings ablaze to drive the prey out for more convenient extermination.

Jack threw the launcher away and got his pistol out. He and Bela dove straight at the Invid, firing and hitting, but having no effect.

Over by the fire pit, Kami backed up, Dardo and the others behind him, as Hellcats closed in all around them. The Owens gun was dead, out of power; Kami yanked its cable free of the backpack, threw the backpack aside, and held the gun as a club.

The recon party's shuttle had last been seen losing altitude, plummeting away to the east. Kami hoped dully that they had survived the crash. In any case, there was no hope of evacuation now.

The 'Cats' eyes seemed as bright as lasers; for some reason of their own, they spread out and began herding Kami and the helpless children toward the fire they had built—a pit eighty feet across, now carpeted with burning Sekiton. Kami, exhausted and still half caked with mud, could feel it singeing the fur on his tail. The cubs had thinned out in a ring one or two deep, all the way around the fire. Hellcats hemmed them in at every turn, forcing them back into the inferno.

His heightened senses shrieked torment and nightmare at him—agony was like a fog all around him, and gruesome death like electricity shooting up into him from the very ground under his feet.

"I'd rather die fighting than roasting!" With that, Kami raised the club wearily and began to totter straight at the 'Cat confronting him, preferring a quick death from claws to a slow one from flame . . .

Suddenly the 'Cat was bashed aside as something immense and heavy hit it like a multiton lineman. It took Kami a moment to realize that it was a Veritech, an armored Alpha in Battloid mode—white with red markings.

Battloid and Hellcat tumbled and fought, the feline's claws ripping at its foe, but the Battloid's big armored fists pounding and pounding at the 'Cat like huge pistons, staving in its sides, shattering one of its eyes.

The other 'Cats turned to throw themselves into the fight, but were prevented when Battloids began dropping from the sky on them, back thrusters blaring—Betas and Logans mixed in with the Alphas. Kami skipped back out of the way as the red Alpha and the 'Cat it had jumped tumbled and tore and beat at one another.

The Skulls had arrived.

In Guardian and VT configuration, they swooped at the Inorganics over in the barracks area, driving them back or blowing them sky-high. Even the Hellcats who broke and fled found that their speed wasn't enough to save them; a second attack wave, diving from high altitude, overtook the things and chopped them down with missiles and cannonfire.

More Invid bipeds, rallying from outposts and patrols, headed for the camp by way of a canyon to the west, forming up to steamroll into the rescuers. The first problem with that plan was that the Wolff Pack was there, and met them head-on.

It was no open-country tank battle; it was a murderous set-to in a limited space, both sides throwing themselves into it without restraint, like a knife fight in a commophone booth. Tank and Gladiator mode didn't offer enough agility, so the Wolff Pack went to Battloid and grappled, fired, kicked, and punched. The Invid met them with claws, tentacles, chelae, and feet, annihilation disks and explosive globes. The valley was a slaughterhouse, but the heavier and more numerous Hovertanks began pushing back the tide inch by inch.

Kami watched as the Hellcat rolled to the upper position, determined to bite the Alpha's throat out or rip its head off with those enormous fangs.

But the Alpha got one forearm under the 'Cat's jaw, slowly levering it away. Then the Battloid had both hands on the feline's throat, squeezing with Robotech strength. The 'Cat screamed and went wild, tail thrashing, but it couldn't free itself. Alloy groaned and squeaked as it gave way, crushed. The light in the 'Cat's remaining eye slowly dimmed.

Then all at once it was dark, and the thing's body went limp and lifeless. The Alpha rose to its feet, lifting the Hellcat up, then threw it to the ground with an impact that made Karbarra quake under Kami's feet. The Invid mecha was a shapeless mass of smoking scrap.

The Skulls had turned things around in minutes. The ground was littered with the remains of Invid mecha, and no enemy was standing. But there were VTs down, too, and their fellows were attending to them.

The functioning Veritechs deployed repair servos that snaked forth on metal tentacles to fix what damage they could. Many of the disabled mecha were beyond such help, though, and would require the facilities of a full Robotech engineering bay.

But some of the damaged Skulls would never rise again, and their pilots had paid the final price. The living descended from their ships for the wrenching and ghastly duty of gathering up the remains. In several cases there was simply nothing left.

The red Alpha turned and walked over through the drifting smoke of battle to look down at Kami. A female voice said over an external speaker, "Sorry we cut it so fine, my friend." It was Miriya Sterling.

Kami could still smell his own singed fur. "It could have been much worse—by several seconds." She laughed. Then he thought of something. "The shuttle! It disappeared over that way!"

Miriya paused for a moment—perhaps informing Max of the situation—then blasted away through the air on her back thrusters, quickly mechamorphosing to true Veritech mode, and heading like a missile in the direction Kami had indicated.

At the landing site, each second seemed like an hour on the rack to Lisa. The Destroids had redoubled their efforts to hold out and, in a few places, had even retaken a little ground. But the Invid were pressing hard again.

Suddenly there was a crackling noise over the command net, and Max spoke, sounding choked up. "We got the kids, Lisa. They're all okay. Do you roger? I say again, all hostages are safe."

Max was starting to talk about arrangements to get the cubs to safety, but Lisa cut him off. "Max, things are deteriorating here. Leave a security force and then get back here with every VT you can spare. Repeat, I need you here ASAP with every mecha you can—"

"Cap'n! Look!" A Spherian tech was pointing through the vast blister that roofed the bridge.

"What—" she said, ignoring Max's efforts to get her to finish her sentence.

All through the city, doors and windows and access panels were opening up on roofs and other vantage points, and intense fire was pouring forth, mostly Invid-style annihilation disks and beams. From what she could see and what she began hearing over the tac net, Lisa concluded that all the fire was directed at the Invid. It was as if the whole city had been turned into one giant shooting gallery. Caught from behind or above and sometimes even from below, the Invid army was being wiped out before her eyes.

She told Max, "Wait one, Skull Leader!" Then she got Crysta, who was with Jean Grant in the GMU, on the ship's internal net. "Crysta, what's happening?"

"I—I knew my people were secreting weapons against this time," Crysta answered. "But Lron and I—we had no idea!"

It's not wise to make an enemy of your armorer, it occurred to Lisa. "Crysta, when did they start—how long have the Karbarrans been preparing for this?"

"Since the hour they took our children," Crysta answered.

Lisa watched the weapons fire incandesce as the Karbarrans had their revenge.

"Baker!"

Karen Penn went straight for him as he sat there nonchalantly on the rump of a defunct Hellcat, looking off into the distance as if he didn't have a care in the world.

That stunt he pulled! Deserting his post in time of battle! Karen just wanted a little piece of him before Admiral Hunter went to work on him.

Of course, part of her anger was the ignominy of being carried back to the compound in the shuttle by three Battloids, like some kind of broken-down commuter craft. That wasn't the heart of it though, and she couldn't have explained just *why* she was so furious.

To top it off, he was sitting there with a stupid grin on his face, *whistling*! "Baker, say your prayers, because I'm gonna—"

He turned to her with a beatific look on his face. "Hi, Karen. Have a seat and enjoy the show; you'll never see another one like it."

She was clenching her teeth, but decided to see what he meant before the fight commenced. "Huh—Oh!"

Down the hill a bit, the Karbarran children were being coaxed out of hiding by Dardo and his buddies. Battloids had put out most of the fires, and then stood back; the cubs had good reason to be wary of giant mecha.

But Dardo and the rest had the hostages coming out now, in droves. Most of the freed cubs were looking around blankly, but some of them were already beginning to caper and skip, jumping for joy.

Without thinking about it, Karen sat down next to Jack to watch. The cubs rushed around in the sunlight, romping and giving in to elation over their rescue. "I'd rather see this than get a duffel bag full of medals," Jack said soberly.

Karen looked at him for a second, then back at the cubs. "You have your moments, Baker, y'know that?"

"*Et tu*, Penn."

A little while passed. They saw Lron arrive, wading through the cubs, to lift up his son and fling him aloft. The cubs got braver where the mecha were concerned, and some of them were playing ring-around-a-rosy about the foot of Max Sterling's Battloid.

"What was that you were whistling?" Karen asked suddenly, without looking at him. "I sort of recognized it."

Still watching the cubs, he began again, a half smile touching his lips. After a few notes, Karen found herself laughing and shaking her head at him in exasperation.

It was "The Teddy Bears' Picnic."

CHAPTER
TWENTY-ONE

> *A tragedy worthy of the Greeks, to be sure, or Shakespeare. A Universal Force or righteous Deity had forged a ring of iron, the Sentinels' leadership. And yet somehow a flaw had been tempered in.*
>
> *One is tempted to paraphrase, "Look upon these frailties, ye mighty, and be humbled."*
>
> Ann London, *Ring of Iron: The Sentinels in Conflict*

IN THE AFTERMATH OF THE SENTINELS' FIRST TRUE CONquest—while the Karbarrans were still exacting their fearsome revenge and the cubs had yet to be calmed down for transport back to their parents—there were details that slipped through the cracks. Trying to bring order out of the chaos, and make sure they had really *won* the day—that there were no Invid backup divisions waiting in the wings —was keeping almost everybody busy beyond any reasonable demand.

And so no one noticed when Burak of Peryton rather than the regular duty officer showed up at the head of the security squad that was supposed to take Tesla back to his cell.

Burak was certainly on the roster as being able to commandeer a security detachment; he was within his rights as a principal signatory of the Sentinels to take custody of Tesla. But he had chosen this time because he didn't want to be interrupted, didn't want to be overheard, while he spoke to the enemy. Once Tesla was back in irons, the aurok-horned young male of Peryton dismissed the mixed unit of Praxians and Spherians, and stood regarding the captive.

Tesla had turned away, but it came to him that Burak was still there. "Well? Can't you leave a helpless victim of war to his misery? I've given you what you wanted." An Invid stronghold was in flames, dashed under an invader's foot, and he, Tesla, had been instrumental in that. "Go away! Or, kill me. I no longer care which." He fingered the gorgeous collar with its hidden explosives.

"I want to save Peryton," Burak got out at last. "And if you don't help me, I *will* kill you."

Tesla saw that he meant it; a young Perytonian, scarcely more than a boy, he was as headstrong as any from the planet where there was still an annual ceremony in the rubbing off of the velvet from the males' horns and where fights over females still frequently led to death.

So, here was Burak, determined to short-circuit the Sentinels' judicious timetable because he suspected, not without reason, that it wouldn't address Peryton's crisis in time. "How do I save Peryton, Invid?"

Tesla saw that Burak had somehow gotten the detonator switch for the collar around his neck. But for once, Tesla wasn't afraid—no, not at all. Standing there in his grand robes with the shimmering gems draped from his neck, he saw that the key to Burak was that *Burak was vulnerable: Burak needed knowledge*.

A certain *kind* of knowledge, but that didn't matter. That kind of craving put any seeker at a disadvantage if the teacher was unprincipled enough. And conniving was Tesla's specialty, even before he availed himself of the Sentinels' hospitalities.

Tesla came up close to the bars, so close that Burak

backed away a step, one hand holding the detonator and the other a little firearm that seemed to be made of white ceramic and hammered brass.

But as he neared the front of his cage, Tesla settled down. He folded his tree-bough legs and sat in a meditative pose, the level of his gaze still higher than Burak's. Tesla's thoughts were like drowning rats, seeking any avenue of escape, marshaling in vaguest terms things that Burak might want to hear.

"The answers lie more within you than within me," Tesla intoned. "My powers tell me that your hour comes near. You have been chosen by Destiny to free your people from the curse under which they live second to second, constantly. This source of such pain to you has made it your Destiny. You have been aware of this for some time now."

Tesla could barely keep himself from dissolving in laughter. What blather! What transparent ego-stroking! Surely, the very Regent, end-all of egotism, would have struck Tesla down for saying such things.

But Burak was an untried youth whose planet was near disaster, and to him it was something of a miracle that he hadn't been swallowed up by it already.

He sat down, cross-legged like Tesla but safely out of the Invid's reach, on the other side of the bars. "Teach me what I need to know, and I'll free you."

Tesla had already anticipated that, and knew that he had to up the ante. Besides, the robes and the gemstones and the turn of events had him thinking along new pathways now.

He tried to think up something suitably muddled and nebulous, something appropriate for a hazy Sentinel mind. "Free? All beings are free. It is only distorted awareness that imprisons them."

Tesla was beginning to enjoy this. "But there are specific things, things like the process for reversing the damage that has been done to Peryton, and freeing all your people from their terrible curse."

Tesla leaned toward the bars with what he calculated to be the correct fervor. "And *these things are not so difficult!*

I shall help you accomplish them. And you will deliver up your people."

Tesla assumed what he hoped looked like a prayerful attitude. "I don't ask you to free me. Nor even to trust me. I only ask you, Burak, to *listen* to me."

Burak stayed back out of range, but he leaned closer.

Rick Hunter had been thinking about taking some disciplinary action against Jack Baker until he found him gathered with most of the rest of the scouting party, sitting there on the rump of the dead Hellcat overlooking the Teddy Bears' Picnic.

Lron was still down among the cubs, and transports were on the way to lift the Karbarran youngsters out now that Lisa and the others in Tracialle had gotten the dome open and the last of the Inorganics were dead.

Rick moved toward them, just in time to hear Bela avow, "He's got the guts of a Praxian! Jack Baker's just like a daughter to me!"

She didn't seem to understand why several people were guffawing and Jack was turning pinker than usual. *Maybe he's been punished enough*, Rick thought; it was a line that would pursue Baker for the rest of his military career. Sackcloth and ashes could be no worse.

Bela spit in her palm and held it out. Jack spit on his and clasped with her, arm-wrestling style, then winced a bit when she inadvertently crunched his fingers together.

Kami was there, too, and cubs kept running up to him with every sort of minor update on what was going on, or simply to hold onto a tuft of his fur. He had freed them, and his pelt was a lot more familiar to them than all the armor and uniforms they saw around them. Several had found their way up into his lap, even though Karbarran cubs were big for a Gerudan to hold.

Rick forgot all about his official duty and just stood to one side, watching. If he went over to join them, things would change. The issue of rank would appear.

So he leaned against the corner of the bunker and

watched. Gnea put a well muscled arm around Rem and gave him a buss on the cheek, yelling something about Hellcats. Halidarre, like something from the *Arabian Nights*, reared a bit every now and then, beating her wings slowly.

He left them to their moment and went off to get a lift back to the capital. He just didn't feel like it was a win yet; he had to hear it from Lisa, see it on her face.

Things about love you hadn't quite anticipated: lesson 207, he thought wryly.

Lightning like this would shake any Human's faith in God, Breetai thought as a passing observation, while one of the rolling, rainless storms of Fantoma lit the sky, exciting the chancy tectonics of the planet and resounding against the hard sides of the mining machines and armored workers.

Here in the thicker medium of the unbreathable Fantoman atmosphere, great Breetai gazed down on a place out of memory.

Zarkopolis!

The history of a people, a *race*, all stemming from the first awakenings there; the things that had been blanked from neuron altogether but somehow, stubbornly, remained in marrow and soul—the past was washing in on him and he could no more sort it out than pick a handful from a wave.

With the mining operation safely established, Breetai had flown back for a look at Zarkopolis, the city where the Zentraedi had begun. *A haunted world*, he thought yet again, for the latest of times past counting.

Breetai took a step forward, to go down and look at the Zentraedi past. The officers who accompanied him made that same step, like shadows.

"Stay back," he bade them. "You may return to the camp; I wish to be alone." They hesitated, then obeyed.

There were only two Zentraedi from those days still alive, the ultimate survivors, and Exedore was now a happily diminutive little *Human*. The thought was unkind, but he couldn't help it; only Breetai was left.

With his vast strides, it didn't take him long to make his

way down into the deserted city. He saw the high, fluted spires that had been erected by his people in defiance of the terrible gravity, not to announce their greatness so much as to affirm the Zentraedi ability to endure, to overcome, through sheer stubbornness and backbreaking hard work. How different a legacy from what the Robotech Masters had given them!

As a memory-wiped warrior for the Masters, he had always felt contempt for the scurrying, insect-colony industriousness of subject races—of workers. But now he looked upon Zarkopolis, remembering the pain and striving in each chisel mark, each laboriously-raised slab.

And memories began returning to him, recollections of what his people had been at the outset: builders and strivers, who had more in common with the Micronians of Earth, and Macross, and SDF-1, than the Robotech Masters had dared let the Zentraedi know.

It is no wonder to me, now, that we were moved so deeply by Minmei's songs, he thought. *At last, at last, I understand!*

With that there came a measure of peace within him.

Now he plodded down—the soil falling *so* fast, and abrading his boots with its weight—toward the stand of cream-colored bunkers and low domes and hunkering complexes that had been the center of all Zentraedi life so long ago.

He stopped. Why return to the source of so much pain and regret and resentment? But—he couldn't hold himself back, despite his iron will.

He had to go down yet again into the weathered, haunted precincts of the Zentraedi workers, and the multitude of voices that spoke to him across the ages. He didn't know why, knew only that he must stand there again, in the center of it all.

"My lord?"

He turned more slowly than he would have under lesser gravity; sudden moves could injure even the mightiest Zentraedi here. Kazianna Hesh was catching up with him, moving with unwise haste in her modified Quadrono suit.

She was again wearing those *cosmetics* the Human females favored. It confused him, seeing her features behind the tinted facebowl of her helmet. He said, "What do you want here? You should be at your work."

She was a little out of breath. Kazianna panted, looking at him earnestly. "My work is done and I am off shift, my lord. I—I had hoped that you would tell me why Zarkopolis obsesses you so, and show me the city where once the Zentraedi dwelt."

He looked down at her and wondered how old she was. In the heyday of the Robotech Masters' empire, the life expectancy of a clone warrior was less than three years, and it was virtually certain that she was one of the hordes brought forth to fill the empty spots in the ranks.

But—whence this curiosity? This disturbing *presence* that she seemed to have? Breetai turned to look out upon Zarkopolis and suddenly understood that these characteristics were things manifest in *all* Zentraedi, in times past. That they should surface again now was, it could be argued, a very good sign.

"Very well; I shall." He started off again and she fell in with him. Breetai led the way down into the city, pointing this way and that, telling her the things that had come buzzing back into his head with the return to Fantoma and, all of a sudden, not hiding in the gaps in his memory.

"In that hall we met to thrash out problems, all of us; it took a very long time to cut the stone columns perfectly, so that they would support the weight of the roof, and even longer to assemble the roof."

A little further on, "Here, the clones were grown, coming forth when they were ready for work, descending those steps over there to adulthood." Steps he had never walked until recently; Breetai antedated the city, had helped raise it.

And so they went. Breetai was pleased, for reasons he couldn't name, to have someone with whom to share his memories. At last they came to a nondescript little house in a tract of them. It was only slightly more prestigious than the mass barracks in which most Zentraedi had lived.

Breetai pressed a button with an armored finger; the airlock swung open. Kazianna could see that it had been refitted to function again after a span of centuries. She had no doubt that Breetai had done it. Lightning was breaking again, and the odd, emphatic thunder of three-g Fantoma was sounding as the outer hatch slid shut.

Inside, the place was unprepossessing, the quarters of a worker/engineer. He had cleaned up the mess, but there were still a few models left, still a few mounted sketches, from the days when a different Breetai had dreamed larger dreams than all the Robotech Masters' fantasies of galactic conquest—dreams of building.

Breetai saw Kazianna looking around, and realized how spartan the furnishings were. In the age since he had lived in that place, he had learned to deceive, but he spoke the simple truth now. "I was the biggest and the strongest of the miners, the first of them," he said. "Only our leader, Dolza, was bigger than I; only he and Exedore were older.

"But—I had few friends—no life, really, except in my work. It seemed to me that they all thought me—"

He stopped, astonished, as she cracked the seal on her helmet and threw it back. Of course, her suit's instruments would have told her there was breathable atmosphere in the tiny quarters—atmosphere he had put there. Only he hadn't seen her check her instruments, and suspected she had done it on what the Humans called "instinct."

"They all thought you *what*," Kazianna Hesh encouraged him, walking around, glancing at his sketches, opening the other seams in her armor. "Thought you too stoic, thought you too formidable, great Breetai? Treated you so that you felt easier when you were either working or alone?"

She had always been deferential toward him, but now she sounded somehow teasing. She had made her circuit of the tiny living room and stopped now to flick the control that broke the seal on his own helmet. "They didn't see what was there inside?"

She unsealed his helmet and lifted it off, having to rise

on her tiptoes to do it even though she was tall. The reinforced floor groaned beneath them. Breetai was too astonished to speak, and the wall was behind his shoulders so he couldn't retreat.

"Couldn't see the real Breetai?" she went on. "Well, my lord, I can." She pulled his head down to her, like some *Human*, and he found himself being thoroughly kissed. How had she learned about things like this, forbidden to the Zentraedi?

Many of his race had spent time Micronized to Human size. Maybe that had affected her somehow, or she had seen or heard something.

But he had little time to wonder about that. A kiss; the sight of such an act had almost debilitated him once, when Rick Hunter and Lisa Hayes performed it on a Zentraedi meeting table. He was awkward at first, self-conscious, but Kazianna didn't appear to mind and in fact didn't seem to know a great deal more about it than he.

When the kiss ended, he would have caught her up in his arms for more, but she held him off and began alternately popping the seals on his suit and her own.

It suddenly came to him what she had in mind. "You . . . this is proscribed."

"By whom? By Robotech Masters who have fled beyond the stars? By laws that were never really ours?"

Breetai thought about that, and considered his hunger for her, too. The bed was refurbished; he had slept there once or twice on his off-duty hours, waiting for the past to filter into his mind once again.

Breetai put his arms around Kazianna and kissed her carefully, very happy about it but aware that he had a great deal to learn. Then he took her gauntleted hand and led her to his sleeping chamber. Since he had built the house back in the early days of the Tiresian Overlords who were to become the Robotech Masters, no one else had ever been in that room.

CHAPTER
TWENTY-TWO

In spite of her resistance, he presses her. His great evil is attracted to her illuminating goodness, like some primal circling of forces.

Does he sense that he only continues to live on my sufferance? I believe so; something in him is too animalistic to miss the emanations. But he has only a little time to mend his ways.

Otherwise, I shall kill Edwards in the next day or so.

REF
#666–60–937

"A LITTLE TO THE RIGHT. NO, NO! *MY* RIGHT!"

The enlisted men hanging the REF SERVICE CLUB sign were certain that it was centered and even, but not surprised that Minmei wasn't satisfied. The club had been her obsession ever since the council had given her the go-ahead. Her headache and her firstborn, all wrapped up in one.

Minmei tried to be patient and remind herself that the techs had volunteered their own time to help. But the sign was just about the last thing to take care of; the club would open that night. And she had been through a lot to see her dream come true. But soon—in hours—she would be standing under the spotlights again, singing out to the dim sea of faces, making contact with fellow Human beings in the only way that had ever been possible for her, really. . .

Speaking of ongoing problems—General Edwards's military limo pulled up right behind her, almost tickling her bottom with one of the flags mounted on its front fenders.

Edwards, in a rear seat bigger than some living quarters, lowered his window with the touch of a button. "How's our nightingale's cage coming along?"

She wished he would stop talking like that, but Minmei knew she was walking a fine line again. Offending him would no doubt make him withdraw his support from the project, and that might very well be the end of things.

On the other hand, she didn't know how much longer she could keep him at bay. Since that very first interview he had kept her on the defensive, and Minmei was running out of excuses—why she couldn't have dinner with him, give a private recital for him, attend a diplomatic function on his arm, or take any one of a dozen other first steps on a path that ended at his bedside.

"Top drawer, sir, as you can see. The doors open at 2000 hours SDF time." She saw a flicker of frown cross the exposed half of his face; she still wasn't using his first name.

Edwards pressed another button and the door lifted out of the way, brushing against her. Minmei started for the club entrance as if she had something to do, but he caught up with her in moments. The volunteer techs watched the two enter the club, looked at one another, then began fixing the sign into place.

Edwards took her elbow as if to assist her through the doorway, but in reality he was simply grabbing her—was just barely restraining himself from shaking her. He swept a hand at the club's main lounge—the stage and tables and chairs.

"Are you going to keep pretending *this* is going to make you happy? When it didn't before, when applause from audiences all over *Earth* didn't?"

He dropped her arm in disgust, the visible part of his face flushed. "You're a fool, Minmei. This club of yours —it was a minor gift from me, haven't you figured that out yet?"

The cold metal of his half cowl contrasted with red anger on the rest of his face. "But before long I'll give you things that *will* satisfy you, things that only the greatest power and glory can command!"

He almost told her about the Living Computer, and what use he meant to make of it. Minmei had come to fill his waking thoughts and his dreams. Somehow evading his advances, somehow immune to the charisma and power he had plied so often before, she had only made him want her more. Especially since she had once been Hunter's!

I will not be thwarted in this, he vowed. But in some way that he was at a loss to explain, the upper hand had slipped to Minmei. Edwards had roused himself wrathfully, not to be frustrated by this waifish little spellbinder; and in the all-out effort to make her love him, he had somehow made her the embodiment of all his desires and dreams. He saw that now, but it was too late to change things.

Be that as it might, some iron core of self-preservation and caution kept him from confessing his plots to her. Instead he leaned close, with a look on the exposed half of his face that made her cringe.

"Is it that ass Wolff? Is *that* who you think's going to come home like a white knight and give you some sort of happily-ever-after? If so, you hear me well, Lynn-Minmei: Wolff isn't fit to stand in my *shadow*!

"*I'm* the one who'll give you what you want and fulfill you at last! *I'm* the one who'll stop the aching in your heart!"

He vaguely knew that he was raving, dimly understood that whatever sorcery it was that Minmei had cast over all the others had been cast over him, too. Only, he was T. R. Edwards, and he was not about to meet some lovelorn fate.

He grabbed her arms, and Minmei felt such power in the grip that she knew it was useless to fight. He pressed his mouth to hers; she didn't resist but she didn't cooperate. He might as well have been kissing a corpse. He thrust her from him, and she landed on the floor with a small cry.

"Go on, then, Minmei! Pine for him, while *he's* thinking about the wife and child he left back on Earth! Do you really suppose you're anything but a hardship-tour convenience for Wolff?"

Then he was kneeling by her, lips drawn back from his teeth as if he might devour her. She put the back of her hand to her mouth and shrank away from him, but couldn't take her eyes off him.

"Perhaps I can't give you some doglike devotion, or whatever it is that you think love is, Minmei. But power and immortality and passion—those are what drive me, and you and I *will* share them."

She thought dizzily that he was going to grab her again, or—or something else, something she couldn't put a name to. Instead, as if he were teetering on the brink of an abyss, Edwards pulled himself back, rose, and stared down at her with all emotion closed from his face.

"And you no longer have any choice in the matter," he told her. Then he turned on his heel and strode from the club.

He had barely gotten out the door when his driver came rushing up to him. "Sir, a code 'Pyramid' signal from the Royal Hall."

Edwards didn't break stride. "Get me there. Now."

In the catacombs under the Royal Hall, past room after room of inert Inorganics stacked like cordwood, Edwards hurried to the chamber where the deactivated Living Computer drifted at the bottom of its tank.

On a nearby communications screen, Edwards saw an image.

The Regent, of course; he had seen photos and sketches from the intel summaries, had taken a good look at Tesla, and could extrapolate from there.

The Regent, for his part, glared down at the half-masked Human and drew conclusions of his own. The Living Computer hadn't been destroyed, nor had the Inorganics. Yet this couldn't be the leader of the Human expedition; there was a furtiveness about the way in which the Regent's communications signal had been received.

Ah, good! A schemer! Luck was with him again at last.

Bad luck had certainly had its run. The Regent had only received a few spotty reports of the Sentinels' onslaught before his commo links went dead. He had grown bored with inflicting horrible fates on advisers and, more to the point, it didn't accomplish much but diminish the available pool and make those around him very nervous.

Then came his master stroke: pretend to sue for peace! He cursed himself for not having thought of it before. Freeze the battle lines now. Call for negotiations and draw them out, and stall as long as possible while he rebuilt his armies and prepared to launch a sneak attack.

But instead of the REF council, he found himself staring at this half-flesh, half-metal face—the Human they called General Edwards. "Call back the forces that have launched this unprovoked sneak attack on my realm," the Regent blustered, "or I shall utterly and completely wipe them out of existence!"

"Can I rely on you to be thorough?" Edwards asked.

The Regent realized the game he was playing wasn't the one he had counted on. "Is there some semantic problem, or do I understand you to mean that you do not care that the pitiful Sentinels will be crushed like vermin?"

Edwards smirked. "You and your boys haven't been doing so well, huh? Mmm, here's something you might want to keep in mind, next time."

Edwards turned and grabbed a memory disk holding the full G-2/G-3 analyses of the *Farrago*, including its one glaring Achilles' heel.

The Regent could scarcely believe what he was seeing, and personally looked at an indicator there at the Home Hive to make sure all this critical information was being recorded. The key to destroying the Sentinels.

"Haven't you got anything for me?" Edwards asked disingenuously, with a nod toward the somnolent Living Computer.

The Regent was still recovering from his phenomenal success. "Hmm. Yes, yes, I do, provided that your information is accurate. I think that you and I must talk, General Edwards."

"By all means. But let's do it here on Tirol, eh?" Edwards's tone didn't brook much debate.

The Regent thought about that. "Indeed we will, friend General, indeed we will. Let me make arrangements and get back to you on the matter."

Edwards made an ironic salute with a forefinger. "Don't take too long; there's a lot to do."

"As soon as I've attended to the Sentinels," the Regent agreed.

"If they beat your boys on Karbarra, they'll be headed for Praxis next."

"Ah. Thank you. I look forward to communing with a, um, kindred spirit."

Edwards inclined his head in a courtly fashion, then blanked the screen. When he straightened, he saw Ghost techs looking at him in some shock.

"Wipe those looks off your faces!" Edwards jerked a head at the screen, and by implication at the Regent. "When the time comes, I'll handle him, too."

With a new lease on life, the Regent swaggered through the soaring halls of the Home Hive issuing orders and dictating memos. He had had his doubts about the Earther's veracity, but a battery of Living Computers verified what Edwards had told him, and the Regent was ready to gamble.

Even with the strategic data Edwards had given him, it might not be easy to destroy the *Farrago*.

Then there was the matter of this visit to Tirol. It was beyond the realm of possibility that the Regent would place himself in danger, and yet this gullible Edwards creature seemed to assume it would be normal. Perhaps there was some way to—The Regent stopped so suddenly that a hapless adviser plowed into him.

The Regent flung the adviser aside in a carelessly nonlethal way, and began talking excitedly to his attendant Scientists. "Are my wife's Genesis Pits here on Optera still functional? Well, find out! And if they're not, make them ready for a project of monumental proportions! Divert workers and technicians and Scientists from other projects; bring them here by starship if need be!

"Oh, what a joke on the cursed Humans!" the Regent hooted. *So, the Regis thinks I lost my sense of humor when I decided to devolve, eh?*

Burak sealed the hatch and slipped into place, seated before Tesla's cage. There were a few Karbarrans on guard outside in the passageway, but they had been joined by friends for a kind of victory feast, and nobody was being very . . . very "strac," as the humans called it.

Tesla said nothing, only sat looking like an immense Buddha. Burak reached inside his robes, eyes averted, his horns dipping.

He came up with three luminous perfect spheres, as green as a breaking wave, as green as molten bottle glass. Seeing them, Tesla almost broke his guru pose and reached, but knew that he would only receive a shock charge from the bars of his cage for his troubles.

"The Fruit of the Flower of Life, as grown on Karbarra," Burak said.

"So." Tesla sat, looking down at the three.

There was legend among the Invid, and among many other cultures as well, about consuming the Fruit of the Flower. The implication was that the consumption of Fruit from all the worlds Especially Touched by Haydon—all the worlds, it happened, from which the Sentinels came—would bring forth some larger, more magnificent manifestation of the one who consumed it.

Tesla had spent a lifetime steeped in this occultish lore; he was convinced that there was a scientific basis to it.

"Give those to me," he said, "and give me Fruit from the rest of Haydon's Worlds, the other worlds of the Sentinels."

"I don't trust you," Burak said.

"I don't expect you to," Tesla shot back. "Why do you think peace is so difficult to achieve?"

Burak slammed his fist on the deck. "Stop talking around it! Can you take the curse off Peryton or not?"

Tesla saw a bulge in the waist rope of Burak's robes and knew a pistol was there, knew what his fate would be if he couldn't sway Burak right here and now.

"I can. But you're going to have to help me. Trust me. And I'll help you win back your family, Burak, and your planet, and everything you've lost. Because you're the one fated to be Peryton's messiah."

Burak sat trembling for a long time, looking at the deck. Then he dipped his head once, horns swaying, nodding in agreement.

CHAPTER
TWENTY-
THREE

Why did Jonathan leave me? How come Lisa's bouquet came right into my hands after the wedding and yet everything's gone wrong?

It all started off so beautifully.

The diary of Lynn-Minmei

THE KARBARRANS THREW THEMSELVES INTO THE EFfort to get the Sentinels ready for the next step in their war with the same energy the ursinoids had shown in destroying the Invid garrison.

Unfortunately, a good deal of the capital's industrial area had been razed. There were shops capable of repairing most of the damaged VTs and tanks, and spaceship yards where *Farrago* could be put back in full battle-worthiness, but no new mecha could be built anytime soon.

Some Sentinels argued that it would be better to wait, to

build new war machines and perhaps even construct more ships, but Rick and Lisa, among others, argued that lives would probably be lost on Praxis in the meantime, and the decision to continue on to the amazon homeworld became unanimous—except for Burak's stubborn abstention.

The vote was one of the few things Rick and Lisa *did* agree on. Though the mecha were being repaired, there were gaps in the ranks of the Human fighters, casualties who had left unmanned machines behind. The two were silent on the subject until the night, in their private quarters, when he admitted, "I'm going back on combat duty with the Skulls, Lisa. They need me. And we still won't be able to get every VT manned."

She rolled over and looked at him for a long moment. "I wish there was something I could say that would stop you. But there isn't, is there?"

He shook his head. She lay back down and they both stared at the ceiling for a time. "You're just so damned cavalier with a life that's important to *me*," she said at last, and he could hear the tears in her voice. "It hurts, Rick."

He reached over to take her hand, but she moved it away. She wanted to lie there and see if she could think of some way that she could change things so that she wouldn't be hurt ever again.

Jonathan Wolff returned to his quarters after twenty-one straight hours of meetings, briefings, consultation, training, and planning sessions. He had forgotten what a bed felt like.

But as he lay down, his eye caught something—a small locket lying on his night table. That type of locket was popular among REF personnel; many carried such a keepsake. He picked it up and activated it; the little heart-shaped face opened like a triptych.

A tiny hologram of Minmei hung in the empty air. "I hope this makes you feel near to me, Jonathan, because I feel very near to you, and I always will. Come back to me

safe and soon, darling. I'll be waiting for you, however
long it takes."

"It's very kind of you to act as our guide," Cabell said,
as the Karbarran skywain sailed through the afternoon sunlight.

"Oh, we love going out to the monument," Crysta
gushed, and at the controls, Lron nodded agreement. Off to
one side, Rem and Dardo paused in the pattycakelike game
Lron's son was trying to teach. "And how old is the monument?" Rem asked.

"Centuries, ages," Lron rumbled. "No one's exactly
sure. History says it was erected right after Haydon visited
Karbarra, and that was long, long ago."

The skywain began its descent, alighting on the top of
one of the higher mountains overlooking the city. Rem
asked again if Cabell would be warm enough; the old sage
reassured him.

Lron and Crysta led the way, up to an open pavilion
carved from the living rock of the mountaintop. There, in
the middle of an acres-wide floor, stood a statue that reared
up and up—a colossus a thousand feet high.

It was of Haydon. It had been carved by Karbarrans,
and time and weather had eroded it, but the figure appeared
to be a humanoid male, wearing flowing robes and poised
with an air of nobility and wisdom.

"It was Haydon who taught our ancestors the secrets of
Sekiton," Crysta said. "Just as he breathed life into the
crystals of Spheris and created Baldan's people, and decreed that the Praxians' should be an all-female planet."

"And Haydon taught the Gerudans how to think," Dardo
said, reciting his school lessons. "And some people even
say he gave the Flower of Life to the Invid!"

Cabell already knew all that, of course, but he tried to
look impressed by Dardo's erudition—Crysta and Lron
were so proud of the cub, after all.

Rem stood staring up at the stone face now worn to

anonymity. Haydon, certainly one of the galaxies' great enigmas, fascinated him just as Haydon fascinated so many others. Where had the bringer-of-miracles come from? What had prompted him to spend a Golden Age in this sector of space, traveling among local worlds and working his magic?

Rem had always vowed that if he got to travel among the stars, he would do his best to find out. And now that time had come. Rem stared up at the smooth visage, wishing it could speak to him. He swore to himself at that moment that before his travels were done, he would know what face belonged on the monument.

"Red alert," whispered one Ghost Squadron yeoman to another. "Stay out of the Old Man's way!"

The second yeoman nodded and did his best to look busy as Edwards marched from his office with a murderous look on his face.

The Sentinels had won a smashing victory on Karbarra! Edwards tried to suppress his fury, but wasn't having much luck. To make matters worse, when he had called Minmei, she wasn't at the club. Nobody seemed to know *where* she was.

This, after he had been there at a ringside table every night to hear her sing, had wined and dined her, had made sure the council listened to her and that her service club was a success. Yet each time he was sure he was making her forget Wolff, she was sure to bring the halfwit's name up.

Edwards stopped in midstride. He suddenly knew just where she would be.

Sure enough, he found her there, looking at the posted casualty reports along with many others, searching the alphabetized lists of KIAs and WIAs. The names would go on the REF broadcast screens momentarily, but there were a lot of people who couldn't bear to wait. There was quite a press, and those at the back were calling out names for those in the front to check.

Just as the general came up behind her, Minmei turned with a thousand-watt smile on her face. "Oh, General! He's not on it! Jonathan's not on the lists, so he's all right!"

Edwards forced a smile. Yes, Wolff had survived Karbarra, but the Sentinels would be headed for Praxis soon, and the Regent was aware of it.

"Yes; he's a lucky man." He showed her what he had brought for her.

"Oh, they're beautiful!" Minmei took the bouquet and held it to her face, inhaling the sweet, exotic alien scents. She was delighted, and pleased with the good news about Jonathan; even though he could be cold, almost cruel at times, Edwards had been such a help, had been there whenever she needed someone to listen to her or reassure her...

Without pausing to reconsider, Minmei put her free arm around his neck and kissed him once, quickly, on the lips. Then she was racing off for a rehearsal.

Edwards watched her go, thinking of the day when he would comfort her in her grief over the death of Jonathan Wolff.

When Edwards got back to his HQ he was in visibly better spirits, but not for long. Adams entered, looking grim, and cued up a recording. "The internal-security people monitored this with the bug we put on Lang's private commo rig," Edwards's aide told him. "It went out earlier today, before Tirol Base lost contact with Karbarra."

Lang was saying, "General Hunter, I'm not opposed to the building of more starships per se; SDF-3 will not be ready for a return voyage to Earth for a prolonged period, and we might very well need this armada that General Edwards keeps pushing for.

"But I must tell you in confidence that I have my doubts about Edwards's motives."

Rick's face, on the other half of the split screen, looked drawn and tired. "Just what are you saying, Doctor?"

"That Edwards may very well be furthering his own ends. I think a coup attempt is a quite plausible danger at such time as this armada is ready."

Rick considered that. "If the other Sentinels' worlds can be liberated as quickly as Karbarra, we'll be back long before the armada is finished, Doctor. And we'll have plenty of Sentinel allies to help us make sure Edwards is checkmated. But after what we've seen—I'm more convinced than ever that the Invid have to be rooted out of these planets they're occupying."

Lang nodded. "I agree, Admiral, but I wanted you to be aware of the gravity of the situation here."

Adams stopped the recording. "What are we going to do, sir?"

Edwards leaned back. "For the time being, nothing. We need Lang to build that fleet and get SDF-3 fully operational. And once the Sentinels show up at Praxis . . ."

He allowed himself a thin smile. "Once they're out of the way, the REF belongs to me completely."

When he returned to Tracialle, Rem was surprised to find Janice Em waiting for him.

They hadn't spent much time together in the rush of the Karbarran campaign. Now, she took his hand and said, "I thought we were friends, Rem. Have I done something to offend you?"

His brows knit. It was sometimes hard to understand what Humans were getting at. "Of course not! What makes you say that?"

She showed a slight pout. "I was beginning to think a gal's got to be a butch weightlifter to get any attention from you."

He realized that she was talking about Gnea. "Hmm? Gnea and I are friends, of course—we went through a lot on that scouting mission." He *had* been spending considerable time talking to the young amazon, learning about her life and her world.

Jan had both his hands in hers now. "If you want me to step aside, just come out and say so!"

He shook his head in confusion. "What? No, no I—"

Janice was suddenly in his arms with a happy laugh. "Oh, I'm so glad! You—you've become kind of important to me, you know."

It felt very good to have her embracing him, brushing her lips against his cheek, his neck, his lips. Very unsettling, but simply wonderful. "Let's go somewhere and be alone," she said.

He yielded as she drew him away. "And you can tell me all about this expedition you took to the Haydon monument," Janice added. "What did Lron and Crysta have to say about this Haydon, anyway? And Cabell; what was *his* reaction?"

Why was she nattering away about *Haydon*, of all things, when she was back with Rem at last? But Janice felt something puzzling, something that made her curious about the subject, and about Cabell and the Sentinels' plans too. And there was something about Rem that excited her and made her want to be with him and know everything about him.

Maybe that's what love is, she shrugged to herself.

On Praxis, the Regis flung her hands high, throwing her head back crying, "Hear me, O my Children!"

Wherever they were, whatever they were doing, her half of her species paused to listen to her.

Just as no subject of her husband's could eavesdrop on her mental link, so none of the Regis's children bore any further allegiance to him.

She looked more Human than a Haydonite, though she was fully as tall as her mate—some twenty feet. And yet there was something ethereal about her, an alienness that showed in her cobalt eyes. Slender and hairless, she wore a full-length robe and curious, tasseled five-fingered gloves. Four emerald-green sensor scarabs, like beautiful brooches or oriental masks, decorated her robe's collar and neck closure.

"Hear me!" she cried again. "My investigations here tell me that the answer I seek is to be found on Haydon IV! There at last I will learn where the Robotech Masters have gone, and what has happened to the last Protoculture matrix, the treasure that we must have in order to carry out my Great Work!"

And an age of deprivation and conflict would be brought to a close. Still shielded in her thoughts, like a hot cinder, was that night so long ago in the Flower gardens of the paradise that had been Optera.

There she had surrendered at last to the emotional enticements and seductive intellect and form of Zor—had surrendered herself to him and surrendered the secrets of the Flower as well.

And was discovered in the act by the Regent, who flung himself off on the descending spiral of devolution. But soon, all those torturous memories and misdeeds would be behind her, and her Children.

"Therefore, prepare yourselves, my Children! Gather and make ready, for we abandon this planet at once, for Haydon IV!"

In the Genesis Pits abandoned on Optera by his wife, the Regent peered into a cloning vat. Work on his project had not been without its problems; his biogenetic workers were less adept than the Regis's, and had been forced to start from scratch after the first abortive attempt.

But now things were going well. The workers had used the most perfect egg available, an unquickened one from the clutch that had spawned the Regent, feeling it was the ultimate perfection of Invid plasm.

The Regent gazed into the vat as into an aquarium. What floated there was no ordinary Invid clone, though. It had a cobra hood like his own, a row of eyelike turbercle sensors that mimicked his.

It was a new Regent, a false one.

"I am pleased," he said. "Make certain that it's ready by the time I've crushed the Sentinels."

Karen found Jack in one of the training areas the Sentinels had set up near their temporary groundside billeting area. She had been looking forward to teasing him about being compulsive in his training, but the look on her face changed when she saw he wasn't alone.

Bela was with him on the firing range, showing him how to use the Praxian crossbow. He was getting the hang of it, and put a quarrel within a foot or so of a bull's-eye at twenty paces.

"Ah, Karen Penn," Bela smiled. "You once asked me about our weapons; now you see they're so easy that even a male can use them. Jack here is making fine progress; would you care to try?" Bela clapped Jack on the shoulder in comradely fashion and gave him a sisterly hug. She towered over him, a full head taller.

Karen made no effort to keep the frosty tone out of her voice. "No, thank you. Lieutenant Baker, I'm just here to let you know that your request has been approved; you've been reassigned to Hovertank duty in the Wolff Pack."

"Hey, that's great!" He had studied Jonathan Wolff's style, and decided he wanted to serve under the man. "Did you get what you wanted?"

She looked at his grin and felt like belting him. He didn't even understand that she was sore at him. "Yes. I'm going over to Commander Grant's GMU staff as of tomorrow morning."

"Congratulations! Let's go celebrate. Bela, want to join us?"

But Karen was shaking her head. "No. I'm sure you two have lots of—exercising to do. And I wouldn't want to intrude."

As he watched her walk off, Jack said, bewildered, "Did I say something wrong, Bela? I don't think I understand what just happened."

Bela shrugged and recocked the crossbow with one

swift, powerful pull on its forestock grip. "Personally, I often find it difficult to comprehend your species at *all*."

At last, after weeks of frantic preparation, training, re-equipping and rearming and reorganizing, the *Farrago* was ready to lift off.

The original plan for a Karbarran starship and fighting force to accompany the Sentinels had had to be abandoned; the Invid had disabled all Karbarran ships, and the new ones on the drawing boards wouldn't be ready for months yet.

"The new production lines for VTs and other mecha will be fully operational in another six weeks," the senior Karbarran administrators had assured the Sentinels. "When you've freed the women of Praxis, we will be ready to help them become an army."

The word was that the Invid garrison on Praxis was much smaller than that on Karbarra, and the Sentinels were hoping for a brief campaign. The Karbarrans cheered as the Sentinels lifted off and passed through the open wedge of the dome. Lisa looked down on the planet and thought that in spite of the pain and losses the war had cost so far, the sight of a liberated planet and a free people made it worthwhile.

Still, she breathed a prayer that the worst was behind them.

> *In a way, the very things I've counseled the others against are what the Sentinels' mission is all about: hurling one's self into the midst of the Shapings and taking the risk that their design will not turn to one of utter tragedy.*
>
> *And yet, in the Sentinels there is that added dimension that most of the species on Farrago are from Haydon's Worlds. I pray, for them, that it brings out the most benign manifestations of the Workings of the Protoculture.*
>
> Dr. Emil Lang, *The New Testament*

THIS TIME, *FARRAGO* WENT IN READY FOR TROUBLE, finger on trigger. The ship emerged from superluminal drive even further from Praxis than it had from Karbarra, since Lisa wanted to get a handle on the situation before any shooting started.

Encountering no immediate opposition—in fact, no sign that the Invid had detected the ship's arrival at all— Lisa moved fast to consolidate what she hoped was the advantage of total surprise. VTs launched to fly cover and screen any enemy attack; the strike forces readied for their go signal. The flagship bore in toward the planet and still there was no sign of a response.

"Nothing in the air, zero activity on the ground, no commo, no power sources—nothing," a tech officer reported from the GMU. "Captain Hunter, if they're playing dead, they're doing an amazing job. It looks to me like there might be nobody home."

"Oldest trick in the book," Lisa heard Jonathan Wolff murmur over the command net. But what if Wolff was wrong? She had learned to expect the unexpected from this war, and surely an uncontested landing would be the most unexpected thing of all.

She warily brought the flagship in close, but not too close, staying beyond the orbit of the outermost of Praxis's two small moons. The next move wasn't hard to figure out, but it brought her a personal pang of regret.

"Skull Leader, we're going to need recon; pick your elements and tell 'em to watch their tailerons down there."

"Roger," Max Sterling answered.

It had come as a bit of a surprise to Lisa that Rick, in returning to combat duty with his old unit, hadn't attempted to step into the command slot. But the Skulls, like the oldtime Israelis and Swiss before them, didn't let mere rank or seniority determine who flew lead.

That was decided by who had the most experience with the particular mecha, knew the current situation and tactics best, had the superior performance record, and so forth. And right now, Rick Hunter, admiral or not, was far from the top of the roster. So, he had swallowed his pride and taken his place as wingman to a young lieutenant commander who had been in high school when Rick Hunter was Skull Leader.

Still, there was no question that Rick would be going down on the flyby; with the ranks of the Skulls thinned as they were, and Max preferring to use veterans on an iffy mission like this, it was only to be expected.

At Max's command, several Alphas—Rick's among them—broke formation and mated their tail sections to the rear of the same number of the powerful Betas, forming aggregate ships with tremendously increased range and firepower. The problem was that maneuverability was decreased and mechamorphosis capability was nonexistent.

The Alpha-Beta conjoinings swept out for a pass at Praxis. The rest of the Alphas, Betas, and Logans fell back to guard *Farrago* under Miriya; Max had led the overflight, of course.

The mission elapsed-time counters ticked off tense minutes. But there was nothing to report, beyond the stillness on the planet and the static of the commo channels.

The Skulls were very low on fuel by the time they finished the low orbit, and *Farrago* moved in to retrieve them. Lisa gave the word that the second recon group go in, this time lower, and had the shuttle stand by with its landing party.

In due course, Battloids trod the deserted streets and countryside of Praxis. A contingent of Wolff's Hovertanks, with Jack Baker among them, was checking one of the largest cities on Praxis—a large coastal town, really—block by block, house by house, for use as a base of operations. Technical teams from the shuttle swore that there was nothing on or under the planet's surface higher up the evolutionary ladder than native wildlife. There were plenty of indications of Invid occupation, but the fortifications and temporary Hives were abandoned.

There was no sign of the women of Praxis.

"But—why would they leave with the Invid? What use would that be?" Gnea was close to tears.

Bela patted her shoulder. "I don't know, warrior, but we're going to find out. And woe to the Invid if we don't find our sisters well and whole."

Lisa had those same fears for the Praxians, and other problems besides. Without the firing of a single shot, the Sentinels' war had been brought to a shuddering halt. The Praxians weren't likely to budge until they had some idea what had happened to their people, but at the same time, each hour used up by delay gave the enemy a chance to regroup and redeploy.

She couldn't afford to spend much time there if it would be to no advantage.

It was at such times that Lisa wished dearly that the *Farrago*'s bridge was small, like the SDFs'. She longed to sit in the command chair she had installed, as Henry Gloval was wont to do on *his* bridge, perhaps with a uniform cap visor pulled down over her eyes, and try to mull her way out of her current fix.

But she didn't have that luxury, and every hour was a precious resource she couldn't replace. The senior Sentinel leaders, Baldan and Veidt and the rest, wanted to confer about what to do next—even though Bela and most of the other Praxians refused to even leave the surface of their planet and return to the flagship.

Lisa exercised her authority as captain and, at this stage of things, de facto overall commander. She got Vince Grant on the horn.

If the Praxians won't come to Mohammed . . . she thought.

"We're going to make one low pass with the flagship and drop the GMU; GMU will begin an intense study of the situtation on Praxis and attempt to reach some logical conclusion while I convene a full meeting of the principal Sentinels. Give me a shopping list, Vince; what will you need?"

Most of what he needed was already aboard the Ground Mobile Unit; the rest of it was quickly transferred. It was also becoming obvious that there were no hostile forces or booby traps on Praxis; for that reason she began to fear for the flagship's safety. Lisa ordered that a minimal force of VTs and Hovertanks be assigned to ground duty, but that most surface security would be the job of a small detachment from the remaining Destroids. All but a few of the Skulls would be pulled back to protect *Farrago*.

She had a sudden thought as she was about to conclude the call, and said, "Vince, there's one more thing that might come in handy. Tell Jean to make sure she's got her

Invid lie detector; I'm going to have Tesla transferred to the GMU."

The architecture of the Praxians seemed like a cross between classical Japanese and Dark Ages Nordic. They used mostly woods and rough-cut stone, and somehow there was the impression that they were used to structures catching fire or crashing down in a quake, and had come to accept it—didn't feel they had to build for posterity.

They also tended to fortify places, even though the last of their generations-long feud-wars—epic bloodbaths of tremendous strife and cruelty and valorous deeds—ended centuries before. But the fortifications were at lower levels, and the higher stories of the amazons' structures could be opened to the air, with mosaic walls or panels of inlaid wood that moved aside or could be lifted.

The local castle at the GMU landing site was the summer palace of the planet's elected ruler. Bela showed some hesitation, in the spacious throne room; then, as senior warrior of her people, she took her place by the foot of the throne. She did not sit down, however.

Other Sentinels had gathered there among the huge ancestral images and holy statuary. This high up, one could see the green, restless bay filling the vista to one side and gray mountains with blue-white caps of snow to the other.

According to Praxian custom, all the war mecha had been stilled, shut down, so that peace and quiet would reign. Even the GMU was powered down, its Protoculture engines inert.

Jack Baker, there as an observer and Wolff's aide, watched Bela falter as she called the meeting to order. *She's really just a kind of ranger, a backwoods cop*, he thought, *thrust into the spotlight by events.* For once, he figured, events had picked the right person.

Bela's confidence grew quickly, especially with Gnea and the other Praxian women there to back her up. Halidarre was standing to one side, stamping just a bit and snorting from time to time, acting more and more like a real animal with each day she served Bela.

Bela threw the first pitch without a windup. "I'm not as good at coming around sideways to things as are the diplomats," she allowed. "I know a lot of you want to go on to the next front in this war. In some ways I don't blame you, because there are no enemies to fight here. But the women of Praxis aren't about to leave until we've tried our best to find out what happened to our people.

"If you can't wait for us, we wish you well. But something's happened on our planet that we have to puzzle out before we're ready to make our next move." She said it in a way that brooked no contradiction.

That left everybody silent and thoughtful, including the senior Sentinels. Karen grudgingly reflected that the Southern Cross Advanced Leadership Program could have learned a thing or two from Bela.

But it was Burak who stepped out of the crowd, out onto the richly polished red hardwood floor of the throne room. "My heart goes out to my sisters from Praxis," he said. "But the question is, *Do theirs go out to the rest of us?* It's time to make rational decisions.

"We sought mecha on Karbarra but came away from there with a grievous net loss. We sought new recruits on Praxis but find an untenanted world. When will the leaders of this campaign see the obvious? There are no fighters on Haydon, no war machines on Geruda! Peryton, *Peryton* is the key here! Let us bypass this and other worlds that cannot advance our cause, and free Peryton from its curse! Then we'll have *legions!*"

Rick, listening, wasn't sure what had changed in Burak, but something was giving him a new and more penetrating gaze, a ringing note to his voice, a larger-than-life aspect to his gestures. It was as if Burak had come into a sense of personal destiny. Rick had seen that sort of thing before, and the memories didn't make him feel comfortable.

Veidt somehow made a sound like the clearing of a throat, even though he had no mouth with which to speak.

"Burak, I've already told you in private why I think it is essential to let Peryton wait until our forces have grown— why I think it is suicide for the Sentinels to try to address themselves to your planet now. The difficulties involved are—"

Burak interrupted, slashing the air with his horns. "I've heard that too often, and too easily, from you! And I say this to the Sentinels: you care so little for Peryton? So be it! The *Farrago* comes apart even more easily than she went together! And the module that is my ship is mine to do with as I please; that was our compact.

"So then, bid me farewell; for today, this very hour, Burak of Peryton leaves, to pursue his own quest and bring salvation to his world, whether you are with me and my people or not!"

There were mutterings, and a dozen voices were raised to try to mollify him, but Burak was having none of it. The few other Perytonians there, stone-faced, fell in behind him and trooped toward the exit.

Lisa jumped as her wrist communicator beeped piercingly for her attention. All over the throne room it was the same, distress calls reaching Sentinels in a variety of ways.

"*Farrago* under attack by large Invid force," was all most of them heard. Then the transmissions stopped.

It was his hour, the beginning of a new age; the Regent resolved to decree a new calendar with that sublime moment as its starting point.

He had stripped outposts and far-flung garrisons, put together a force even greater than the one he had assembled to send against his enemies on Optera.

And this time fortune was with him. His fleet emerged from superluminal at just the correct angle of attack, in good formation and proper deployment. Scouts and Pincers rocketed off, this time under competent veteran commanders, to join combat with the enemy mecha trying to protect their flagship.

And the flagship! How long he had hungered for *that*

morsel! A Living Computer in the Regent's command ship matched it up with the specifications Edwards had given him, and with exquisite precision the Invid sensors penetrated down and down into it until they found the junction and the components Edwards specified—the ones Lron had explained to the REF and Lang when the Sentinels first appeared.

Lacking the grand slam of the GMU's cannon, the *Farrago* turned to its lesser weapons, gamely firing and firing, weapons crews staying at their stations even though things seemed hopeless. Most of them had been in Invid cages, and had no intention of being there again, whatever the price of freedom—even if it was death.

But luck wasn't with them this time. The Regent's techs and scientists had prepared a super cannonbolt in accordance with the things Edwards had revealed to them; they fired it now.

It struck to the heart of *Farrago*, sending a pulse throughout the ship's structure. In another moment the flagship was *coming apart*. The forces that unified it had become forces sundering it.

The Regent watched, one fist under his chin, wondering if there was some lesson here. Then he roused himself to bellow at his communications drones. "Haven't you contacted the Regis yet? *Well*?"

Ah, what a sweet victory this would be! To wipe out the approaching enemy in the nick of time, to humble the Sentinels and destroy them forever here, where his mate could see it all—and be won back by him by this proof of his strength at war and military brilliance! A true, savage, devolved stroke of greatness.

Farrago was ripping itself to pieces; shields were down, power systems were failing, communications were all but nonexistent. Always a patchwork ship, she was being driven apart by the Regent's single bolt.

A string of explosions opened a power conduit all along a main passageway, like something being stitched by a monster sewing machine, inflicting awful casualties among the crewbeings trapped there. The last of the explosions sent shrapnel and fire into Mr. Blake, Lisa's trusted bridge officer.

He had almost made it; the Spherian module was before him, the last that was intact. There was no one aboard the Spherian; at least, no one alive. Concussion, blast, fumes, and flying debris had downed them all.

Blake barely dragged himself inside; he was losing consciousness and had lost a tremendous amount of blood. Yet he somehow held himself up with one hand on a commo box and reached through the hatch, feeling for the emergency release.

He had to strip off the safety seal, ripping fingernails loose in the process but scarcely feeling the pain. Tiredly, he took the little quartz lever there and pulled it down. A crystal tone began to sound in the empty Spherian ship as its hatch closed and the strange repelling forces generated by the Regent's volley began to separate it from *Farrago*.

But another internal explosion blew out that whole part of the passageway and penetrated the Spherian hull, killing Blake instantly and damaging the Spherian ship. It would never make its programmed rescue run; it broke in half, the drive section tumbling off on a vector of its own, the rest consumed, along with Blake's body, by another huge detonation from *Farrago*.

The VTs, taken by surprise and surrounded by a horde of Invid mecha, closed ranks and tried to defend themselves as best they could. A few elements tried to break through and run for Praxis, but the Regent's forces were deployed to stop them. The Skulls re-formed and got ready for a fight to the death. There were some garbled transmissions from the Invid, something about surrender, but the fighter jocks had all heard the tales from the Sentinels who had been prisoners, and decided they weren't interested.

Outnumbered five to one, and at times ten to one, they flew from second to second, and died at full throttle. A few joined Alpha to Beta and catapulted themselves into the enemy midst; others got into tight flight elements and rat-raced, skeeting enemies until their own number was up.

They were the best Earth had to offer, people who had contended with cramped living conditions, low pay, and a long separation from home to serve a cause greater than themselves. And no one was there to thank them as they died in the gun turrets, the flight decks, the cockpits. But they hadn't signed on for thanks, and hadn't expected them.

Farrago came apart, its outlashing throwing portions and scraps of it toward unreachable stars. The teeming Invid swarmed in to slay the last of the VTs and strafe the flagship's remains.

"Still no contact with the Regis?" the Regent howled, shaking a gargantuan fist. "Has she no idea what I've accomplished?"

A drone technician looked stricken, realizing that he might die in the next few seconds. "Oh, All-Powerful One! The Regis is no longer on Praxis! The readings we receive indicate that she may be on her way to Haydon IV with her half of our race, but—there are no Protoculture readings on Praxis, no power sources, no movement—nothing!"

The Regent screamed aloud, but it would have been too much of an inconvenience to leap from his throne and smite the technician. Instead, he tried to wipe the taste of disappointment from his mind.

"A waste, a waste! Did you record every bit of my victory, so that she may see it? Then, make ready to depart!"

"To Praxis, my lord?" an Enforcer asked.

The Regent cuffed the Enforcer aside, and the Enforcer's armor buckled against the deck with the impact of it. "No, of course not to Praxis! Back to Optera! I'll find that female and *make* her see the truth, *make* her appreciate me!"

He felt acceleration around him even as he issued more orders. "Send a small observation force to Praxis in case any of my enemies return; this place is of no use to me now. Have them set up a transmitter to warn me if there's trouble here again. And then back to the Home Hive!"

There was his alter ego to groom, and set on its pathway. Enough of these meddling Humans; he would send in his simulagent double to do away with the Tirol base, then consolidate the near stars at his leisure. And when he held all the cards, he would bring the Regis to heel.

A sudden thought struck him. If he could produce a copy of himself, why not a copy of the Regis? Yes! One who would be dutiful and compliant and a proper wife? Meek and obedient and ... *receptive* to him. The very image of that made him feel rather paternal and husbandly at the same time.

But no; he snarled at the realization that the Regis was gone, and she had taken all detailed biogenetic models of herself with her. Even more to the point, possessing a mere image of her wouldn't be the same as possessing *her*, of bending his mate to his will; he would always be aware, on some level, that the real thing was out there in the universe somewhere.

"Why are we dawdling?" he bellowed. The command ship blurred forward to superluminal speed.

CHAPTER
TWENTY-FIVE

We should protect the Seed,
or we could all fade away
Flower of Life
Flower of Life

Song of the Tiresian Muses*

*D*AMN HER!

T. R. Edwards tried to tell himself that he didn't care anymore. Wasn't his staying away from the ringside table tonight proof enough of that? The storied Lynn-Minmei enchantment had no power over him, and now the world knew it. Oh yes, the world knew it . . .

He hadn't meant to have more than that one jigger of Tirol-made bourbon with Adams and the others, but it had gone a little beyond that, and while he wasn't unsteady on his feet, it was time to go home. The planning of a coup

---

*lyrics (c) copyright 1985 Harmony Gold Music, Inc.

d'état took a sharp mind and unrelenting work. To bed, then.

Except—the door to his quarters was slightly ajar.

He silently drew the pistol that was with him day and night, entering without a sound. He could have called security, but tonight he was in the mood to kill someone.

He edged in, peered around a corner—and froze.

"Come on; sit down quick, before it gets cold." Minmei blew out a long match as the candles on the improvised dinner table filled the room with a warm glow.

She threw the dead match into the fireplace, looking as awkward as a teenager. "This is just home cooking." It was almost a whisper. "The guys at the club got me the ingredients, but I'm a good chef, T. R.; from way back. Worked in my folks' restaurant."

She swallowed and watched him. Edwards felt like doing something violent; the idea of having feelings this strong for anyone was anathema to him.

"Do you really love me?" Minmei asked him all at once. "I have no way of making you, but *please* don't lie to me! Can you love me—"

She was cut off by the beep of the special commo apparatus in his study. Without saying a word, he unlocked it by retinal scan, went into it, and locked the door, making the room a secure, soundproofed facility.

He was glad he was sitting down when he keyed the call. It was a patch-through from the loyal Ghost Team techs manning the Invid equipment beneath the Royal Hall. The Regent stared out at him. "You take your time about answering a transmission."

Edwards found his voice. "My apologies. Had I known, I would have—made arrangements." Not "been waiting"; he had to keep a certain parity here.

The Regent made an annoyed gesture. "There are other arrangements you *don't* have to make; the Sentinels are destroyed, one and all."

Edwards felt the color rise in his face, and the grip of

his hands as he made triumphant fists, but he gave no other sign as a silent victory cry rang through him. "And now it is time you and I met face to face," the Regent continued.

Edwards's eyes narrowed. "Surely, you don't expect me to, to—"

"Come to Optera? No; you wouldn't, would you? But *noblesse oblige*, and all that; *I* will come to *you*, this one time. Do us all a favor, Human, and see that you make it worth my while."

The Regent broke the connection and Edwards sat there, his head swimming. *My rivals are dead. The would-be Overlord of the galaxy wants to cut a deal with me.*

Edwards instantly began trying to figure out ways to gull, use, and betray the Regent.

Minmei looked up as Edwards came back into the candlelit dining room. "Good news, I hope?"

"No news at all." He had his hands on his silvery headpiece, straining a bit. "But . . . where were we? You said please don't lie to you; you said please tell you if I can love you."

He drew the half cowl off his face, letting her see him there in the soft light.

Once, the face had been handsome; but now there were raised white scars in a violent, puckered crisscross, a slash from his hairline to the bridge of his nose and from there a reverse angle to the heel of his jawbone. The eye was scarred shut, with only a little prosthetic fitting showing now. A half-devastated face that gave him a doomed look.

"Do you really love me?'" he quoted her own words to her. "'I have no way of making you, but *please* don't lie to me!'"

Where did the act end and truth begin? If she rebuffed him at this moment, Edwards resolved to launch his coup now, taking her as his first hostage and the one he would never let go.

She reached out tentatively, touching the ravaged side of his face. He had never endured that touch from anyone. He returned the touch but otherwise sat like a granite statue. Then she was around the table, in his lap, kissing him.

"*Farrago* destroyed," Vince Grant said. "But it doesn't look like the Invid are coming after us; something's happening."

The rest of the Sentinels stood around him, repressing their questions; they had already learned that it was bedlam when they all talked at once.

They were gathered in a deactivated GMU; the Praxian requirement that all mecha power down during the meeting in the castle had been an unexpected godsend.

Is this where our luck turns? Gnea wondered.

The Invid fleet above suddenly let forth a myriad of minor sensor "paints," then accelerated for superluminal.

The small observation force of Pincers and Scouts and armored Shock Troopers swept down confidently to take up their places. They quartered the globe that was Praxis. They isolated the important civic-commercial centers, and came in for landings.

The VTs rose up to meet them, having received the word that the Regent was gone. Wolff's Hovertanks fired as Gladiators, or flew on back thrusters as Battloids, dragging the enemy from the air. Again there was that total environment of warfare, so insane—and yet so emphatic that it seemed to the fighters that it was the only time they were truly alive.

"Skull Ten, you got a bogey; scissor right!"

"Skull Six, Skull Six, scissoring; get 'im off my back, Max!"

And the GMU cannon fired, its first round hitting the Invid command ship. There would be no distress call to the Regent.

The Invid threw themselves into the engagements with utter ferocity. But they were met by young Earth soldiers who were angry about Karbarra and confused and scared about Praxis: in a certain sense, the Invid had made their enemies too scared to give in and too scared to lose.

Neither side could withdraw, and so the fighting went on. One by one, the VTs fell, despite their high kill ratio. The mecha hunted one another across Praxis, the VTs using up ordnance and fuel. Both Rick and Max were forced to land when their mecha began to lose power; Miriya had been forced to eject earlier, her VT too shot up to stay in the air.

When the Invid were also forced to take to the ground, the Destroids and the Wolff Pack moved in, with other Sentinels on Hovercycles and in flitters, and riding whatever else they could get into the air. The Invid still had the advantage of numbers, but the Hovertanks and REF irregulars were comparatively fresh. In a half-dozen separate, desperate actions, the Invid were surrounded and annihilated, but at terrible cost.

In the aftermath, the principal Sentinels gathered—stunned and bloodied by what they had abruptly endured—and realized what had happened to them.

The two or three surviving VTs had landed, spent, no longer capable of lifting off Praxis. Only a handful of Hovertanks and Destroids had survived the no-quarter fighting.

Hundreds were dead, in addition to the thousands who had perished with *Farrago*. The GMU was their only resource; they had no way of communicating with Tirol, or any other potential source of rescue.

Bela came by to help a weary Jack to his feet as he sat near the GMU; he had barely escaped his burning Hovertank, and it looked like he was plain old leg infantry again, at least for the foreseeable future.

He was filthy and tired. He had just come in from two sleepless days and nights of recon patrol, trying to make sure there were no Invid left and to find something, *any-*

thing, that would help the Sentinels get out of their dead-end dilemma. And he and his squad had come back empty-handed.

Bela was leading Halidarre, one of the few operating mecha left. "Admiral Hunter wants to see you, old son," she said. He groaned wearily as she pulled him up, and shouldered his Wolverine.

"Where are you headed?" he asked. She and the Robo-horse were laden with gear and weapons, and so was Gnea, who was hurrying up to meet her.

"To scout the planet for Hunter, and for myself. Jack, they can't all be gone." Bela turned and put her hands on his shoulders, Halidarre's rein drooping from her grasp. Her face, with its hypnotic raptor eyes, held him, its lines pulled into fierce but frightened lines. *"They can't all be gone!"*

He reached up and thumped her shoulder with his fist. "We'll *find* 'em, sis. You'll see."

She gave him a hug, kissed his cheek, and rumpled his hair. It felt a little like an affectionate mugging. Gnea hugged him too, and then both Valkyries were on their winged horse. Halidarre reared and gave a whinny so real-istic that Jack wondered if something wasn't going a little strange with its engrams.

Then Halidarre was away, into the sky, and Hagane, the malthi, went zipping and zooming after like a humming-bird. The rallying cries of the Praxians drifted back, sounding sad now, all alone in the emptiness.

In the GMU, Karen, with Jan Em's surprisingly capable help, was bending over readouts to tabulate what resources were left: there were very few.

Major Carpenter was standing by; with the TO&E all but obliterated, he was a rising star, an all-around fixer. Jack didn't quite like his can-do-even-if-it's-hard-on-the-lower-ranks-*sir* style, but at least the guy was trying to help pull things back together.

Admiral Hunter was starting to look pretty grizzled, like Jack himself. "I want you to take a team out and check on a possible Invid base for me," Rick told him.

"Sure thing, sir," Jack answered. "But I think we should go belowdecks and apply a welding torch to that Tesla first, and get a little more intel information out of him."

Then he realized Lisa was about to brief those assembled. Jack nodded understanding to Rick's hand signal, and took a seat to listen.

Another recon, Jack thought. *Wish I had a flying horse.*

"All right, there's no getting round it. We're—we're *stuck* here," Lisa was telling Vince and the Sterlings and the principal Sentinels.

We might be here for the rest of our lives, it occurred to Jack. He found himself stealing another look at Karen, but she was busy.

"But *that's just for the moment*," Lisa went on forcefully. They all seconded her, from varying places on the emotional spectrum: anger, growing misgivings, stoic determination, or, in Burak's case, a kind of starry-eyed disregard of reality.

We'd better get out of here, Jack Baker thought. *'Cause I'm not so sure how long we can last all thrown in together like this.*

Lisa outlined new strategies, new possible solutions. After the group had broken up, she drew Rick aside. "I'm afraid I'm not very good at dog-and-pony shows."

"You did fine."

They left the GMU, headed for their quarters at the palace. At least there was no shortage of living space, or food; a vacated Praxis provided plenty of those.

Halfway there, Lisa stopped and began pounding her fist on a stone wall. "We've got to get things moving again, before the Sentinels fall apart and everybody settles down to become subsistence farmers, or hunters. The Invid aren't going to leave us alone forever; you *know* that."

He put his arm around her waist and they went their way again. "Everybody's gonna realize that, Lisa, once they get a chance to think. Believe me."

"Rick, they *must*!"

She drew an uneven breath. "Listen, tell me: what were you thinking about when you were standing back there with Baker, during the briefing? You had a peculiar look on your face."

He clicked his tongue. "Unworthy, maybe, but I was thinking that at least we're together, and . . ."

She didn't let the hesitation go on long. "And what?"

"And if one of us had had to go with *Farrago*, I'd rather it would have been me. Because I couldn't have faced this or anything else without you."

Lights were coming on with the dusk, in the GMU and the palace.

The following chapter is a sneak preview of DEATH DANCE—Book III in THE SENTINELS saga.

> *It was as if the Expeditionary Mission was fated to strike a
> truce with someone, and the Regent just happened to be the only
> enemy in residence. In another five years the Robotech Masters
> would arrive in Earthspace, followed three years later by the
> Regis and her half of the Invid horde; but in 2026 (Earth-relative)
> this was still speculation, and for a few brief days there was talk of
> peace, trust, and other impossibilities.*

> Ahmed Rashona, *That Pass in the Night: The SDF-3 and
> the Mission to Tirol*

A FLEET OF INVID WARSHIPS EMERGED FROM THEIR
trans-temporal journey through hyperspace into the cool ra-
diance of Fantoma's primary, like so many shells left revealed on a black-sand beach by a receding tide. The
mollusklike carriers positioned themselves a respectful distance from the moon they had captured then lost; only the
fleet's molet-shaped flagship continued its approach, menacing in its sealed silence.

At the edge of the ringed giant's shadow Tirol's guardian, the SDF-3, swung round to face off with the Regent's
vessel, the crimson lobes of its maingun brilliantly outlined
in starlight.

Aboard the Earth fortress, in the ship's Tactical Information Center, Major General T. R. Edwards watched as a transport shuttle emerged from the tip of one of the flagship's armored tentacles. Edwards trusted that the Regent was aboard the small craft, accompanied certainly by a retinue of guards and scientists. The presence of the Invid fleet made it clear that any acts of aggression or duplicity would spell mutual annihilation for Invid and Humans alike.

Admiral Forsythe, who commanded the SDF-3's bridge in the wake of Lisa Hayes's departure with the Sentinels, was now in constant communication with the Invid flagship. It was the Regent who had taken the initiative in suggesting this extraordinary visit, but Forsythe had insisted that the fortress remain at high alert status at least until the Regent was aboard. Disillusioned by decades of war and betrayal, and hardened by the grim realities of recent reversals, it was the Human race that had grown wary of summits, distrustful of those who would sue for peace.

Scanners and camera remotes monitored the approach of the Regent's shuttlecraft and relayed relevant data to screens in the fortress's cavernous Tactical Center, where techs and staff officers were keeping a close watch on the situation. Edwards moved to the railing of the command balcony for an overview of the room's enormous horizontal situation screen. Studying the positions of the Invid troop carriers in relation to the SDF-3, it occurred to him how easy it would be to fire at them right now, perhaps take half of them out along with the Regent himself before the Invid retaliated. And even then there was a good chance the fortress would survive the return fire, which was bound to be confused. Numerous though they might be, the Invid seemed to lack any real knowledge of strategy. Edwards was convinced that their successful strike against the SDF-3 almost six months ago had been the result of surprise and old fashioned blind luck. More to the point, he felt that he had an intuitive understanding of this enemy— a second sense birthed during his brief exposure to the brainlike device his own Ghost Squadron had captured on Tirol.

Edwards reminded himself of the several good reasons for exercising restraint. Apart from the fact that the actual size of the Invid fleet remained unknown, there was this Regis being to wonder about; her whereabouts and motivations had yet to be determined. Besides, he sensed that the Regent had something more than peace negotiations in mind. In any case, the data Edwards had furnished the Invid regarding the Sentinels' ship had already linked the two of them in a separate peace. But Edwards was willing to play out the charade—even if it amounted to nothing more than an opportunity to appraise his potential partner.

He dismissed his musings shortly and returned to the balcony console, where he received an update on the shuttlecraft's ETA in the fortress docking bay. Then, giving a final moment of attention to the room's numerous screens and displays, he hurried out, adjusting his alloy faceplate as one would a hat, and tugging his dress blues into shape.

The docking bay had been transformed into a kind of parade grounds for the occasion, with everyone present as decked out as they had been at the Hunters' wedding extravaganza. There had been no advance notice of what if any protocols were to be observed, but a brass band was on hand nonetheless. The impression the Plenipotentiary Council wished to convey was that of a highly-organized group, strong and decisive, but warlike only as a last resort. The twelve members of the Council had a viewstand all to themselves at the edge of a broad magenta circle, concentric to the shuttle's touchdown zone. A majority of the Council had ruled against the show of force Edwards had pushed for, but as a concession, he had been allowed to crowd the bay with rank after rank of spit-shined mecha —Battloids, Logans, Hovertanks, Excalibers, Spartans, and the like.

The shuttle docked while Edwards was making his way to a pre-assigned place near the Council's raised platform; since he had been the Council's spokesperson in arranging the talks, it had been decided that he represent them now in the introductory proceedings. Edwards had of course both seen and fought against the enemy's troops, and he had met face-to-face with the scientists Obsim and Tesla; but neither of these examples had prepared him for his first sight of the Invid Regent, nor had the Royal Hall's communicator sphere given him any sense of the XT's size. Like the lesser beings of the Invid race, the Regent was something of an evolutionary pastiche—a greenish, slug-headed, bipedal creature whose ontogeny and native habitat was impossible to imagine—but he stood a good twenty feet high and was crowned by an organic cowl or hood, adorned, so it seemed, with a median ridge of eyeball-like tubercles. Dr. Lang had talked about *self-generated transformations and reshapings* that had little to do with evolution as it had come to be accepted (and *expected*!) on earth. But all the Protoculture pataphysics in the galaxy couldn't keep Edwards from gaping.

A dozen armed and armored troopers preceded the Regent down the shuttle ramp (a ribbed saucer similar in design to the troop carriers), and split into two ranks, genuflecting on either side of what would be the Regent's carpeted path toward the Council platform. Recovered, Edwards stepped forward to greet the alien in Tiresian, then repeated the words in English. The Invid threw back the folds of his cerulean robes, revealing four-fingered hands, and glared down at him.

"I learned your language—*yesterday*," the Regent announced in a voice that carried its own echo. "I find your concepts most . . . amusing."

Edwards looked up into the Regent's black eyes and offered a grin. "And rest assured we'll do our best to keep you amused, your Highness." He was pleased to see the alien's bulbous snout sensors begin to pulsate.

Edwards's one-eyed gaze held the Regent's own for an instant, and that was all he needed to realize that something was wrong—that this being was *not* the one he had spoken to via the communications sphere. But he kept this to himself, falling aside theatrically to usher the Regent forward to the Council platform.

The Plenipotentiary members introduced themselves one by one, and after further formalities the Regent and his retinue were directed to the amphitheater that had been designated for the talks. The Regent's size had necessitated a specific route, along which Edwards had made certain to place as many varieties of mecha as he could muster. Each hold the summit principals passed through found combat-ready Veritechs and Alphas; each corridor turn another squad of RDF troops or a contingent of towering Destroids. While onboard, the Regent's every word and step would be monitored by the extensive security system Edwards had made operational as part of his Code Pyramid project—a system that had also managed to find its way into the Council's public and private chambers, and into many of the fortress's Robotechnological labs and inner sanctums.

There was a smorgasbord of food and drink awaiting everyone in the amphitheater's antechambers; the Regent nourished himself on applelike fruits his servants brought forth. Edwards noticed that Lang was doing his best to attach himself to the Invid leader, but the Regent seemed unimpressed, refusing to discuss any of the topics the Earth scientist broached. In fact, only Minmei succeeded in getting a rise out of the Regent. Edwards noted that the Invid could barely take his eyes off the singer after she had completed her songs, and he retained a slightly spellbound look long after the introductory addresses had commenced.

Terms for a truce were slated for follow-up discussions, so civilians and members of the press were permitted to enter the amphitheater itself. Edwards saw to it that Minmei was seated beside him in the front row, where the Regent could get a good look at the two of them.

The alien's initial remarks put to rest any doubts that may have lingered in Edwards's mind concerning the ongoing impersonation. The Regent spoke of misunderstandings on both sides, of a desire to bring peace and order to a section of the galaxy that had known non-stop warfare for centuries. He claimed to understand now just what had prompted the Human forces to undertake their desperate journey, and he sympathized with their present plight, hinting that it might be possible to accelerate the timetable for the Human's return trip to their homeworld—providing, of course, that certain terms could be agreed upon.

"It's a pity there has been so much loss of life," the Invid continued in the same imperious tone. "Both in Tirolspace and during the so-called 'liberation' of Karbarra. But while we may have no cause for further quarrel with your forces here, it must be understood that no leniency could be expected for those of your number who chose to join the Sentinels. And despite what you may have been told by the Tiresians, those worlds—Praxis, Garuda, and the rest—belong to me. The reasons for this are complex and at present irrelevant to the nature of these negotiations, but again we wish to stress that the Sentinels' cause was a misguided one from the start. It was inevitable that they fail sooner or later."

A charged silence fell over the auditorium, and Edwards had to restrain himself from laughing. The Sentinels had not been heard from for four months now. Official word had it that the *Farrago* was maintaining radio silence for strategic reasons. Then, recently, there was open speculation that the ship had been badly damaged during the battle for Praxis. But Edwards knew better. He felt Minmei's trembling grasp on his upper arm. Colonel Adams, also seated in the front row, leaned forward to throw him a knowing look.

"We have only recently lost contact with the *Farrago*," Professor Lang was saying. "But I'm certain that once communications are re-established and an accord of some sort is enacted, Admiral Hunter and the others will abide by its terms and return to Tirol."

The Invid crossed his massive arms. "Yes, I'm sure they would have honored it, Dr. Lang. But I'm afraid it's too late. Four months ago the Sentinels' ship was destroyed— with all hands aboard."

A collective gasp rose from the crowd, and Edwards heard Minmei begin to sob. "Rick . . . Jonathan," she said, struggling to her feet, only to collapse across Edwards's lap.

Someone nearby screamed. Lang and the rest of the Council were standing, their words swallowed up in the noise of dozens of separate conversations. News personnel and members of the general staff were rushing from the room. Edwards snapped an order to his aide to summon a doctor. Adams, meanwhile, was shoving onlookers aside.

Edwards held Minmei protectively. Once again he sought out the Invid's lustrous eyes; and in that glance a pact was affirmed.

But on Praxis the dead walked—those Sentinels who had escaped the destruction of the *Farrago*, and, unknown to them, a deadly host of archaic creatures returned to life in the bowels of the planet's abandoned Genesis Pits . . .

"Take a look for yourself," Vince Grant suggested, stepping back from the scanner's monitor screen. Rick Hunter and Jonathan Wolff leaned in to regard the image centered there: an intact drive module that had been blown clear of the ship and fallen into low orbit around Praxis. Vince was reasonably certain the module's Protoculture-peat engines were undamaged.

"And there's no way to call it down?" Rick asked. "A hundred miles or so and an Alpha could reach the thing." Normally, one could fly a Veritech to the moon and back, but not one of the Sentinels' all-but-depleted Alphas was capable of attaining escape velocity.

Vince shook his head, his brown face grim. "We barely have enough power to keep the nets alive."

"Then it might as well be a million miles away," Wolff thought to add.

Vince switched off the screen and the three men sat down to steaming mugs of tea one of the Praxians had brewed up from some indigenous grass. After four months it had come down to this: the GMU's stores were nearly empty and foraging had become one of the group's primary activities. And in all those months they had yet to come up with an explanation for the disappearance of the planet's native population. What was left of the central city and all the surrounding villages was deserted. But whether what Bela called "the Praxian Sisterhood" had *chosen* to leave had not been ascertained.

Puzzling, too, were the tectonic anomalies and quakes that were continuing to plague the planet, as often as three times a day now. The quakes had convinced the Sentinels' Praxian contingent that Arla-Non—Bela's "mother" and the leader of the Sisterhood—had struck a deal with the Invid to move the planet's population to some other world. Rick wasn't sure if he bought the explanation, but it certainly served a therapeutic need if nothing else.

"Look," Rick said, breaking the silence, "they're probably already searching for us. Lang's not about to write us off. And even if the mining operation is *close* to on-schedule, they'll have at least one ship readied with the capability for a local jump. We just have to hope the Invid have lost interest in this place."

The horde's absence these months bordered on the conspicuous; and what with the quakes and deserted villages, Cabell had speculated that it was possible the Invid knew something the Sentinels didn't.

Rick's optimism in the face of all this had Vince smiling to himself. *Rick would always be a commander whether he liked it or not.* "It's not Lang we're worried about," he said, speaking for himself and Wolff.

Rick caught his meaning. "Edwards has to answer to the Council." There was an edge to his voice he didn't mean to put there. Lang had warned Rick about Edwards during one of the last links the *Farrago* had had with Base-Tirol, and it was difficult to keep the memory of that brief deep-space commo from surfacing.

"Don't underestimate the man's ambitions, Rick," Wolff cautioned. "I'm sure they're going to come looking, but I'm willing to bet that Edwards will have the Council eating out of his hand by then. Maybe one of us should have—"

"I don't want to go over old ground," Rick cut him off. "The only thing that interests me right now is a way to reach that drive module."

Grant and Wolff exchanged looks and studied their cups of tea. Rick was right, of course: there was no use dwelling on the choices they had made, individually and collectively. Wolff liked to think that at least Vince had Jean by his side and the precious GMU under his feet. But Rick had all but resigned his commission, and Wolff himself had left his heart behind.

A rumbling sound broke the silence now, causing the mugs to skitter across the tabletop. The tremor built in intensity, rattling the command center's consoles and screens, then subsided, rolling away beneath them like contained thunder.

No one spoke for a moment. Wolff wore a wary look as he loosened his grip on the edge of the table and sat back to exhale a whistle. "Course Praxis could do us in long before the Invid or Edwards."

"Pleasant thought," Vince told him.

Rick gave them both an angry look. "We're going to get to that module if we have to pole vault there."

Tactical concerns (and personal preference) had kept Vince Grant and Rick somewhat anchored to the GMU (which had been moved inland from its original seaside landing zone); but the rest of the substantially reduced Robotech contingent, along with the XT Sentinels, had opted for Praxis's wooded valleys, the planet's often glorious skies, and rolling hills. Max and Miriya's Skull Squadron had spent most of the past months reconning remote areas, hoping to come upon some trace of the vanished Sisterhood; but they had only succeeded in further depleting already critical reserves of Protoculture fuel. Consequently, the Wolff Pack stuck close to base, Hovertanks shut down. Bela and Gnea and the other Praxians had voluntarily detailed themselves to serve the group's logistical needs, and were assisted in this by the bearlike Karbarrans and vulpine Garudans. Cabell had all but isolated himself, disappearing for long walks from which he would return with samples of native rock or flora. Still a bit uncomfortable with the Humans and not yet fully accepted by the XTs, the Tiresian was often found in the company of Rem, Baldan, Teal, and the limbless Haydonites, Veidt and Sarna. Janice, too, had become an unofficial member of Cabell's eldritch clique, much to Rick and Lisa's puzzlement.

Presently, Cabell and Janice were off together on a long walk; they were on a forested slope about fifteen miles from the mobile base when the tremor that had shaken the GMU struck. The minor quake did little more than knock them off-balance and loosen some gravel and shale from nearby heights; but it was the morning's second shakeup and it brought a severe look to Cabell's face.

Janice had thought to take hold of the old man's arm and utter a short panicked sound as the ground began to tremble. It was a performance worthy of Minmei's best, although Janice could hardly appreciate it as such—any more than she could fully understand just what had compelled her to seek out Rem and Cabell's company in the first place. That this should somehow *please* Dr. Lang was a thought as baffling to her as it was discomforting.

"There, there, child," Cabell was saying, patting her hand. "It will be over in a moment."

They recommenced their climb when the tremor passed. Janice disengaged herself and urged Cabell to go on with what they had been discussing.

"Ah, yes," he said, running a hand over his bald pate, "the trees."

Janice listened like a student eager for As.

"As you can see, they're nothing like the scrub growth we found on Karbarra—far healthier, much closer to the unmutated form." He motioned with his hand and went up on tiptoes to touch the spherical "canopy" of a healthy-looking specimen. The tendrils that encased the solid-looking sphere and rigid, near-transluscent trunk seemed to pulse with life. Gingerly, Cabell plucked one of the verdigris-colored, applelike fruits, burnished it against his robe, and began to turn it about in his wrinkled hand.

"Even the fruit they bear is different in color and texture—although still a far cry from the true Opteran species. Nevertheless, it may tell us something." He took off his rucksack and placed the sample inside. "Look for the ripest ones," he instructed Janice, as she added a second fruit to the pack.

Cabell was straightening up when a sudden movement further up the slope caught his eye. Janice heard him start, and turned to follow his narrowed gaze.

"What was it?"

Cabell stroked his beard. "I thought I saw someone up ahead."

"A Praxian?" Janice asked, craning her neck and sharpening her vision.

"No," he said, shaking his head. "I would swear it was *Burak*!"

Later, a stone's throw from the grounded GMU, inside the wooden structure that had been designated both quarters and cell, Tesla wolfed down the fruits Burak had picked from the sinister orchard Zor's Flower of Life seedings had spawned on Praxis.

"Yes, yes, different, ummm," the Invid was saying in a voice tinged with rapture.

The young Perytonian tried to avert his eyes, but in the end couldn't help himself from watching Tesla as he ingested fruit after fruit. Moist sucking noises filled the cell.

"And you think they may have seen you?" Tesla asked him.

"It is possible—Cabell, in any case."

Tesla scoffed, still munching and handling the fruits as if they were wealth itself. "Cabell is too old to recognize the nose on his own face. Besides, they know I can't subsist on what you call food."

Burak said nothing. It was true enough: the Invid's food stock had been destroyed with the *Farrago*, and the Sentinels had agreed to place Burak in charge of securing alternative nutrient plants. But Cabell, who was anything but a doddering old man, and perhaps fearing the very transformations Tesla was beginning to undergo, had suggested that the Invid's fruit and Flower intake be regulated—this in spite of the fact that Tesla had to some extent ingratiated himself with the group since their victory on Karbarra. Each evening, Cabell and Jean Grant would look in on Tesla. Burak had been asked to furnish them with a daily log of the amounts gathered and ingested; and the devilish looking Perytonian was complying—in as much he would file a report. But the report was hardly a reflection of the actual amounts Tesla consumed. Fortunately, though, the Invid's transformations had been limited to brief periods following his meals, when neither Cabell nor Jean were present.

"More," Tesla said now, holding out his hands.

Burak regarded the Invid's newly-acquired fifth digit and pulled the basket out of reach. "I think you've had enough for today." Burak had heard it said that extraordinary powers could be gained from ingesting the fruits of Haydon's worlds, but he had never understood that to mean physical transfiguration, and the Invid's recent changes were beginning to fill him with fear.

Tesla's eyes glowed red as he came to his feet, taller by inches than he had stood on Karbarra. "You *dare* to say this to me after all we've been through? You, who sought me out before fate landed us in this despicable situation? And what of your homeworld and the curse you were so feverish to see ended—have you given up hope? Would you renounce your destiny?"

Burak took a hesitant step toward the door, the basket clasped to him. "You're changing!" he said, pointing to Tesla's hands. "They're going to notice it, and what then?

They'll cut back on the amounts, put someone else in charge of you. Then what becomes of your promises—what becomes of Peryton?"

Tesla continued to glare at him a moment more, transmogrifying even as Burak watched. The Invid's skull rippled and expanded, as though being forced to conform to some novel interior design. Gradually, however, Tesla reassumed his natural state and collapsed back into his seat, spent, subdued, and apologetic.

"You're right, Burak. We must take care to keep our partnership a carefully-guarded secret." His black, ophidian eyes fixed on Burak. "And have no fear for your tortured world. When the time comes for me to assume my rightful place in these events, I shall reward you for these efforts."

"That's all that I ask," Burak told him.

The two XTs fell silent as a gentle tremor shook the building.

Tesla stared at the floor. "I sense something about this planet," he announced, his sensor organs twitching as his snout came up. "And I think I am beginning to see just what the Regis was doing here."

ABOUT THE AUTHOR

Jack McKinney has been a psychiatric aide, fusion-rock guitarist and session man, worldwide wilderness guide, and "consultant" to the U.S. Military in Southeast Asia (although they had to draft him for that).

His numerous other works of mainstream and science fiction—novels, radio and television scripts—have been written under various pseudonyms.

He resides in Ubud, on the Indonesian island of Bali.